FLIGHT OF FANCY

VICKI THARP

FLIGHT OF FANCY

Flight of Fancy is a work of fiction. Names, characters, places and incidents either are the product of the author's imagination or are used fictitiously, and any resemblance to actual persons, living or dead, business establishments, events, or locals, is entirely coincidental.

Original Cover Design by Designs EE

Editing by: Amy Duli

Proofreading by: EK Editing

ISBN 978-1-948798-37-2

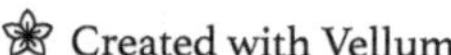 Created with Vellum

1

Milo Malone's hand started sweating as he waited for his call to connect. Every year his body responded this way. The damp palms. The rapid heartbeat. The sinking feeling in his stomach. With this being his seventh call, you would think it would get easier.

It hadn't.

The line clicked, and instead of the expected, 'Second Life, this is Janet,' Janet's warm voice said, "Hello, Milo, it's good to hear from you."

The change of greeting took him off guard until it clicked that Second Life must have installed Caller ID.

He wasn't entirely sure Janet was happy to hear from him, but her soft, empathetic voice almost made her sound believable.

"H-Hey. I was just... just calling..."

Spit. It. Out.

"I'm very good at my job, Milo." He heard the indulgent smile in Janet's voice. If she had sounded annoyed. He wouldn't have blamed her.

"I-I know that. I wanted to make sure you got the card and—"

"I forwarded it four days ago. The family should have it by now."

Milo's heart thumped so hard that sometimes he feared it would break right through the scar running down the center of his chest, even though the doctors had long ago told him he'd completely healed.

"Have you gotten anything back?" He could have probably answered that for himself. All the previous years, the answer had been no. He shouldn't expect a different answer this year.

Still, Milo had hope.

But not an expectation.

"No. I'm sorry, Milo. This is how it goes sometimes. It can take years for a donor's family to respond to a recipient's letter. Sometimes, they never do."

Milo had heard this all before and hoped that if his donor's family read his cards, that they took comfort in knowing how much the gift of a heart had meant to him, even if they couldn't bring themselves to reply.

But he also knew that some people didn't need the reminder because they lived with the loss of their loved one every day.

Because of that, he'd kept his cards to once a year, mailing them two weeks before his *alive day*—the anniversary of his heart transplant, hoping his Organ Procurement Organization, OPO, would forward it in time for the anniversary.

Though he still had a hard time squaring it in his head that the best day of his life had been someone else's worst.

Which probably had something to do with how he'd been drifting through life ever since he'd blown out eighteen candles on a lopsided German chocolate cake and left home.

"Milo? Are you still there?"

"What? Yeah. Sorry. I spaced. What did you say?"

Her soft chuckle came as soothing as honey in the hot tea his mother used to make. The honeyed tea hadn't kept his heart from failing, but it had been like a warm hug in a cup.

"I asked how you were doing."

Foss—aka Foster Torres—best friend, and most annoying roommate, thumped Milo on the back of the head as he passed Milo in his nest of blankets on the couch. "Come on. I want to get there before traffic gets too bad or the trails get too packed."

Milo held up a finger, but Foster just rolled his eyes and shouldered his hydration pack.

"My friend and I are hiking along the coast to celebrate my alive day."

"So, you're good?"

If you called couch surfing and being jobless—again—good, then that's what he was. But he didn't want to get into that with his coordinator. "Hey, look. I've got to go. I also wanted to give you my new address in case you got a reply."

Milo rattled off Foster's address. Even though the whole couch-surfing thing was supposed to be temporary, Foster would let him know if anything showed up in the mail for him later.

"Thanks for the update," Janet said. "And I'll be sure to forward anything we get as soon as it comes."

Most people probably didn't stay in contact with their OPO coordinator seven years after their transplant. But Janet had worked with him and his family in the months before his transplant and had become a vital part of his support network. "Thanks."

"And, Milo?"

"Yeah?"

"I'm really glad you're doing well. Enjoy your day. It's a beautiful day for a hike."

Milo chuckled. "It's Southern California. It's always a beautiful day."

They said their goodbyes, and Milo extricated himself from the blankets on his temporary bed. He quickly dressed, trying to shake off his melancholy. Which at times seemed harder to escape than the La Brea Tar Pits.

His donor's family had already given him the ultimate gift. Was it selfish of him to ask for more?

Maybe it was better that he hadn't heard back. This way, the family would never know that he had done so little with his life since his transplant. At times he wondered if maybe his heart should have gone to someone else. Someone more worthy. Someone who would make something of themselves.

Milo tied the laces on his hiking boots and grabbed Foster's spare hydration pack.

"I filled the water bladders and stuffed some nuts and beef jerky in the zippered pockets. I know what a little bitch you can be when you're hangry," Foster said.

Of course he had. Foster had that fabulously annoying way of being overprepared and five steps ahead of everyone else. Which was probably what made him the golden boy at his company.

"It's only, like, a five-mile hike."

"I'm not taking any chances that your blood sugar drops, and you start whining about breaking a nail."

Milo held up both hands, the backs of his hands toward Foster, his fingernails chewed short, his black fingernail polish badly chipped or worn completely off. "These are too short to break."

"Which only means you'll find something else to whine about."

Milo lowered all his fingers except his middle one, making Foster laugh.

When they got to the door, Foster stopped Milo with a hand on his shoulder. Milo turned.

Foster's face had one of those grim, sympathetic smiles. "I'm sorry your donor family hasn't responded. I really am. I wish I could make this easier for you. But for what it's worth..." Foster released his shoulder and tapped Milo in the center of his chest with the meat of his fist. "I'm so fucking glad you're still in this world, my friend."

Foster's voice thickened, and his eyes misted, making Milo's water as well. Milo gave him a playful shove back. "Stop, you're going to make me fucking cry."

Foster caught him in an affectionate chokehold and placed a platonic smacking kiss to the side of his head. "Let's go. We've got a lot to celebrate."

Joss Kincaid sat at his kitchen table with seven unopened cards. Blue, red, green, orange, white, purple, and yellow. All with his address on the front. They'd been forwarded from Second Life, the OPO who'd handled Dan's organ donations.

The last one, the green one, came the same way they always did a few days before the anniversary of the worst day of Joss's life—and the last day of Dan's.

Year after year after fucking year.

An excruciating reminder of everything Joss had lost.

Derek Watts came through the front door of the apartment Joss and Dan had built inside their airplane hangar and kicked up his aviators to the top of his head. He wore a blindingly white designer T-shirt and a pair of jeans that probably cost more to distress than it cost Joss to fill his Twin Otter plane with fuel.

"Sorry I'm late. Who'd have thought it would be so hard to find these stupid little suckers anyway?"

Derek dropped the toys onto the table—seven little army men with the plastic parachutes. One for each year since Dan had been gone.

It was Joss's annual way to commemorate Dan's last fateful jump.

Joss dropped the card on top of the rest and stood. "I really appreciate you getting these for me. I usually find them ahead of time, but this year..."

Joss let the sentence trail off because he couldn't think of an excuse that didn't make him sound pathetic or might make someone wonder when he'd get the hell over Dan's death.

As if that would ever happen.

Derek clapped him on the shoulder and gave it a squeeze. "It wasn't a problem."

"What are these?" His friend picked up one of the cards, flipped it over, and glanced at the unopened flap.

"Sympathy cards." Joss didn't know exactly why he'd lied. But if he'd told the truth, he'd also have to tell Derek about Dan's organ donation, and that had always felt like such a personal thing that he hadn't shared it with anybody.

Or maybe you didn't want all those good meaning people who didn't know what to say to tell you that 'at least something good came from Dan's death.'

Because in Joss's world, Dan's gift was like a lick of new paint over a crumbling, dry-rotting core. It only made things on the outside look better.

"If you want, I can read these for you."

Joss took the envelope out of Derek's hand and dropped it on the stack. "I don't want you to read them. Nothing anyone can say can make any of this any better."

"I know that, but—"

Joss leveled Derek with a caustic look that shut him up. It took a lot to shut up a guy like Derek, a man who had policed some of the roughest neighborhoods in LA back before he'd been forced into a career change.

"Right. Okay," Derek said as he took a step back. He clapped his hands together. "Let's hop into that gorgeous new bird of yours. What do you say? She's the only girl I can never wait to get my hands on."

"She'd be the *only* girl you've had your hands on."

"Besides Ashley in middle school," Derek said with an irrepressible grin. "But in my defense, that was before I became a connoisseur of dick."

Despite the day, Joss chuckled and shook his head as they headed out to the grass runway behind his hangar. His property sat on a rare flat spot in the foothills of the San Gabriels. When he and Dan had first found the long, thin strip of land, it had been begging for an airstrip. And the two of them had pulled every cent they could beg, borrow, steal, or con, to buy it.

Okay, the con was a bit of an exaggeration, but Dan had been born knowing how to sweet-talk people into getting his way, and investors had found it impossible to tell him no.

The same way Joss had.

Joss carefully went through visual preflight on the outside of his plane. A task he never let himself rush. Then he pulled the wheel chucks and climbed into the cockpit. Derek settled into the copilot seat, and they both put on their headsets as Joss finished preflight and started spooling up the Otter's twin engines.

Derek put his hands on the yoke in front of him. "Oh, baby. Come to papa."

Joss adjusted the idle speed and said, "She's not like one of your hookups. She's not going to fall at your feet and let you have your way with her with nothing more than some smooth-talking."

"Hookups?" Derek gave him the side-eye. "You make it

sound like I'm twenty again and taking anything horny and hard back to my bed."

Joss increased his throttle speed and started taxiing to the end of the runway. "Hey, no judgment here. Horny and hard is starting to sound good these days."

Using his private airstrip, he didn't have to wait on a tower to give him clearance, but he would radio LAX as he approached their airspace on his path toward the Pacific Ocean.

They bumped down the grass strip, and the earth fell away as they caught air, the sky bright blue and cloudless. Another perfect day in Southern California. He never tired of the hum of the engines in his ears and the vibrations it sent through the frame to his body, as if he and his bird were one.

He hadn't had her nearly as long as his old Cessna 182, the first plane he and Dan had bought back when they'd started their life and adventures together. Of all the places in the world, Joss felt closest to Dan when he took to the air.

He veered north, essentially taking them in a big circle from the San Gabriels, up past Santa Clarita, across through Bardsdale to Ventura, then following the coast south before making a long arc and cutting across at Huntington Beach before finally turning north again.

Since he only had toy parachutists and not the real thing, he didn't have to climb nearly as high. When he leveled off at around five thousand feet, he handed over the controls.

"She's all yours," Joss said.

Derek grinned, his hands on the yoke confident and light for a man who seemed to love flying as much as Joss.

"Oh, man," Derek said as he flew the plane. "She handles so much better than Betts."

Betts. The Cessna 182 he had in parts in his hangar. A project he and Dan had always planned on doing together. Joss had only started the work in the past year, deciding he needed to finish what he and Dan had wanted to start.

"For a guy who loves flying as much as you, I'd have thought you'd have gone for your commercial pilot's license instead of becoming a private dick when your old gig dried up."

"One," Derek said, without taking his focus off the sky in front of him, keeping an eye out for other air traffic. "The way you say 'private dick' makes it sound like I stand out on the street corner at night and sell myself. Which is fine if that's your jam. And two..."

Derek glanced at Joss for a fraction of a second, his friend's expression hard to read with his eyes hidden behind his reflective aviators, but the hard, thin set of his lips gave Joss a hint. "And two, my 'old gig' didn't dry up. I was forced out. Big difference."

And obviously, still a sore subject. Even after his private investigation agency had become a huge success. Anyone in the valley—hell, in Hollywood and the greater Los Angeles area—knew there was only one private investigator to hire if you wanted results and you wanted them fast.

They were almost to the coastline, and Derek started his long, slow turn to the south.

"Sorry. I didn't mean—" Joss started.

"We're coming up on the spot soon. You should be getting ready, yeah?"

Not for another five minutes or so, but Joss could take the hint. He of all people understood it when others didn't want to talk about a subject that left them gutted and raw.

Joss pointed to the GPS coordinates that matched the drop zone for Dan's last jump. Dan had wanted to land on a less populated stretch of beach. It had always been his favorite place to land, even if he had to navigate missing Highway 1 and the pounding surf.

On those days, Joss would find Dan on the beach after he'd landed the plane and driven all the way across the damn valley to get to him. Dan would be still damp after jumping in the water, the sun kissing his skin, and a face-splitting grin on his handsome face.

"Give me a one-minute warning on the jump lights."

"Sure thing."

Joss unbuckled and worked his way to the back of the plane. Instead of regular seats, he had two long rows of benches so people could straddle them. They worked great for the newbies who had to jump tandem or the more experienced skydivers.

He stepped into a harness and clipped himself in before rolling up the side jump door. He sat on the floor, his legs dangling out of the plane. He glanced up, the red 'no go' light to the right of the door had turned to yellow, telling him to stand by.

Taking the parachute men out of his pocket, he removed the rubber bands holding the parachutes in place. Down below, he could make out the narrow hiking path along Sycamore Canyon. And if he held on tight and leaned out far enough, he could barely make out the sandy beach and surf on the other side of the plane.

The wind whipped at his clothes and hair, and he squinted his eyes against it. He glanced up. The green 'go' light came on as they reached the exact location of Dan's last jump. Chest tight, and with a lump in his throat, Joss released the men one by one and said the words Dan had always said before he jumped out of a plane. "Time to fly."

2

MILO AND FOSTER HIKED THE SYCAMORE CANYON TRAIL ALONG the coast. If they stopped walking and held their breath, they could hear the surf pounding in the distance. If Milo walked backward, he could see the haze of smog hanging over Los Angeles to the south, but where he was, the air seemed clear and fresh.

Below, cars zoomed by on the Pacific Coast Highway, many with their tops down. On the beach, people walked or sunned themselves. A few braved the frigid waters and played in the surf.

But Milo preferred to be higher up. One of the many small things that had changed since his surgery. He tried to chalk it up to his new lease on life, but sometimes he wondered if there was something more to all of his new idiosyncrasies.

A couple came up the trail from the other direction, a big beefy guy and his girl, hiking the trail hand in hand. They nodded to Milo and Foster. They nodded back. But Milo couldn't help himself. He turned and pulled his sunglasses down his nose and scoped the guy out after they'd passed.

Foster bumped him in the shoulder. "Since when do you like the big bears? I thought the twinks were more your speed?"

"I can look, can't I?" No need to go into how his taste in men had done a complete one-eighty. A change he could probably chalk up to getting a little older himself. Nothing strange about that, right?

"I don't know," Foster said. "Maybe we can do more than look."

Foster took a step toward the couple as if he were going to track them down and ask if they were interested in a four-way, and Milo put a staying hand on Foster's arm. "Stop. That guy's straight."

Foster slapped a hand to his heart as if mortally wounded. "The guy could be bi. We exist." He held his hands out, his expression said, 'Hello, can't you see me?' "Bisexual is not just a temporary stop from straightland to gayland."

Milo swatted him with the back of his hand. "Yeah. I know that."

"So—"

"So that doesn't mean we're going to proposition every guy with a girl in case he's bi."

Foster shrugged. "Your loss." Then he cocked his head and scoped the guy out from his wide shoulders, to narrow waist, to muscle-builder ass. "You sure we can't ask this one time?"

Milo rolled his eyes and tugged until Foster turned and followed him up the trail.

"I knew allowing you to stay with me would cramp my sex life. I should have said no."

"I'm not planning on staying long. A few days, a week or two tops, just until I get my feet on the ground and find a job."

"You're never going to be able to afford a place on minimum wage. Not here."

"I'll figure something out."

"Maybe you can go back to college, and—"

Milo pressed his hands over his ears and picked up his pace, the air sawing in and out of his lungs. Foster jogged to catch up and pulled one of his hands away from his ear.

"You don't want to listen because you know I'm right. If you'd have stayed in college, you would already have a degree and a career, and you wouldn't be begging friends for couches to sleep on."

The anger came lightning quick, something he still wasn't used to, even after seven years. He stopped in his tracks. "College was an even slower death than my bad heart. I couldn't stay."

"Fine. College isn't for everybody. I get it. But you need to find *something*."

And as quickly as the anger arrived, it abated. "You're right. I know that. It's..."

"It's what?" The patience in Foster's eyes was something Milo didn't think he deserved. He'd about used up everyone's patience over the years. When would Foster reach his limit?

How did he explain how unsettled he felt? How free and tied down he felt? The dichotomy, something he couldn't explain or find a workaround. He'd thought when he got the call from the OPO that they had a heart for him, that all his troubles were over. He'd had zero idea that it would be the start of a whole knew set of problems.

"I don't know what it is," Milo said at last. "And today of all days, I'd rather not have to think about that."

Foster nodded. "Fair enough." He bobbed his chin toward the trail. "At the top of that ridge, there's a spot with a great view. We can stop there for a bit. Drink. Have a snack."

"Fuck you," Milo said with a laugh. "I'm not five."

"Coulda fooled me with that little temper tantr—"

Foster didn't even get the rest of his sentence out before Milo chased out after him. For a guy who spent most of his time behind a computer in a nearly windowless office, Foster was quite fast. Even with the new heart, Milo didn't have a chance of catching him.

By the time they'd made it to the lookout, Milo had caught up with Foster, too out of breath to do anything besides rest his hands on his knees and suck air in and out of his lungs. His quads and calves burned with the lactic acid buildup, and his heart thumped in his chest, this strong, steady rhythm that he still couldn't get used to.

Before, when he'd been this out of breath, his lips and the skin under his fingernails would turn a faint shade of blue. But beneath the chipped paint on his fingernails now, his nail beds were a rosy, healthy, beautiful pink.

Foster, of course, was hardly breathing hard, because he carried that same perfection from other aspects of his life into his physical fitness as well. Foster sucked on the tube of his hydration bladder, then shucked the pack and started digging food out of the zippered pockets. Milo did the same.

They pulled off their shirts and sat on them. Milo eased closer and closer to the edge of a rocky outcropping, until his feet dangled over the drop-off. A hundred or more feet below, a trail wound down toward the ocean.

"What the hell are you doing?" Foster asked. "You're terrified of heights."

Milo waited for that all too familiar roll in his stomach and the nausea to hit, but it didn't happen. His heartrate picked up, but not from fear—from exhilaration. "I'm okay. Come over here. The view is killer."

Foster crab-walked until he sat beside Milo.

"Breathe," Milo said. "You're not going to fall."

Foster shook his head. "I don't get you. First, a beefy guy turns your head, and now, you're inches from a drop-off that's scary as hell. And I'm not afraid of heights. Who are you, and what have you done with my friend?"

Milo shrugged. It's not that he hadn't noticed some of the subtle changes, but... "That's what people do, right? They grow out of childhood fears. Their taste in men changes. *They* change?"

"I don't know." Foster eyed Milo as if he expected him to pull off his human mask and reveal the alien lurking beneath.

They'd been best friends forever, but they hadn't spent every day together since they'd left high school and gone their separate ways. Milo supposed that even though they'd visited each other and kept in contact by phone, text, and Facetime, many of his more subtle changes probably hadn't showed.

"You've changed, too," Milo pointed out as he opened his snacks, not wanting the focus on himself. "You and your fancy clothes, your sporty car, your—"

"If my parents had had the cash when I was in high school, I would have had the designer clothes and the flashy car back then. I'm lucky that my job pays well enough for me to afford those things. But deep down, I'm the same person."

Milo didn't like to think that Foster had a point. "So am I."

Foster nodded, but it didn't give Milo great confidence that Foster believed him.

Far below, hikers made a dangerous dash across the highway to get to the beachside. Over the water, a banner trailed behind a plane advertising a popular beer.

He munched on a handful of mixed nuts as the shimmer of sweat quickly dried on his skin. The wind whipping up from sea level buffeted them, but the cool breeze felt refreshing on a late summer day that was turning out hotter than expected.

They sat in companionable silence for a while, taking in the sights and sounds as the seagulls cried out overhead. Milo ripped off a piece of beef jerky with his teeth and chewed as a hawk flew overhead, circling on the hot air currents.

He felt Foster's eyes on him. When Milo turned his attention toward his friend, Foster said, "What's that on your ribs?"

Self-conscious, Milo slapped a hand over his left side. "Nothing."

"I'm calling bullshit. If you don't tell me, I'm going to keep asking, so you might as well get it over with now."

"*Fiiine.*" Milo raised his left arm over his head to showcase the tattoo on his ribs. And when people warn you that having a tattoo over your ribs hurts like a bitch, you'd best believe them.

Foster leaned in closer and ran his finger down the length of the tattoo, as if touching it would bring clarification. "I don't get it."

"It's a tattoo. You know, body art. What's there to get?" Maybe if he sounded casual enough, Foster wouldn't ask too many questions.

"I get the tattoo. I don't get why you would get a tattoo of a skydiver. You're afraid of heights. At least you were."

"It's not a skydiver. It's an umbrella."

"Oh. Yeah. Right." Foster nodded as he rolled his eyes. "I totally get that."

"You're such a dick."

Foster grinned. He had one of those smiles that made you want to be his friend so you could watch the way it lit up his face. It made you want to smile along with him even if you weren't in the mood to smile. "Explain it to me then."

"Explain to you why you're such a dick?" Milo asked. "I mean, I could, but it would take so long that it would get dark and we'd have to hike back without flashlights and—"

Foster stared at him over the top of his sunglasses.

"Okay. Okay." He hadn't had the tattoo for long. No one had asked about it before, so he hadn't had to explain. "When I woke up from surgery, I'd had this dream. I couldn't really remember it, but there was this umbrella, and I sketched it out on my tablet."

"I remember the tablet. You took it everywhere."

"It helped me pass the time. Waiting rooms. Hospital rooms. They're the worst. Anyway, I could never get that image out of my head. I thought it must mean something important. I got it tattooed on my side so I wouldn't forget."

"But you don't know what it means?"

Milo shrugged.

"Maybe it's protection from the storms life throws at you?"

It was as good of an explanation as anything Milo had come up with. "Maybe."

"You about ready to head back?"

"Sure." Milo started packing away his trash and stood.

Foster did the same, then hitched his thumb over his shoulder. "I'm gonna take a piss."

Milo glanced around. For a popular hiking trail, it hadn't been that busy, and he couldn't see anyone coming from either direction. With the low scrub brush, the area was wide open. Foster jogged down the trail where it dipped a bit and offered a modicum of privacy if someone popped over one of the rises.

Milo shouldered his pack and stepped to the very edge of the outcropping of rock, the toes of his hiking boots even with the edge. He held his arms straight out to his sides and let his head fall back. The wind rushing up buffeted his body, making him feel like if he jumped, he could fly.

Far below, the waves rolled in, and in the distance, he heard the buzz of a small plane engine. Planes had flown all up and down the coastline while they hiked, like a swarm of mechanical dragonflies, and he'd paid them no mind.

"Time to fly," Milo said to no one.

One second, Milo stood on the edge of the drop-off, and the

next, he lay on his back on top of Foster, the hard landing knocking the wind out of him.

He coughed and sputtered and rolled onto his back on the rocky ground. It took him a minute to catch his breath. When he had, he said, "What the actual fuck, Foss?"

Foster pressed the heels of his hands into his eye sockets, then lifted them away. "I thought you were going to jump."

"What? Why would you think that?"

"*Why?*" Foster's tone reached a high pitch that any drag queen would be proud of. "I come back from taking a piss, and there you were standing on the edge, your arms outstretched as if you thought you were Superman. And then you said that thing about flying and fuck, man, I thought you were going over and I—"

"I'm sorry. I get it. I—" The red that rimmed Foster's eyes stole Milo's breath again. Milo had frightened the crap out of him. "I'm not suicidal. I wasn't going to jump. I'm sorry if I scared you."

"*Scared* doesn't even begin to describe it. I was knee-knocking, heart-plummeting, breath-stealing *terrified.*"

Milo rolled onto his back as a plane flew by overhead, its rear door open and a guy dangling his legs over the side. If anyone looked like they were about to jump...

The man dropped something out of the plane one by one, and Milo watched as the objects bobbed and weaved on the currents. One of them caught a downdraft and floated his way. He glanced over at Foster, but he had his arm thrown over his eyes and a hand over his stomach as if he were trying to keep from heaving.

Milo rolled to his feet.

"Where're you going?" Foster asked.

"Nowhere."

He walked down the trail a little bit to intercept the object.

He shielded his eyes from the sun and caught it before it landed. He turned it over in his hand.

Footsteps came up behind Milo, and Foster looked over his shoulder. "What is it?"

"It's a parachute man."

3

MILO SAT AT THE KITCHEN TABLE EARLY MONDAY MORNING IN nothing but a pair of ratty sweatpants he couldn't bear throwing away. He had his tablet open to a local job-hunting website. After sifting through job after job, realizing he wasn't qualified for anything that paid more than minimum wage, he stopped looking. He clicked off the page of entry-level jobs he'd planned on applying to and opened his drawing app.

He drew more of the same images that he'd drawn ever since that morning he'd woken up from his transplant surgery. The urge to draw and make sense of his dreams was strong. Seven years later, none of it made any sense.

Foster walked in, heading straight for the coffee pot and his supersize travel mug. For a computer geek at a startup that had begun making a name for itself, Foster didn't look the part. With his carefully gelled hair, his designer button-up shirts and dress slacks, he looked like he should be one of those slick motivational speakers who promised to help you get your life on track.

He leaned against the counter, crossing his legs at the ankles, and taking a sip of the black coffee. Foster didn't like his caffeine diluted. Milo was surprised he didn't chew on the coffee beans and skip the whole water part.

"What are you doing up so early?"

Milo glanced up from his sketch. "Looking for a job. I wasn't kidding when I said I only planned on staying here for a short time. I don't want to overstay my welcome."

"As long as you'll clear out on the nights I want to bring someone home, you can stay as long as you like. I enjoy having you here. The two musketeers back together again."

Milo chuckled. "I feel more like Robin Hood. Stealing from the rich to—"

"I'm not rich," Foster said, "and you're not a mooch. You're going to find a job, and if you don't, if you want to go back to school, I can find a two-bedroom apartment, and I can help you out until—"

"You're not my mom or dad. And college definitely isn't for me."

"You're too smart to waste your talents at a dead-end job."

Milo bobbed his head toward his tablet. "According to JobSearch's questionnaire, I have no marketable talents." He glanced down at the doodles of clouds and fan blades on the screen. "I don't think this chicken scratch counts."

Foster pulled a business card out of his pocket and set it on the table, his hand over the top of it as he braced both hands on the solid wood surface. "Don't be mad," Foster said, but he didn't give Milo a chance to respond before he continued, "but I made you an appointment today. It's at two. The consult is free."

Now Foster really had Milo worried. Was it for a shrink? He didn't need a mental health consult. He just needed to figure a few things out.

"I appreciate that, but..." Not only did he not need a shrink, he also couldn't afford to pay for one if he did. And no, running to mom and dad for money wasn't an option. They already paid for his health insurance.

"It's not for a psychologist if that's what you think."

Milo sat back, the wash of relief unexpected. "Then what's it for?"

Foster straightened and slid the business card over to him with one finger. "It's a local PI. He helped a buddy at work find his adoptive parents." Foster shrugged. "If he found them, he might be able to find your donor."

Milo's mouth worked, but no sound came out, probably because his lungs forgot how to perform a basic, life-saving function. They kicked back in as black spots started forming in his peripheral vision.

He had to draw in a couple of breaths before he could speak. "I'd never thought about that. Do you really think he could find out who it was?"

"Dunno," Foster said with another fortifying swig of his coffee. "But don't you think it's worth a try?"

Milo didn't want to show how tempted he was. He pushed the card back. "If the family wanted contact with me, they would have answered my cards by now. Besides, I don't have that kind of money."

"It won't hurt to go for a consult. He may not even be able to help. And nothing says you have to contact the family. You can know who your donor was without doing that. And if you need to borrow a little bit of money, buddy, I'm here for you. Whatever answers you're looking for, I want to help. Go. Please."

For the second time in as many days, Foster had brought Milo to the brink of tears. He cleared his throat before he spoke. "Yeah. Okay. Thanks."

Foster clapped him on the shoulder as he went by. "I might have to work late, so don't wait up, honey."

Milo laughed. "Fuck you."

"And call me after the consult. I want to know what he says."

Milo didn't know what he'd expected from a private investigation firm, but it wasn't the tiny brick building he'd walked up to. If it had room for more than one office, he'd be shocked. The building stood on a corner of two streets with a hair salon one building over and some sort of small manufacturing company on the other side of the four-slot parking lot.

A sleek black Mercedes AMG Roadster sat parked in one of the slots.

Luckily, the bus stop hadn't been too far, and he'd only had to transfer once, so he wasn't a sweaty mess by the time he got there.

Ten minutes early, he opened the door, expecting a waiting area and a receptionist, only to find he'd walked straight into the man's office. Milo pulled up short. Maybe he was in the wrong place.

But the man behind the desk motioned him inside and offered a quick, calming smile as he talked on the phone. Milo tried hard not to listen in, but it wasn't easy. Something about if the person needed a PI to hack into a database, he wasn't the right man for the job.

The man quickly finished up the call and stood, reaching his hand across the desk. "Derek Watts," the man said.

"Milo Malone."

"Have a seat. What can I do for you? Your friend didn't give me many details when he set up the appointment last week."

"I don't know if you can help me, or even if I can afford your fee." Milo glanced around the office, the desk and file cabinets came from a high-end office supply store, and despite the small size of the building, the floors were solid wood. Next to a door that Milo assumed was the restroom was a kitchenette with a sink, coffee maker, microwave, and a mini fridge beneath the counter. The leather couch on the wall opposite the door where Milo had entered had a bed pillow against one armrest. Maybe the man camped out at the office on occasion. "I'm thinking I'll be wasting your time."

Milo started to get up, but Derek shook his head. "The consult is for thirty minutes. Why don't we spend that time seeing if we're a good fit?"

That Derek hadn't taken one look at him in his jeans and clean, but older, T-shirt and not kicked him immediately out said something about the man. Milo had already spent the bus fare getting there, so he might as well follow through and see what his options were.

"I'm looking for someone."

"Most people who contact me are."

"The person I'm looking for is dead."

That got a raised brow out of Derek. Milo could see his interest spark. "Go on."

"I had a heart transplant seven years ago. I want to find out who my donor was."

Derek's eyes didn't drop to the center of Milo's chest the way a lot of peoples' eyes did after he dropped that pearl of personal information. Milo liked Derek more and more by the minute. Though for a man in his what? Early forties? In his line of business, Milo should have expected the self-control and the steady, unflappable manner.

"The transplant center won't give you the information."

It wasn't a question, but Milo answered anyway. "I can send cards and letters to the donor's family, and if they agree, we can meet. But they haven't responded to me."

"What are you hoping to get out of this? Of finding your donor or his family?"

Milo had been asking himself that from the moment he'd mailed his first card. He couldn't expect that they'd be a second family. He didn't even need that. His own family was plenty good. "This may sound stupid, but ever since the transplant, I've been at loose ends. Which is weird, because before, when my heart was failing and I had little future to look forward to, I was so focused on what I wanted to do, what I wanted to become... and now..."

Milo shrugged, not knowing how else to finish that train of thought. "It's different now is all."

"And you think finding out who your donor was will help?"

"Maybe. I don't know anymore. I can't stop thinking about them. Wondering what their life had been like. Who they loved. Who loved them. Were they a good person? Would I have liked them? Would we have been friends?" Milo fell silent, and Derek sat with him in that space, his eyes warm and steady while he waited for Milo to continue. "Most of all, I guess I wonder if I'm worthy of their gift."

That last bit came out on a breath. Something Milo had thought long and hard about but had been afraid to voice. A hollowness remained where the secret words had been hidden. Not a painful, aching void, but a lightness Milo hadn't expected.

Derek nodded, more to himself than to Milo it seemed as he absorbed his words, his truth, and sat with them.

"And if I agree to find this person. His family, perhaps. What are you planning on doing with the information?"

"I don't know." Would having a name be enough? Could he accept and respect that the family didn't want contact once he had that information? Or would he take the information and show up on some unsuspecting family member's door and ruin their day?

Or you could make their day. What about all those videos online of donor families meeting their recipients? It could be like that.

Except those families had chosen to have contact. Milo's donor's family hadn't.

"Okay," Derek said at last. "I'll take your case if you're interested."

Hope clogged Milo's throat, and he had to swallow it down before he could speak. His heartrate kicked up, and he still couldn't get used to the fact that he didn't get lightheaded anymore when his heart sped up the way it would with his old heart. "Okay. Cool. I mean, yeah. I want you to, you know, find them or what you can. I..."

"Is there a problem?"

Milo hated talking about money. Probably because he'd never had much of it. Every last cent he had to his name was balled up in the pockets of his jeans. "What are your rates?"

Milo audibly gulped when Derek told him. At least he was able to keep from laughing in the man's face. He might as well have set his rate at a thousand dollars an hour. It wouldn't have seemed any less unattainable. But if Milo found a job and saved up for a while, then maybe he could come back next year and hire him.

He stood to leave, not wanting to waste Derek's time. He should have left as soon as he'd arrived and saved them both the trouble. "Thanks for your time. If I can pull the money together, I'll give you a call."

Derek leaned back in his chair. "How much do you have?" It looked like he was as surprised by the question as Milo was.

Milo pulled out his wads of bills. A few twenties, a couple of tens, some fives, and a bunch of singles. His face heated. Derek would probably think he worked at one of the strip joints with all those ones. Which, if Milo thought anyone would pay to see him naked, he might have given stripping a try. He could have used the fast cash.

"That's all you've got?"

"Yeah." The flush crept all the way up to Milo's hairline, the flash of heat so strong he might have thought he'd lapsed into sudden menopause if he hadn't known any better. He started picking up his cash and stuffing it back into his pocket along with the change for his bus fare home. "I appreciate your time. I'll give you a call when I can swing it."

Derek reached for a one-dollar bill, flattened out the crinkles, and slipped it into his wallet. Milo cocked his head but didn't say anything.

"My retainer," Derek said. "I'll poke around in my spare time. See what I can find. If something comes up, we'll work something out for the rest of my fees."

Milo couldn't believe what he'd heard. He had to keep from sticking his finger in his ear and giving it a thorough scrubbing to make sure he'd heard Derek right. "Why? Why are you doing this?"

Derek slipped his wallet back into the back pocket of his charcoal gray slacks, a wry smile on his face. "Beats me."

Walking around his desk, Derek took a clipboard off the top of his credenza under one of the windows and pulled papers out of various folders in his file cabinet. He handed it all over to Milo along with a pen from his desk. "Fill these out. When you're done, you can tell me everything you know to get me started."

For the second time that year, Joss had Ol' Betts' engine cowling—a 1986 Cessna 182 that he and Dan had bought for their first plane—on the floor of his hangar, prepared to do more work on the engine. At this rate, his new Twin Otter would never see the inside of the hangar.

Back when they'd first purchased the Cessna, he and Dan

had emptied their bank accounts and eaten far too many ramen noodle meals before Dan had the plane running in tip-top shape for an old bird. Finally, they were able to make some money, taking people up for their skydives.

The two of them would switch off who piloted and who got to do the tandem jumps, though if they'd been keeping a tally of the logbooks year after year, Joss slowly started flying more, while Dan took more of the tandem jumps with the newbies.

Now, Joss finagled a box wrench around a nut he could feel but couldn't see. Sweat dripped down his spine and ran into his eyes. He couldn't get much leverage on the seized bolt, spending the better part of an hour trying to break it loose. He lay across part of the engine, the metal pressing uncomfortably into his gut. From one of the old hoses, hydraulic fluid leaked onto his hand.

He grunted, pushing on the wrench with all his strength. A knock came on the people door to his hangar, but he ignored it. If someone were delivering a package, they could leave it on his doorstep. He wasn't going to answer the door and have to spend another ten minutes contorting himself back into position.

The knock came again.

"It's fucking open!"

He gave the wrench one more solid shove. It gave way, the wrench came off the nut, and Joss's knuckles slammed into a sharp edge. He dropped the wrench, and it fell to the concrete below with a ringing clatter.

Cussing to himself, Joss worked his way off the engine and stood on the short scaffold, his knuckles aching as blood dripped down his fingers.

He pulled a greasy rag from his back pocket and wrapped it around his hand as a man walked through the people door.

"Um, hey," the guy said. "I'm looking for Joss Kincaid."

"That's me." Joss climbed down and offered his bloody,

bandaged, greasy right hand.

The guy—more of a kid really—stared at the offered hand and shoved his own into the front pockets of his dirty jeans. His hair looked like he'd forgotten what a comb was for, and if Joss found out he'd showered sometime in the past week, he'd be surprised.

"I'm Freddy. I called about the job." Freddy didn't seem too excited to be there. In fact, the more Freddy looked around, the more his eyes got wide, and Joss had a feeling the kid might turn on his heel and run. "Um... were you robbed or something?"

Joss glanced around the hangar at the array of Cessna parts under his plane, at the workbench with tools strewn about, at the long table where he had a pile of parachutes that still needed to be packed.

From where he stood, he could see into his office on the other side of the hangar with the mountain of paperwork sitting on his desk that needed filing.

"I haven't been robbed. I need someone to help organize and run this place. I can only do so much."

Freddy scrunched up his face. "You mean *I'd* have to clean all this up?"

This wasn't a good start. "Yes. As well as book flights, and jumps, and wash planes, and help me with maintenance and repairs, among other things."

The small step back Freddy took should have told Joss to send him on his way. He didn't have time to waste on someone who wasn't willing to work.

"And what's the pay?"

Joss told him. One and a half times minimum wage wasn't a bad deal, he didn't think, for basically a job that didn't require many skills besides a little organization and the ability to not be an asshole to clients.

Freddy didn't seem too impressed.

"Plus, a room if you need it."

"Can I see?"

Joss pointed and headed toward the room next to his office. The kid followed, his gaze continuing to sweep through the hangar. Turning on the room's light, Joss stepped back to give Freddy room to walk through.

"There's only a twin bed."

"And a dresser. And a bathroom by the storage room. But it has a shower. And you can use my kitchen if you want to cook your meals."

"What's there to do around here at night?"

That made Joss laugh. "If you're looking for nightlife, you're going to have to go back to the valley."

"I don't have a car," the kid said. Then his eyes lit, and Joss knew he'd spotted Joss's Harley sitting in the hangar. "Could I borrow that?"

"Not on your life."

Freddy deflated. If he thought he'd get his hands on Joss's baby, he was sorely mistaken.

"You interested?" Joss didn't have a lot of confidence Freddy would work out as a long-term employee, but he needed a warm body before the work swamped him.

The kid shrugged. "What have I got to lose?"

"Come with me. I'll show you how to schedule appointments."

Freddy trailed after him to Joss's office next door. Joss showed him how to log into the system and after a short training session, had Freddy schedule and cancel a few mock flights and jump trips.

Joss blew out a breath of relief. The kid caught on fast to the system, though it was fairly intuitive for even newbies to use. He handed Freddy the portable phone off his belt. "When we get a call, you answer 'Kincaid Air, how can I help you,' yeah?"

"Sure. It's not like it's rocket surgery."

Rocket surgery? Joss couldn't tell if the kid was joking or if he'd mashed two sayings together without knowing. "Right. Come with me. You can help me with the Cessna."

Joss set Freddy up on the scaffold within easy reach of all the tools so Freddy could hand them to Joss, and he wouldn't waste all his time searching for what he needed.

Joss contorted himself again, pleased to find that at least he'd managed to break the nut free when he'd rapped his knuckles. He quickly removed the bolt and stuffed it into his pocket. He held out the box wrench he'd used to Freddy and said, "I need the Phillips head screwdriver."

He stood there with his empty hand out, his body over the engine waiting for a screwdriver to land in his hand. Nothing. He waited. Still nothing. Finally, something landed in his hand, and he brought it up to the screw.

Fuck.

He pulled up and wiped his sweaty forehead on his sleeves. He handed back the driver Freddy had given him. "This is a T-20, not a Phillips."

The kid blinked at him. "Uhhh..."

Joss quickly went through the names of all the tools on the tray. "Got it?"

"Yeah, sure."

Joss scrutinized Freddy harder, waiting for a nod of affirmation, but only got a bored, blank stare. *Fuck his life.* He grabbed the Phillips head screwdriver and unscrewed a grounding wire.

The business phone rang, and Joss stopped working to listen to Freddy's end of the call. Freddy answered the way Joss had instructed. So far, so good.

Freddy didn't say anything else at first, then he said, "No, man. We don't have anything at that time. Yes, I'm sure. I'm not stupid. I saw the schedule for tomorrow. There's nothing I can do. If we're booked, we're booked. I'm sure there're plenty of other skydiving outfits you can call."

Joss struggled to worm his way off the engine before Freddy lost him business.

"No, I don't have their numbers. You've got Google, don't you?"

Joss snatched the phone out of Freddy's hand. "This is Joss Kincaid. If you give me a minute, I'll personally recheck the schedule and see what we can work out."

Joss glared at Freddy as he stepped to the ground and headed for his office. "No. It's not a problem at all."

After apologizing profusely, sweet-talking the new client on the other end of the phone, and offering a newcomer's discount, Joss scheduled the man and a couple of his friends for two days out.

When he'd finished, he thumbed through one of his apps and made some arrangements before walking back out to the Cessna—where Freddy was taking selfies with the plane's engine in the background.

Joss pulled two twenties out of his wallet, which was much more than the kid deserved for twenty minutes of 'help,' but if he never had to see Freddy again, it would be money well spent.

"Take it," Joss said.

Freddy took the money. "What's this for?"

"Call it severance." When the kid looked at him goofy, he added, "You no longer work here."

A car honked out front. The rideshare operator must have been close. "That's your ride. Get lost."

Freddy shrugged, and Joss couldn't tell if he were feigning indifference, or if indifference was his default setting. Either way, Freddy wasn't Joss's problem anymore.

But finding a decent employee was.

4

A week to the day after the first time Milo had spoken with the PI, Milo stepped back into Derek Watt's one-room office on his way to turning in a couple of job applications.

Milo had found he did much better applying for jobs face-to-face at businesses looking to hire than he did with a quick online application. He'd dressed the part in a pair of Foster's hand-me-down chinos and a periwinkle blue button-up.

Periwinkle. Foster's word, not Milo's. In Milo's world, blue was blue was blue.

The dress shoes pinched Milo's little toes, and he'd have one hell of a blister on the back of his right heel when the day was done, but if he found a job, it would be worth it. The sooner he could get off Foster's couch, the better.

Derek glanced up from the computer and stood, greeting Milo with a handshake and an expression Milo couldn't read. The morning had been unseasonably cool, and despite the walking he'd done, Milo hadn't been sweating until now.

As they both sat down, Milo swiped at the beads of sweat on his upper lip. "You said you found something?"

Derek nodded, his lips pursed in thought. "I did."

Milo's heart took flight, soaring and doing acrobats in his chest. "And?"

Derek's lips went flat, and he blew out a breath. Before Derek could speak, Milo said, "Is there a problem?"

"Not a problem, *per se*." Derek leaned his forearms on the edge of his desk and steepled his fingers. "I'm in a bad spot here."

"How so?"

"Turns out, I knew your donor. And his family. Or I guess I should say what's left of it."

That soaring feeling in Milo's chest stalled out and went into freefall. He was seconds away from finding his organ donor, but the conflicted expression on Derek's face made him wonder if Derek would tell him.

You could demand the answer.

Milo laughed to himself. Right. Like a dollar retainer gave him any kind of leverage. Then again, if Derek could find his donor, certainly another investigator could as well. Instead of pressing further, Milo stood. "I get it. You don't want me stirring up trouble for your friends. I'll—"

"Sit down." Derek left no room for argument. Milo sat. "Before I give you a name, I need some assurances from you."

"Anything."

"If you meet your donor's family, if they give any indication they don't want anything to do with you, you leave and promise not to ever contact them again. No showing up on their doorstep, no phone calls, no *cards*. Nothing." Derek leaned forward and gave him a look that Milo could only describe as the evil-eye, except instead of malice behind it, there was a deep concern for his friend's family. "Are we clear?"

Milo nodded, his heart rate restarting and leveling out. "Why are you doing this?"

"I have my reasons."

"Fair," Milo said. "I don't even know what I'm going to do with the information. Ever since the surgery, I dreamed of finding my donor, but... I never expected to find him. Or her."

"*Him*." Derek leaned back and pushed a manila file folder toward Milo. "Daniel Devine. It's all in there. His bio, etc. There's a link to his social media page. His partner has kept it alive over the years."

Milo tripped on one word. "*Partner?*"

Derek's brows drew together. "Dan was gay. That going to be a problem?"

Blowing out a huff of disbelief, Milo said, "Not at all."

"I added information about Dan's partner because one look at the social media page, and you'd be able to figure it out. His name is Joss Kincaid. He's local to the valley. He's a good man, Milo. It's taken a long time for him to come to terms with Dan's death, so don't go marching into his world and screw everything up."

"I don't want to do that." Milo took the folder and stood. "How much do I owe you? I haven't found a job yet, but I'm looking really hard and—"

"Keep your promise to me, and I'll call us even."

"Th-Thank you."

Derek nodded, and Milo made his way to the door. The information in the file burning a hole in his hand. He couldn't wait to dive into the information, but he didn't want to be rude and do it in Derek's office.

Plus, a silly part of Milo worried that Derek would change his mind about giving up the information and snatch the file out of his hands.

At the door, Derek called out, "And Milo?"

Milo turned, his hand on the knob, the folder gripped tightly in his hand. If Derek came around the desk to take it back, he'd have a tug-of-war on his hands. Not that Milo stood a chance in hell of winning. "Yeah?"

"Don't fuck with Kincaid's emotions."

"Got it." Milo turned to leave again and turned back, chancing one more question. "Dan. What kind of man was he?"

The question knocked Derek back in his chair. "The best kind."

Outside Derek's office, Milo glanced at the Notes app on his phone and plugged in the address to the next location he'd planned on applying for a job.

A ten-minute walk.

He lowered his sunglasses as the building heat rose off the pavement under the high noon sun.

Milo didn't make it to the next place of business. In fact, he only made it as far as the closest burger joint. It was lunchtime. His stomach grumbled. He could eat and glance at the file, and then he'd continue his job hunt.

He placed his order at the counter and tapped his toe while he waited. When his number came up, he filled his cup to the brim with cola and settled into a two-seater table tucked into a corner. The buzz and hum of a busy restaurant faded away as he tucked into his food and lost himself in the information Derek had provided.

Two hours later, with his cup empty and his bladder over-full, a notification popped up on Milo's phone. He was out of data.

Fuck.

He'd poured through Dan's social media page. Read all the comments. All the anecdotes friends had left as a memorial. He felt like he'd known Dan all his life, yet there was still more to learn. He dug his remaining cash out of his pocket, having taken the time the night before to organize it, so it didn't come out in his hand in a messy wad.

Counting the bills, he counted sixty bucks and some change. If he bought more data, he'd be nearly out of money. Without a job, what money he had needed to last. Hell, he shouldn't have even spent what little he had on the meal since Foster had food back at his apartment.

He walked past a cellular store on his way to put in his next application, but the overwhelming need to find out everything he could about Dan Devine almost had him saying fuck it and pulling open the door to the cellular store. One of the buses that would take him within a mile of Foster's place pulled up at the stop on the street ahead. Within forty minutes, he could be back at Foster's and get on his tablet and continue his deep dive into Dan's life.

Milo hopped on the bus. He could always come back and put in the applications tomorrow. What difference would a day make?

It wasn't lunchtime anymore, but the traffic in the valley didn't know that. The bus inched along and stopped, waiting for the light to change. Milo read the name above the cemetery off to his right. The light changed, and the bus's brakes squeaked as the driver lifted his foot.

"Stop!" Milo shot out of his seat and ran to the front of the bus. "I've got to get off here. Please."

The bus driver didn't give him an earful about not being at a designated stop, probably because he had about five seconds before the traffic in front of him moved enough for him to start forward. The man opened the door, and Milo hopped out.

He walked through the wrought-iron gates of the Valley View cemetery and opened the map to Dan's grave that Derek had provided.

At the back of the cemetery, under a massive old Mimosa tree, was Dan's plot overlooking the valley and the San Gabriel mountains in the distance. A fresh bunch of flowers sat in a vase at the base of the headstone.

Milo sank to the ground, not caring that he might get his borrowed pants dirty or scuff the polish on Foster's too-tight shoes. He sat cross-legged and plucked at some of the lush grass at the foot of the grave.

"Hey, Dan... it's me," Milo said at last when he felt certain his voice wouldn't shake. Though he didn't know why he cared. There wasn't anyone around to overhear. "I guess you and I need to talk."

It was a week and a day since Joss had told Freddy to get lost. And a week and a day since he'd wondered if maybe he'd been too rash.

Freshly back from his morning hop with a group of experienced skydivers from a local club, Joss had quickly changed clothes as soon as they'd left and started working out with his weights. If he wanted to get more things done, he'd need to utilize every bit of downtime to get the important things done.

And to a guy like Joss, getting his workout in was one of them. With the weights or jogging the airstrip, he could let his mind blank for forty minutes, an hour maybe, and only focus on the pain in his muscles and, for a few brief moments, forget about the pain in his heart.

After seven years, the pain of losing Dan wasn't as fresh or as sharp. He could even talk about Dan to their mutual friends and enjoy the old stories without falling apart all over again.

Mostly.

But every time the anniversary of Dan's death rolled around, it ripped that scab open all over again. A raw open sore that festered instead of healed.

He had the front and rear doors of the hangar open to allow the breeze through while he worked out. He stood shirtless at the lat machine on his universal gym, sweat pouring down his body as he counted down the last of his reps.

A car pulled up out front, and Joss dropped the bar and wiped his face with a hand towel. A guy got out and said something to the driver before the driver backed up and left the way he'd come.

Huh. It wasn't one of his scheduled flights. He didn't have another flight until the next day. He wasn't expecting anyone else, except a guy who'd applied for the job, but Joss hadn't expected him for another couple of days.

With his hands on either end of the towel he had around his neck, Joss leaned a shoulder against the open hangar door and caught his breath as the man approached.

Joss's heart tripped mid-beat, and that breath he tried to catch ran away again.

"I'm—"

"You're—" beautiful was the first word that came to Joss's mind. He shook that thought free, ignored his near-instant semi, and held out his hand. "You're Tim McIntyre."

"Umm..."

"Funny, you don't look like a Tim." Joss grinned. Joss never grinned. Not like a love-sick puppy, at least. But damn if his muscles refused to listen. "I wasn't expecting you for a few more days."

"Yeah, well, I decided to come early?"

That Tim's response had come out sounding like a question wasn't lost on Joss, but he was too busy giving Tim the once over without trying to look like he was checking him out. *Fuck*. He'd never get anything done if his new employee looked like that.

Thin, but with an athletic build. A mop of dark hair on his head that he had to brush off his forehead. A pair of mesmerizing eyes that looked innocent yet smart and determined at the same time. A killer combination.

And the chipped black paint on Tim's nails... gay or goth?

Or Tim could be a guy who didn't give a shit what society thought and did what the hell he wanted. Joss could appreciate that, too.

But still...

Please be straight. Please be straight.

No one has given you a hard-on the way this guy has in a long time. Maybe it wouldn't be so bad if he were gay...or bi.

No. He was not banging a potential employee, no matter how much the guy tripped his levers.

Besides, Tim looked way too young for Joss.

He'd have to keep it in his pants, but if it meant Joss had a decent employee, he could manage that.

"You arriving early works," Joss said. "Follow me. I'll show you around the place."

Joss took Tim around the hangar, showing off the work he was doing on the Cessna only because the guy's eyes were wide with wonderment instead of the bored, zoned-out expression on Freddy's face the week before.

The hangar wasn't in any better shape than it had been then, but that didn't seem to deter Tim.

"You're saying if I took the job, I'd have to organize your equipment and..." Tim stuck his head into the office, his assessing gaze immediately landing on the pile of paperwork on Joss's desk.

Joss hated filing with the fiery passion of a thousand suns. He'd rather scrub his Twin Otter with a toothbrush than file papers.

"...file all the paperwork, I'm guessing," Tim said.

Tim had a sweet smile, one that only the hardest of hearts could resist smiling back at. Even as damaged as Joss's was, he wasn't immune. "That's my least favorite job around here. To be fair, I know exactly where everything important is in that stack, but yeah, I need a better filing system than vertical."

"Sounds easy enough." Tim stepped into the office with none of Freddy's trepidation and sat at the computer. "May I?"

Joss leaned over and logged him in, as well as logging the scent of Tim's cologne. It was clean and subtle. Maybe he wasn't wearing cologne at all. Maybe that was how he smelled...

"I use the WorkWise scheduling system," Joss said, "it—"

"No. This is cool." Tim flipped through the application, from scheduling to payment to his regular client database. "It's really similar to one I've used before. The interface was probably designed by the same company."

The phone on the desk rang, and Tim glanced up at Joss. Joss gave him a nod. Let's see how the hot shot handled a customer call.

"Kincaid Air, this is Mi—*Tim* speaking, how can I help you?"

The little slip-up should have tripped the hairs on the back of Joss's neck, but the adept way Tim handled the call, going through each of the questions on the list in the program required to schedule a flight or jump like a pro, had Joss pushing any potential reservations aside.

"I'm sorry we couldn't get you in this week, but..." Tim glanced at the weather app Joss always had open on his desktop. "...the weather report for next week looks amazing. You'll have a great day skydiving, I'm sure."

When Tim hung up the phone and beamed that self-assured smile at him, Joss's heart stalled.

Fuck. He should turn this guy down for the job. Having him around would be *waaay* too dangerous.

Don't be a fucking idiot. Good help is hard to find. Especially help who doesn't run when seeing the work ahead of him and can handle calls like a seasoned professional.

And seriously, someone who didn't answer the phone with a gruff 'Kincaid Air' as if the person on the line was interrupting, could only help business.

"Nice job."

"Thanks."

Whatever lightness Tim's smile had given him, Joss's next thought stole it away. If Tim didn't run when he saw his accommodations, it would be a minor miracle.

"Do I get the job?'

Joss harrumphed. "Wait until you see your room before you make any rash decisions."

Joss took him next door to the room Joss had been surprised Freddy hadn't spat on. He turned on the light and stepped into the room. With him in there, there wasn't much room for Tim to walk around.

"This is for me?" There only seemed to be amazement in Tim's voice, not disgust.

"If you want it. If you have your own place, that's fine, but some mornings start super early, and other days run long. We are a little way from the valley, so it's here if you want it."

"Oh, I want it." Tim sat on the bed and bounced, then lay back, testing the mattress. "Comfy."

Joss averted his eyes. He did not need the image of Tim's lithe body laid out on a mattress cementing itself into his head.

Joss turned toward the door as if to leave, well aware that his athletic shorts would do nothing to hide his growing erection.

Maybe he just needed to jack off more. He'd been so busy lately that his sex life, limited as it had been, had taken a back seat to the business.

Tim followed him out, and Joss walked over to the workbench to hide his semi. No sense scaring the guy off on the first day.

He told Tim the pay and said, "It won't be a nine-to-five gig.

The hours will be long. But I think with overtime the pay is fair. You interested in the job?

Joss's heart hammered in his chest as if he were the one who had the most to lose if Tim said no.

"Yeah," Tim said. "I'm interested. When do I start?"

"Now if it suits you. Tomorrow if you need the extra time."

"Now's good."

Joss blew out a breath, his heart settling back down into a normal rhythm. He plucked one of the phone receivers off the charger on the pegboard above the workbench and handed it to Tim. "Keep that with you, so you don't have to keep running across the hangar to answer calls. There's a headset in the office you can use if that would make things easier. There's also another computer terminal on the other side of the hangar, so if someone needs an appointment, you can use whichever one is closer."

Tim tucked the phone holder onto his belt. "Where do you want me to start?"

Joss led him to the storage room where it looked like it had been ransacked by the DEA on a drug bust. He gave Tim the dustpan and broom and told him how he wanted the room organized. If the kid didn't resurface in a day or so, he'd call in a rescue.

"Thanks again for the opportunity," Tim said, his hand out to shake Joss's. "You won't be sorry."

5

MILO SET TO WORK ORGANIZING AND CLEANING THE STORAGE ROOM to Joss's specifications. His accelerated heartrate and the sweat dripping down his spine had little to do with how stuffy the storage area was and everything to do with the fact that he'd lied his way into a job.

As Milo had suspected, Joss had never opened his cards. If he'd had, he would have recognized him in an instant from the photos he'd included and not mistaken him for the mysterious Tim McIntyre.

How long did he have before Joss found him out? What was he going to do when the real Tim showed up? What then?

You can kiss this job and your new room goodbye, that's what you can do.

That's if Joss flat out doesn't kill you first.

It had taken everything Milo had not to stare at Joss's ass as he showed him around the hangar. And that chest. And those muscular thighs.

And don't forget those biceps that could probably squeeze the life out of him in ten seconds flat.

What the hell are you doing, Milo? You promised Derek you

wouldn't fuck with Joss. And you promised yourself you would introduce yourself and be ready to turn around and leave if Joss didn't want anything to do with you.

And you'd promised Dan.

You sat there on that cemetery lawn, and you gave a dead man your word.

What you weren't supposed to do was assume someone else's identity and their job.

Fuckity fuck fuck fuck.

You are so screwed.

By the time Milo got the shelves organized, the trash thrown out, and the floors swept, his feet were killing him.

He still wore the interview clothes that he'd borrowed from Foster. The dress shoes had that thin leather with zero cushion.

He might be crippled for life. In fact—

"*Hey.*"

Milo jumped and turned to find Joss standing in the doorway.

"I was calling you."

Milo held in his eye roll. Fuck. He'd heard Joss calling 'Tim,' but since that wasn't his name, it hadn't clicked. Damn. He was going to mess this up the first day.

"Sorry. What did you need?"

"I said it's time to quit for the day. I've got a couple of jumps tomorrow, and we might as well take the time to knock off at a reasonable hour while we have the chance."

Milo hung up the broom and dusted the dirt off Foster's nice clothes.

"In the future," Joss said, "nice shorts or jeans and a Kincaid Air T-shirt will do fine." Joss tossed him a couple of T-shirts with the Kincaid Air logo on the left breast and his skydiving logo on the back. "I'd hate for you to ruin your good clothes."

"Okay. Is it all right if I bring my stuff back later tonight?" If

Milo timed it right, Foster might be able to bring him back before he went to bed. As it was, he'd be late getting to the apartment. He'd spent all but his last seven dollars on a rideshare to take him to Joss's, not wanting to show up sweaty and unkempt to meet Joss for the first time.

But the walk back to the valley and the closest bus stop could take an hour or more.

"Tonight's fine."

They stared at each other awkwardly, Milo wanting to say more, but didn't know what.

You could ask him to sit on your face. Maybe if you said pretty please, he'd be more inclined.

He'd stalked his donor's—*Dan's*—social media page. Dan had been so handsome and built like an elite athlete.

No way would Joss ever be interested in Milo.

Milo snorted out a laugh, except it was external, not internal. Fuck.

"What's so funny?"

"Nothing. I'll put these shirts in my room and see you later."

Milo left the hangar with a sick feeling in his stomach. This ruse wouldn't work for long. He should come clean. As soon as Joss asked him to fill out a W-9, the truth would come out. That he hadn't asked already was a damn miracle.

But he also couldn't pass on this opportunity to get to know the man who Dan had loved. To maybe find out more about Dan, without Joss being too guarded thinking Milo wanted more than to know the man who'd given him a new lease on life.

But he knew no matter how careful he was, his deception was bound to come back and bite him on the ass.

***

"*HEY!*" JOSS CALLED OUT RIGHT BEFORE TIM DISAPPEARED AROUND the corner in the road at the end of Kincaid Air's driveway. Tim turned around. "What the hell are you doing?"

"Going home," Tim hollered back.

On fucking foot? Not only was it a long damn walk back to the valley, on a windy road with no shoulder it could be deadly.

Joss waved him back. As Tim approached, the setting sun was at the man's back and shined around his hair like a damn halo. Joss laughed to himself. Tim seemed like a good guy, but an angel was probably stretching it, no matter how good he smelled.

Maybe, but I bet if he wrapped those lips around your cock, you'd call out God's name and hear the angels sing.

"Give me a minute to change, and I'll give you a ride to wherever you need to go."

"It's okay, the bus stop isn't that far and—"

"Don't argue." The words come out harsher than Joss had intended, but it was not a good enough excuse that his nerves and temper had been riding a knife's edge in the time leading up and right after the anniversary of Dan's death. This time of year always made him short-tempered and quick to lash out at people. It wasn't something Joss was proud of, but he hadn't managed to find a way to mitigate it yet.

Tim swallowed hard and snapped back a quick and obedient, "Yes, sir."

What Joss wanted to do was lean toward him and, in a deep, sultry voice say, 'say that again.'

Instead, he did an immediate about-turn toward his apartment in the hangar. *'Yes, sir.' Fuck if the kid knew what those snapped-out words did to him.*

The semi he'd sported since Tim had walked through the hangar's doors was a situation Joss couldn't quite understand. He wasn't a stranger to basic needs, but sex hadn't been his focus for so long that his body's response had taken him by surprise.

Hell, it wasn't like he hadn't been around any sexy men since Dan had died, and he'd hooked up with his fair share of them as the need arose, but this seemed... different somehow.

And the urge to jack off hit hard.

He walked into his apartment and left the door open for Tim. "Make yourself comfortable," he said as he walked past the den, the kitchen, and down the back hall to his bedroom. Closing the door, he stripped and jumped into the shower for a quick, cold wash. Maybe that would cool the heat in his belly and alleviate the heaviness in his balls.

But the shower did nothing to help, and Joss had to tuck himself into a pair of jeans that didn't quite have enough room for him while he was half-hard.

He had nothing against taking himself in his hand and relieving some of the pressure, but he didn't have the time, and it felt wrong doing it with his new, possibly straight, employee on his mind.

In less than ten minutes, Joss came back out of his bedroom, his motorcycle boots clomping on the stained concrete floors to find Tim standing in front of the wall of pictures behind his kitchen table.

"What are you doing?" Joss barked.

Tim jumped—even though technically he hadn't been doing anything wrong—and slunk away from the wall, his eyes big and doughy, the way a puppy's might be after eating the corner of the couch.

Tim put his hands up as if fending off an impending attack. "I was only looking."

Fuck, Joss had sounded like an asshole. The wall was covered in pictures of him and Dan. Their flights and jumps and adventures. To Joss, it seemed as if it were a private memorial. For *his* eyes only.

But it's in a public part of your house. A public part that you invited Tim into. It's not like he'd pulled a photo album out from the bottom of the bookshelf and started thumbing through the pictures.

Just because you can count on one hand the number of people you've had in this space since Dan died, isn't anybody's fault but your own.

Joss took a mental step back.

"Sorry," Tim said. "It won't happen again."

"Look..." Joss closed his eyes a moment to collect himself, when he opened them again, the vulnerability on Tim's face nearly undid him. "That wall represents some of the best moments in my life, and sometimes I forget that sharing that with others isn't going to take those special moments away from me."

From Tim's confused expression, those words raised a lot more questions than they answered, but Joss wasn't getting into any of that with someone he'd known for only a few hours.

Instead of asking questions, Tim said, "Fair enough. I can still walk to the bus stop. It's not too late if you'd rather not—"

"What's the matter," Joss said as he swiped his Harley keys off the island in the kitchen. "You scared of the bike?"

He hadn't meant it as a challenge, but it came out like one.

And seriously, Joss knew he could be an asshole sometimes, but today he was in rare form.

Tim raised his chin. "No."

He didn't sound convincing, but Joss took him at his word. Joss could have driven him down to the valley in Dan's old Jeep, but he only drove that on the rare occasion that the weather was too shitty to ride. Luckily, he lived in a place like Southern California and not Juno, Alaska.

Joss plucked his spare helmet off the kitchen island where it seemed to live despite having a place for it in the hangar and handed it to Tim.

Tim followed him out, putting on the helmet. He waited by the bike until Joss threw his leg over and got it started.

Joss blipped the throttle when it wanted to die and motioned with his head toward the tiny seat behind him. Good thing the guy was small. He'd heard from enough people that the seat was hard on the ass.

Tim kicked the rear pegs down and climbed on, acting as if he had no idea where to put his hands. Tim sat far back on the seat, and he'd likely fall off the first time Joss accelerated.

Joss lifted his visor and raised his voice to be heard over the rumble and chug of his engine. "Get closer and put your arms around my waist if you don't want to be dumped on the road."

Tim scooted closer, his thighs bracketing Joss's and his arms going around his body, his hands linking an inch above Joss's junk.

Fuck. Maybe he hadn't thought this thing through. But if he wanted to use the Jeep, he'd have to take off the cover and pray the battery hadn't died, or the power steering hadn't run out of fluid, or that the bald tires had enough tread not to blow the minute he took a turn sharply.

You could fix all that with one day of work.

If he had the time.

And *if* he could spend hours working on Dan's Jeep without breaking down and crying like a fucking baby.

You know it's all right to have emotions? You're, like, human. Don't pretend you aren't.

Fuck, if he didn't know that. If he weren't human, there wouldn't be a fucking hole in his chest where Dan used to be.

Tim lifted his visor. "Are we going?"

"We're going. Don't get your panties in a twist."

"More like jockstrap," Tim said.

Jockstrap? Joss walked his bike back then shifted into gear. Did Joss hear him right? Tim wore a jockstrap?

One point in the gay column.

Make that two.

One point for wearing a jockstrap under work clothes. And one point for admitting it.

You don't have to be gay to wear a jock.

No, but...

And if you want to know if he's gay, you should ask him.

Information he absolutely did not need to know. Professionally, it had no bearing on how Tim did his job, and personally... personally, it certainly didn't matter because Joss had no intention of doing anything about the stupid little infatuation he had going on.

He'd jack off later that night. Clear the pipes and be good as new come morning.

Right?

"Have you lost your fucking mind?" Foster paced his den as Milo folded the blankets on the couch. He felt bad he didn't have time to wash them before he left, but Foster didn't seem to care about the blankets right then.

Milo didn't answer right away because he was afraid the truth would come out, and he'd say 'yes.'

Really, what else would explain why he'd lied his way into a job after it became apparent Joss had been expecting someone else? And not only not come clean but kept up the ruse. And let Joss bring him back to Foster's. And then started packing up his things without stopping long enough to think about what he was doing or what would happen when Joss found out who he really was.

Because Joss *was* going to find out. Milo wasn't that good of a liar, and the guilt of his dishonesty was already gnawing at the edges of his conscience.

But he'd worked hard. And needed a job. That hadn't been a lie. Not telling Joss the truth about who he was and why he was there didn't mean they couldn't both benefit from him working there.

Clearly, Joss needed the help.

And Milo needed a job.

Win. Win.

Except for the whole deception thing.

"Are you even listening to me?" Foster had one hand in his hair, his grip tight on the strands as if he were about to pull them out in one big chunk.

"Yeah. No. I hear you. It's just…"

"There's no 'It's just,' Milo. You fucking lied to the guy. If you don't come clean now, it's going to blow up in your face."

"Maybe it won't."

Foster laughed. It sounded dismissive and lacked even the tiniest fraction of humor. "And maybe RuPaul will be your fairy godmother and make everything okay, but I wouldn't bet my life savings on it."

"At least you have a life savings. All I have is this job and seven dollars in my pocket and a whole lot of questions about a man I'll never meet but owe everything to."

"Fuck, Milo." Foster plopped into the leather chair across from him, his forearms resting on his knees. "I know you're curious about your donor, but—"

"*Dan*," Milo corrected. "His name was Dan."

"You should have stuck to your original plan of introducing yourself and seeing if Joss would talk with you."

"Too late now."

Foster leaned back as if deciding further argument was fruitless. "Did you see the size of that guy? I did. He could break you like a twig if you got him mad enough."

Milo batted his eyes and smiled his most endearing smile.

"What's that look? You look like you ate bad shrimp and need to fart, but you're sitting in front of the Queen and you can't."

Milo rolled his eyes. "That was me being adorable and un-twig breakable."

"You might want to practice that in the mirror a few times. I think it needs work."

"You only say that because you're my friend and you're immune to my charms."

"No, I say that because I'm your friend, and I don't want you getting your ass kicked."

"*Psht*," Milo waved him off. "Joss looks rough and gruff, but I'm sure there's a soft, chewy center at the core. He gave me a ride back here, didn't he?"

Foster reached down and started packing some of Milo's electronics into his backpack. "That only means he's not a complete asshole, or more likely, he's happy to have found an employee and didn't want you getting smooshed on the road before he could get a bunch of work out of you."

"See? Soft and chewy center."

Foster shook his head. "Whatever. All I can do is hand out the advice. I can't make you take it."

Milo stood and set the stack of blankets on the coffee table. "I know this must all seem nuts to you, but I've got to see this through. I can't explain it, even to myself."

Foster picked up the blankets to take back to the linen closet, and to be cautious, Milo said, "Maybe you don't want to pack them too far in the back of the closet. I could be back here in a few days if it all goes to shit."

Foster shoved the blankets onto a shelf and had to hold

them back and lean on the door before it closed. "Don't you mean *when* it goes to shit?"

"You done?"

Milo didn't mean was Foster done putting the bedding away. He meant was he done busting his balls.

"For now."

"Are you still taking me back, or do you want me to take the bus?"

"Don't be an idiot. I'm taking you."

Milo grinned and shouldered his backpack. "You want a closer look at Joss."

"I want to know if his photo on his website does him justice, or if he paid someone to airbrush all those muscles onto him."

Milo laughed, glad Foster was allowing him to shift the subject. "Trust me. I had my hands on him as we weaved in and out of traffic. Nothing on him is airbrushed. It's all real and even more impressive in person. Especially when he's all sweaty and has his shirt off."

"*Ooof*. Don't make me jealous." Foster toted Milo's duffel bag, and they headed down to his car. Milo didn't have much in the realm of worldly possessions, which was a good thing, considering the trunk of Foster's sports car could barely hold a six-pack of beer.

"Does he know you're gay?"

"It didn't come up," Milo said as Foster beeped his trunk open and they squished his belongings inside.

But something else certainly did come up during that ride. If his boss wasn't paying attention, if he hadn't already caught on that Milo was gay, Joss certainly could have figured it out when Milo had gone hard with his crotch snugged up against Joss on the ride down to the valley.

They climbed into Foster's car, the low grumble of the engine vibrated throughout Milo's body and, even for a guy who wasn't a gear head, it was hard not to appreciate the power under the hood.

As they drove, the awkward silence lingered.

Foster turned at the first traffic light. "What aren't you telling me?"

"I may or may not have popped wood while riding on the back of his motorcycle."

Foster barked out a laugh. "Are you saying you rubbed your hard-on against your boss's ass?"

"Not intentionally."

"Oh, sweet gay baby Jesus. This is going to be a disaster."

6

Joss slid onto the barstool at Sneaky Pete's, a gay bar in the valley around the corner from Derek's office. To call the bar a hole-in-the-wall would be generous.

But the dim lighting helped keep you from seeing the worst of it, allowing you to suspend your disbelief that one strong blow of the Santa Ana winds wouldn't crumple the place on top of you.

But the beer was cold, the bartenders friendly, and it was one of the few places that he'd been going to for so long that the staff remembered Dan.

Not that the subject of his partner came up often, but occasionally a story about Dan would pop into someone's head, and they'd share it with Joss. It made him feel like he wasn't the only one responsible for keeping Dan's memory alive.

Plus, as difficult as it could be, it was also nice to remember some of the good times, too, and be able to laugh about it.

Besides, it was one of the few local bars you could buy a Preacher Peach IPA, Dan's favorite beer. Joss wasn't a huge fan of the fruity taste, but the smell triggered a lot of memories, and when he wanted to feel closer to Dan, sometimes Joss ordered one.

Derek pulled up the barstool next to him about the time Joss's burger and fries arrived to sop up some of the beer in his empty belly. As big as Joss was, he was a cheap drunk. He rarely drank much because he had to keep his wits about him while driving through the valley traffic on a motorcycle.

Plus, he never had more than a beer the night before a flight. He knew the official rule was no alcohol within eight hours of flight, but he took his and his passengers' safety seriously and was extra cautious.

"Glad to see you venturing off the mountain every once in a while," Derek said as he raised a hand to catch the bartender's eye.

One of the lights behind the bar shined through Joss's glass, highlighting the slight peach hue in the beer.

"Dan?" Derek asked, knowing full well it was.

Joss moved his beer to the other side of his plate, essentially putting it out of reach for discussion. That he'd wanted to feel closer to Dan when his dick had noticed another man shouldn't be that complicated to understand, but it certainly wasn't something Joss wanted to talk about.

When Derek's beer arrived, he took a sip and twisted in his seat, his focus returning to Joss. "What's this about finally hiring a guy? You were kind of cryptic in your text."

Around a bite of burger—and Jesus, it was a good burger—Joss said, "'I hired a guy' isn't all that cryptic. I'm sure an investigator as smart as you could figure that one out."

"Don't be a dick," Derek said, though the words didn't hold any animosity. "Tell me about this guy."

"Not much to tell. He'd contacted me from one of the job sites online. Was moving here from Arizona or New Mexico or something. He seemed keen enough, and I hadn't gotten much interest, so I told him to stop by for an interview when he rolled into town. I didn't really expect him for a few more days, but there he was on my doorstep this morning."

Derek stopped, the bottle half-way to his lips. "*This* morning?" Derek had slipped back into PI mode. Joss wasn't even sure Derek knew he did that, but Joss had known Derek long enough to notice the subtle shift of his body, the slight tension in his shoulders, the focused attention to the question even as he tried to act casual.

Joss didn't think most people would notice, but to him, it was as if Derek had stood on the deck of a ship, waving a couple of semaphores, signaling danger to the other ships in the area.

"Yeah, what of it?"

"What's this guy's name?"

"Tim, something or other."

Derek finally took that sip of beer, shaking his head as he did so. "'Tim something or other?' Is that what he put on his W-9?"

"He hasn't filled out any forms yet."

"*Joss.*"

"I'll get to it before his first paycheck. Dan being gone doesn't mean you have to fill his shoes and nag me about the trivial shit."

"Proper employee documentation is not 'trivial shit.'"

Whatever. He hadn't called Derek down to the bar to give him shit about his business practices. "You want to hear about this guy or not?"

The bartender came over, and Joss waited while Derek placed his food order. For a Tuesday night, Sneaky Pete's was filling up. People crowded them at the bar, but Joss wasn't in any kind of mood to give up his seat and hunt for a table.

"Okay," Derek said, "I'm all ears."

"He's good. At least what I've seen so far. Answered the

phones without pissing customers off, and he Marie Kondo-ed my storage room in only a couple of hours."

"Sounds like a fucking miracle. Does he have a PI brother I can hire? I'm about at the point that I need to find help myself."

"Tell me about it. And I didn't ask about a brother. But fuck, if this guy can hang around long enough to get me organized, then maybe I can start advertising again and bringing in more business. Maybe look into leasing another plane, hire another pilot."

"Dan always had big plans for you guys, but don't think you have to stick with his vision. You're allowed to make Kincaid Air whatever you want it to be."

Joss put his beer down because his throat locked up and he wouldn't have been able to get even a few drops of the liquid down. He took a few breaths, and when he could speak, he said, "I want to make him proud."

Derek leaned in and gave Joss's shoulder a squeeze. "Buddy, he's already proud."

Joss huffed out a self-deprecating laugh. "You say that, but I didn't tell you the part where my dick was acting like a divining rod, and Tim was a long-lost source of water."

Derek almost spit his beer out on the burger the bartender placed in front of him. "You are *not* fucking your employee."

"Fuck, Derek, you don't think I know that? Jesus, I shouldn't have said anything. Any other time of year, when my emotions are more balanced, this never would have happened. But these past couple of weeks, my defenses have been down and—"

And what? What excuse are you going to parade in front of him? Face it, your employee turns your crank. That animal attraction has nothing to do with losing Dan.

"You know, another guy turning you on doesn't mean you loved Dan any less."

"You don't think I fucking know that?"

Anybody else would have shrunk from his outburst, but Derek didn't even flinch, he just leveled him with a steady gaze, a *do you hear yourself?* expression on his face.

"It's not like I haven't dated since Dan. And Vin and I were serious for a while before it became obvious I wasn't the one his heart was stuck on."

"But even that has been what? A couple of years ago now? More?"

Joss didn't bother calculating how much time had passed since he and Vin had broken up. It would only depress him more.

"All I'm saying is that the only thing wrong with what you felt for this guy is that you hired him to do a job, and that job isn't to *do* you."

<hr>

FOSTER TOOK THE WINDY ROAD UP TO KINCAID AIR PRACTICALLY the same way Joss had on the way down, on two wheels.

Milo white-knuckled it the whole way up, while Foster's grin spread wide over his face as his car hugged the curves. Foster pulled up in front of the hangar, Milo's seatbelt catching with the quick stop.

"Fucking hell. You trying to kill me?"

"On the contrary, I'm showing you how to live." Foster rubbed his dashboard, and the engine seemed to purr and growl under his adoring touch.

"And here you accuse me of being suicidal. I've never gripped a door handle so tight in my life."

"I was perfectly safe. This baby never crossed the center line once."

"It was hard for me to tell with the blinding light of my life flashing before my eyes."

The ride down with Joss had been as fast, and they'd leaned hard into some tight curves, but with his arms wrapped around Joss's strong body, he'd never felt unsafe.

"You coming? Or are you having second thoughts?"

Milo glanced up to find that Foster had already exited the car and had leaned back in. Milo popped his door. "I'm coming."

And definitely no second thoughts. What better way to find out more about Joss and Dan than from Joss himself? Social media could only tell you so much about a person.

Milo shouldered his backpack, and Foster retrieved his duffel and closed the trunk.

Foster glanced around. The hangar doors were closed, and there were no lights on in the apartment in the left front of the building. A lone amber security light shined above the man door to the hangar.

"Doesn't look like anyone's here," Foster said. "Are you sure he said you could come back tonight?"

"Positive." Milo tried the hangar door. Locked. Then he knocked on the apartment door. When there was no answer, he tried the knob, but it was locked too.

"We can go back to my place. I can bring you back in the morning if you don't mind being really early."

"Joss gave me his number. I'll text him. He could be close by or something." Milo pulled out his phone and texted Joss. He sat on a concrete parking block in front of the apartment and waited for Joss's response.

He didn't have to wait long. Milo read the message and said, "He's got a key for the apartment in a lockbox around the corner. We can get into the hangar from the apartment. Sounds like he's on his way back."

"We're going through his apartment?"

"Yeah. What's wrong with that?"

Milo turned the on the flashlight on his phone and walked

around the side of the building to a short fence around the air conditioning units.

"I don't know." Foster followed him to the unlocked gate. "Isn't it weird being in your donor's house alone?"

"Dan's house," Milo said, not bothering to look up. He opened the unlocked gate and found the key lockbox on the fencepost where Joss had described and punched in the code Joss had given him. "But it's Joss's apartment too, and he said it was okay, so why are you being so weird about this?"

Foster shrugged. "This whole thing is weird if you ask me. Not the part about you finding Joss, because I guess I facilitated that. But the part where you pretend to be someone you're not."

Milo retrieved the key and left Foster to follow in his footsteps as his irritation with his friend grew. Yes, it was unusual, but fuck, nothing about his life had been *usual*.

He stopped at the door to the apartment and turned to his friend. "What are you trying to say?"

Foster was quiet a moment before finally speaking. "I'm kind of wishing I hadn't stepped in to help."

For fuck's sake. He unlocked the door and flicked on the hall light. The security panel beeped, and he glanced down at Joss's text for the security code and punched it in.

When it deactivated, Milo relocked the door behind him and continued through to the den and the door that led out to the hangar.

"Are you going to say something?" Foster hurried to catch up to Milo's ground-eating pace through the apartment and hangar. "Or are you going to ignore me?"

There were enough security lights in the hangar so that he could make his way to his room without running into any of the workbenches or parts of the Cessna.

Milo stopped short, and Foster bumped into the back of him.

"If you didn't want me to find Dan, why did you send me to a PI in the first place?"

"I was trying to help, but this is crazy, Milo. What's going to happen when he finds out who you really are? What then? I saw how big this guy was. He could really hurt you."

"Joss isn't like that."

"How the fuck would you know?" Foster dropped the duffel and paced away a few steps before coming back. *"You don't know him.* Reading his website and social media pages doesn't mean anything. Everyone knows how whitewashed social media pages are. They only show the good. They rarely show the bad."

Milo picked up his duffel and started toward his room. Even though it was a complete lie, he said, "I know what I'm doing."

Foster laughed. "You keep telling yourself that. While I'm going to be the one who has to scrape your crumpled body off the floor when Joss finds out."

"When Joss finds what out?"

Milo and Foster spun on their heels to see the shadowed form of Joss walking toward them.

"For fuck's sake," Foster muttered under his breath for only Milo to hear. "He's huge."

Joss stopped and held out his hand. "Joss Kincaid, you must be the friend."

Foster whipped his hand out. "Foster Torres. Official friend and driver of Mi—"

Milo jabbed him in the ribs with his elbow.

"Of *my* Tim, here," Foster corrected.

Joss glanced between the two of them. "And what are you worried I'm going to find out?"

Unfortunately for Milo, Joss didn't have a short-term memory problem. "That I don't know much about planes or skydiving, but I keep telling Foster that I'm willing to learn."

"As long as you're willing to put in the work, we're going to do just fine. There's nothing you're going to be doing here that requires special training. Unless you want to learn to pack parachutes. Then we'll talk."

Pack parachutes? "That would be amazing."

Milo's genuine interest earned a small smile from Joss.

Joss nodded to Foster. "Nice meeting you."

"Same," Foster said.

They both stood there, feet frozen to the floor until Joss disappeared into his apartment. A light went on, and Milo saw Joss walk by the apartment window overlooking the hangar.

"That was close," Foster said.

Now that the danger had passed, Milo broke out into a cold sweat and sat down on the bed and leaned back, running his hands down his face.

"Look." Milo glanced up, and Foster held his hand out in front of him. "My hand's shaking."

Milo rubbed his sternum. "I think my sternum's bruised. My heart thumped as soon as I heard his voice. Fuck, I thought it was all over."

Foster sat down on the corner of the bed since the room wasn't big enough for a chair. "You really need to think about what you're doing here."

"Maybe you're right. I... I need a few days to figure things out. The kicker of it is, I like him."

Foster's brows rose to near his perfectly gelled hairline.

"I mean as a boss. And the job could be interesting and—"

"I'm not the one you have to convince. All I'm saying is be careful. I just got you back in my life. I don't want that to change."

"Even if it doesn't work out here, I'm not planning on going anywhere. Though that might mean you may have a mooch on your couch for the foreseeable future."

"I'm good with that. I told you, you're welcome to stay there as long as you need."

"I appreciate that." Milo sat up now that his knees weren't so weak.

Living a lie wasn't his strong suit.

"And thanks for the ride out."

"Anytime."

Milo walked Foster out through the man door of the hangar and waited for him to drive away before returning to his room.

Like Joss's apartment and office, Milo's room had a window overlooking the hangar. It didn't have a curtain, but that could be remedied later. For tonight, the room was perfect.

And being able to sleep in a bed instead of Foster's couch was an added luxury. Milo unzipped his duffel and unpacked his clothes into the dresser, even though his time there would undoubtedly be limited.

If he were going to play the part, he needed to act like a man who planned on staying.

When he finished, he stared down at the drawers. His clothes didn't even take up two of them. But having so few possessions made it easier to travel light.

He laid his tablet on the top of the dresser and plugged it in to keep it charged. He checked his phone, but since he still didn't have any money to buy data and he hadn't gotten the Wi-Fi password from Joss, he couldn't surf the internet.

But it was late. He should take a shower and go to bed. He peeled off his shirt and tossed it aside, catching movement out of the corner of his eye.

He glanced up.

"Knock, knock," Joss said as he came to his open door. Milo couldn't help but notice the way Joss's eyes scanned up Milo's torso, stopping at the long scar in the center of his chest.

Milo wanted to reach for his shirt and cover it up, but it was way too late for that.

"I um..." Joss tore his gaze away and met Milo's eyes. He held out the towels and washcloth in his hand. "I thought you might need these."

Milo walked around the end of the bed and set the towels, washcloth, bar of soap, and a sample-size shampoo bottle on top of the dresser. At least Milo had his own toothbrush and paste. "Thanks."

Instead of ignoring what caught his eye the way most people did, Joss bobbed his chin toward Milo's chest and said, "What happened there?"

Milo's hand immediately went to cover it. More of a reflex reaction than the fact that he had a problem with people seeing it.

He'd had amazing surgeons, and the scar had healed well, the redness of the fresh scar eventually fading out to white.

Now's your chance. Tell Joss the truth. Come clean. Maybe he'll kick you out. But maybe he'll listen.

But when Milo opened his mouth, the lie fell easier than the truth. "Car accident."

"Fuck," Joss said.

Milo shrugged, though he felt anything but indifferent. "It was a long time ago."

"Well," Joss said as if at a loss for words. "I'm glad you're here."

When he said it, it didn't sound like he meant 'here' to mean at the hangar, it sounded as if he meant 'here' as in this world.

Milo choked up unexpectedly, his voice gruff when he said, "Yeah. Me, too."

7

JOSS GOT OUT OF BED THE NEXT MORNING WITH A SPRING IN HIS step that he hadn't had for a long time. He chalked it up to a bright, cloudless day and having two jumps ahead of him.

Any day he had the chance to fly was a good day.

Your good mood has nothing to do with the sexy man sleeping in your spare room? A sexy man that you had a dream about and jacked off to in the shower?

Joss groaned to himself. There was nothing wrong with a little harmless masturbation. Everyone did it.

He rapped on the window to Tim's room since opening the hangar doors and flooding it with early morning light hadn't seemed to wake him.

"Coffee's on in the office," Joss said loud enough to be heard through the door. "First flight's in a couple of hours."

He headed straight out the back of the hangar where his Twin Otter and Dan's Jeep were parked. He pulled off the Jeep's cover and lowered the canvass top.

Despite the dust cover, the bright purple paint had dust all over it. Dan would have been displeased to find his baby neglected like that. Joss would have to do better.

Joss popped the latches holding down the hood and checked all the fluid levels before swinging into the driver's seat and cranking the engine.

It was slow to turn over, then it caught and coughed out a tailpipe full of dark smoke before settling out into a steady hum.

Tim walked out of the hangar, his dark hair still bed-tousled, and a sweet, sleepy look on his face. He took a sip of the coffee from the set of mismatched mugs Joss had left by the coffee pot. This one said, 'World's okayest pilot.'

"What are you doing?"

Joss climbed out and said, "Do you drive?"

Tim's eyebrows drew together. "Why wouldn't I?"

Joss's eyes flicked to Tim's chest, where that hellacious scar lay beneath his shirt. It must have been one hell of a car accident. "I wasn't sure."

"Yeah, I drive. But I can't afford my own car yet."

"Can you drive a stick?"

"Mostly."

Joss laughed. Maybe he'd need to take Tim up and down the airstrip to make sure he didn't hand over Dan's Jeep only to find out the guy would grind all the gears down to nubs.

"What did you have in mind?"

"It would be helpful if you could run errands for me if need be, and there's no fucking way I'm handing over my Harley keys."

"The Jeep works for me."

"Yeah, well, she needs a little work, but I think for short trips into town, it'll be okay. We'll have to arrange to get new tires put on before anything."

"Sounds good. What do you need me to do today?"

"I'm taking up a group of eight this morning. I need you to print off the release forms and pull together the rental equipment for three people. Everyone else has their own stuff. The checklist you'll need is in a file on the computer, along with the release forms. I'll come and double-check your work after I've refueled the Otter."

"Got it." Tim turned on his heel, and Joss lowered his aviators to watch Tim's ass as he walked away.

Fuck... *that ass.*

And in the span of three seconds, his dick acted like that jack-off session he'd had in the shower that morning had never happened.

He shoved the aviators up his nose and hopped into his fuel cart and drove over to the Otter, trying to put that fine ass, and his new employee, out of his mind.

By the time he'd made it back into the hangar after refueling the Otter and completing his external preflight, Tim had the eight release forms on individual clipboards laid out on the parachute folding table, as well as three packs along with their respective altimeters, helmets, and goggles.

He checked each of the release forms to make sure they were the current ones. And checked the parachutes and the dates they'd been packed.

Joss had been the only one packing chutes at Kincaid Air for years now, but he always checked and double-checked that everything was as it should be.

Tim came up beside him. "Everything okay, boss?"

"Looks good. Did you have any trouble finding anything?"

"Only the clipboards. They were buried under a pile of paper on your desk."

Tim's stomach growled, and he laughed. "Sorry."

"You didn't have breakfast?"

"I—well..." Tim glanced away, the red rising in his cheeks. "What?"

"I don't have any food. But it's fine. Foster is going to pick me up after work today and take me to dinner to celebrate getting the job."

No food? Joss stared at him. Then his brain kicked back in. "When was the last time you ate?"

"Yesterday."

Joss narrowed his eyes. "When yesterday?"

"I ate breakfast yesterday before I came out here."

"And nothing since?"

"Well, I hadn't expected getting hired so fast, and then I was working and then I needed to go back and get my stuff and—"

"You hungry?"

"I'm starved."

"Come on. I've got plenty of food in the kitchen."

"I can pay you back once I get paid. Or I guess you can take it out of my check."

Joss shook his head. He hadn't even thought about Tim not having any food, much less any money to buy some, or a way to get any even if he did have the money. It wasn't like there was a convenience store right around the corner.

Tim must have taken that shake of the head to mean that Joss didn't believe that he'd be paid back because Tim then said, "Or I can borrow the money from Foster, and I can give it to you tonight when he gets here."

Joss turned at his apartment door, and Tim bumped into his chest. Joss caught him with hands on his shoulders and held him at arm's length. "You're welcome to whatever I have in the kitchen. You don't have to ask. You don't have to pay me back."

Tim didn't look at him, the red only deepening on his cheeks.

Joss put a finger under his chin until those blazing blue eyes met his. The jolt of his soul-searing gaze would have knocked him back a step if his back weren't already backed against the door. "Okay?"

Tim swallowed hard. "O-Okay."

For a fraction of a second, Tim's eyes fell to Joss's lips, and fuck if Joss didn't want to bring his lips down on Tim's to steal a taste him, if only for a moment.

But Joss forced himself to let him go.

In the kitchen, Joss opened the refrigerator and searched around for options. He really could stand to hit a grocery store himself. "I've got bacon and eggs, I think I might still have bagels in the pantry, and I have some leftover pizza from a couple of nights ago. Pick your poison."

Joss took a step back so that Tim could look.

Tim flipped up the top of the pizza box. There were three slices left. "Ooh, anchovies. Come to papa." He took the box to the kitchen table and started in on the first slice.

"You want a plate for that?"

Tim shook his head, his mouth too full to speak. In the time it took Joss to walk around the island to the table, Tim had scarfed down the first slice and had started in on the second.

Joss sat even though he had a ton of things he could be doing that didn't involve watching his employee eat.

Tim turned the box around to face Joss, tucking a bite of pizza into the pocket of his cheek and said, "Want the last one?"

"Go ahead."

While Tim chewed, his eyes kept straying to the wall of photos on the wall behind Joss. He felt like a total ass having barked at Tim for looking at them the night before. His curiosity was normal, right?

"That's me and my partner, Dan," Joss said. "Kincaid Air was his idea from the start."

Tim swallowed hard. Maybe Joss should get him a drink. "You guys looked so young."

"Young, dumb, and full of cum."

Tim choked on a laugh.

"Fuck, sorry. That was a pretty inappropriate thing to say."

"It's okay," Tim said. "I promise not to report you to HR."

"Noted."

Tim finished off the third piece but left the last of the thick crust. "You two look very happy together."

"We were."

"Were?"

"He died." Joss stood. He didn't want to discuss Dan with a virtual stranger. Especially to a stranger who made him hard and think about making inappropriate advances. If Dan knew, he would—

He would tell you to get the fuck over yourself and loosen up. He'd tell you that your life isn't over even if his is. He'd tell you that you should do whatever you can to make yourself happy.

Fuck happy. Joss would settle on feeling normal again.

In the distance, Milo heard the drone of Joss's plane as he landed after the last jump of the day.

He sat at Joss's desk, attacking the biggest stack of papers on the desk first. He'd started organizing the papers in preparation for filing. Fuel receipts, airplane part orders, and a whole host of things that went along with running a business.

Stuffed way down at the bottom of the stack, Milo had found the seven cards he'd sent Joss over the years. All unopened, which confirmed what Milo had suspected.

Even the newest card was there, as if Joss had shoved them under the stack of paperwork, unable to throw them out, but wanting them to go away.

And they probably would have remained buried there if Milo hadn't come along.

After finding the unopened cards, his stomach had started

churning, and once or twice he almost had to run to the bathroom because he thought he'd throw up.

He hadn't expected it to hurt so much to find out none of them had been opened. But he guessed in some way he understood. Everyone grieved differently, and if Joss wanted it to all go away—the way him hiding them beneath the stack of papers suggested—maybe ignoring them, and Milo, had helped Joss.

Maybe letting Joss know who he was, wasn't such a good idea after all. He liked Joss. And the pay and the job weren't bad.

Who says he ever needs to find out who you really are? Even if he finds out your real name, if he never opens the cards, he'll have no way of knowing how you and Dan are connected.

He picked up the stack of cards, intending to make a file for them later and stuff them in the file cabinet with the rest of the paperwork. He'd label it clearly in case Joss ever decided he wanted to open them, but out of sight, out of mind, right?

"What are you doing with those?" Joss snatched the cards out of Milo's hand.

"I found them while organizing your paperwork. They're unopened."

"I'm aware."

Milo should have left it at that, but that part of him that always seemed to push boundaries had him asking, "Are you going to open them?"

"If I'd wanted to open them, I would have. They're not important. And they're none of your business," Joss said with a curt gruffness Milo hadn't experienced from him yet.

Milo sat back. Heart beating in his throat, he cleared it and said, "Yeah, sure."

Joss's eyes had gone dark and stormy. The kind of intense shift in weather that made you want to hunker down until the brunt of the storm passed.

Except Milo had caused that storm. "I-I could throw them away if you prefer."

The phone rang, and Joss said, "You should get that."

Anything to get out of that awkward situation was fine with Milo. He did his now usual phone greeting, not even stumbling when he used his alter-ego's name. He kept one eye on Joss and noticed instead of tossing the cards in the trash, he stuffed them in the top left drawer of the desk.

Maybe not so unimportant after all.

The ball of nausea in Milo's stomach started to settle, and after Joss left the office, he could finally concentrate on the call.

The woman was asking all sorts of questions about where Joss took them to jump and what altitude, and where they'd land and all sorts of other things that Milo had no clue.

If all she'd needed was a scheduled jump, Milo was her man, but he hadn't been there long enough to learn all the particulars.

"Ma'am, if I could put you on hold for a few minutes, I will get Joss who can answer all those questions for you."

"That would be great, thanks."

He put her on hold and went to track down Joss. He heard Joss's booming laugh coming from out front. There was a familiar car in the parking lot, and Milo froze.

If there hadn't been a call waiting on the line, he would have gone and rearranged the storage room or found some other hole to hide in, but as much as he dreaded the coming confrontation, Milo couldn't lose a client for Joss because he was a chicken shit.

Somehow, someway, he'd bluster and bullshit his way through.

Milo walked out the open hangar doors, his head ducked as he made a beeline for Joss, knowing damn good and well that Derek would recognize him.

"Hey boss," Milo said, holding out the phone, "this lady has a lot of questions I can't answer. Could you talk to her?"

Derek Watts stood beside Joss. Derek crossed his arms over his chest, a blood vessel ticking at his temple. His jaw worked side to side, and Milo hoped he could distract Joss long enough to speak to Derek before Derek ruined everything.

Maybe it should be ruined. This is a dangerous game you're playing, and you're only going to sink deeper into the lies. Like quicksand, you'll soon be in way over your head.

"Sure." Joss took the phone out of Milo's hand. To Derek, Joss said, "This is the guy I was telling you about."

Derek stuck out his hand. "You must be—"

"Tim," Milo said, "Tim..." Fuck, what was his last name supposed to be?

"*Tim* Tim?" Derek asked, an aggressive brow raised. If he were into the whole the good cop, bad cop thing, he'd definitely come off as the intimidating bad cop.

Joss chuckled at their exchange, then stepped back into the hangar to handle the call.

Derek glanced over Milo's shoulder. Joss must have been out of sight because he leaned in and growled, "What the fuck are you playing at?"

And right at that moment, with the evil-eye focused on him, every excuse Milo had been feeding himself vanished. He sputtered, trying to come up with a valid reason why he was working for Joss under an assumed name. A reason that wouldn't get him killed.

Not that he really thought Derek would physically hurt him, but the knowledge that he could made Milo's knees weak. He took a step back to reclaim some of his personal space, but mostly it was so he could lean against the exterior wall and prop himself up.

Milo snuck a quick glance over his shoulder, knowing Joss

could reappear any second. With a whisper, he said, "I'm not playing at anything. I'm working. I'm—"

"You have zero idea what you've done here. When he finds out—"

"Why does he have to find out? Maybe it's not so important that he knows who I am. I got to meet him. He thought I was someone else. I needed the job. Before I knew it, he'd hired me, and here I am not knowing what to do about it."

"What are you after?"

Milo barely stopped the verbal vomit before it got any worse. He took a calming breath. "Honestly, I don't know anymore."

"I'm going to give you a *very* short leash. You need to come clean. He's my friend, and I'm not risking our friendship over your debacle. If you don't tell him soon, I'm going to tell him for you."

"What's going on?" Joss came out of the hangar glancing between Milo and Joss. "Why do you two look like two stray dogs circling each other over a bone?"

Derek was the first to break eye contact, his smile coming easy as he slapped Milo on the shoulder as if they were best buds. "We were just coming to an understanding."

8

THE NEW TIRES FOR THE JEEP ARRIVED BY COURIER LATE THURSDAY night, so Joss was up early Friday morning, putting the new tires on the old rims and remounting them on the Jeep.

He finished tightening the last of the lug nuts with his air wrench when Tim stumbled outside barefoot, wearing a pair of threadbare sweatpants and nothing else, his bedhead untamed, a coffee mug in each hand. He looked sexy as hell, and it only had a little bit to do with the extra cup of coffee in his hands.

Joss wondered again about the scar on Tim's chest but managed not to stare this time. Besides, there were plenty of other things about Tim that caught his eye—the smattering of hair on his chest. The V arrowing down beneath his low-slung sweats. The sexy, shy smile as he squinted, the rising sun in his eyes.

"For you," Tim said, holding out a steaming mug.

Joss stood and took the coffee from his outstretched hand. "Thanks."

"Why didn't you wake me? I would have helped."

"It's all good," Joss said. "This is personal work, not work,

work. Trust me, there will be plenty of odd hours you'll have to work, don't go looking too hard for it."

Joss set his mug on the hood of the Jeep and pulled two hundred dollars out of his wallet. "Here."

"What's this for?"

"After I take my group up this morning, why don't you head into town and get us some groceries. Between the two of us, we've about run my cupboards bare."

Milo ducked his head and stuffed the bills into the pockets of his sweats. "I'm sorry about that. Foster always complained about how much I ate. It seems like I'm never full."

Joss grunted. "Sounds like someone else I knew."

Dan had been a lot like that. Joss had outweighed him by a good forty pounds, but it was always Dan finishing up his meal first at the restaurants and then starting in on Joss's.

"Well, I'd better go get cleaned up. I've got to prep for your jump. I think everyone on this one is renting equipment."

"Plenty of chutes to pack later then. I can give you a lesson tonight if you're interested. Unless you had other plans for your Friday night?"

That same sweet smile flashed again, and Joss's heart did a barrel roll. Jesus... this guy...

"No. No other plans."

"Great."

"It's a date then." Tim's eyes went wide. "I didn't mean a date, date, I meant—"

"I know what you meant." Joss smiled. "It's a figure of speech."

Though a part of him wondered what a date with Tim would be like. Would he be shy? Would he come into his own?

Before you picture him in your bed again, don't you think you should find out if he's even gay?

Though each day that had passed, Joss had about concluded

that while Tim might not be gay, he certainly wasn't entirely straight. Not with the way Joss had caught him sneaking glances while he worked out, or the way Tim's eyes drifted to Joss's junk any time he wore athletic shorts.

Joss watched him walk away, knowing he needed to tamp down on all those salacious thoughts bubbling to the surface and keep telling himself he wasn't looking for a fling.

Or even a boyfriend.

And definitely not a partner.

Been there, done that, couldn't fucking live through that kind of loss again.

What about Vin? He'd meant something. You'd even told him you loved him. Don't think you can't love again.

Can't and *won't* were two entirely different things.

Joss left the keys in the ignition for Tim to easily find later and wandered over to the fuel cart and gassed up the Otter.

Within a few hours, the skydivers had come and gone, leaving a pile of spent parachutes in their wake.

With no other flights scheduled for that day, he cleared off the long, thin parachute packing table and started packing his first chute. He saved a couple of chutes off to the side to teach Tim later.

He heard a car pull in, but from the chug of the engine, it wasn't Tim returning from his shopping trip with the Jeep. He turned and watched a man walk into the hangar. He gave Joss a little wave as he spotted him. Changing directions, he walked over to the packing table.

"Hey," the man said. He was probably in his early twenties, heavy for his size even though he had to be an inch or two taller than Joss. "I'm looking for Joss Kincaid?"

"Found him," Joss said as he untangled and straightened paracord lines, only giving the guy half of his attention. "What can I do for you?"

"I'm Tim McIntyre."

Joss's hands stilled, and he glanced up from the cords in his hands. His eyes narrowed. He couldn't possibly have heard him right.

Right?

"What did you say?"

"Um... I'm Tim McIntyre. We spoke on the phone about a job. It was last week, so..." He shrugged his shoulders as if waiting for Joss to remember their conversation.

And what were the chances there were two Tim McIntyres knocking on his hangar door? What the fuck was going on?

"You were moving here from New Mexico."

Tim McIntyre smiled. The relief showing on his face that Joss hadn't completely forgotten him. "Phoenix, Arizona, actually, but hot and dry so close enough."

"You got ID? Résumé?"

Now you're suddenly all concerned about résumés and verifying identification? Where was this four days ago? Or were you so dumbfounded by the other Tim's beauty that you'd done all your thinking with your dick?

The man in front of him pulled out his ID, verifying his name and an address in Phoenix.

Jesus Christ, what was going on?

Tim McIntyre hitched a thumb over his shoulder. "My résumé's in the car. I'll go get it."

Joss was determined to get to the bottom of this. "Meet me in my office, yeah?" He pointed across the hangar at his office door.

"Sure. Be right back."

Joss scratched his head and rubbed at the tension knotting the muscles at the back of his neck, playing back in his head the few days before when a different Tim turned up on his doorstep.

Joss had been so desperate for good help and ecstatic that

someone had shown up for the job that he hadn't done his due diligence when the first Tim had knocked at the door.

And it chapped his ass that Derek had been right. If *his* Tim weren't the *real* Tim, he would have found that out if he'd checked references or had him fill out a simple fucking form.

Your Tim. Do you hear yourself?

That slick taste of bile rose at the back of his throat, and he swallowed the bitter taste down. He almost reached for his phone to call the real Tim or the fake Tim. Hell, he didn't even know what to call him anymore.

How about calling him the Tim you jack off to every night? Is that a good enough descriptor?

Jesus Christ.

He plopped down into his chair, his elbows on his desk as he rubbed his face with his hands. He glanced at his watch. Both Tims should be walking back into the hangar any minute now.

A knock came on the jamb of his office door, and Joss glance up.

"If you'd rather I come back another time, I—"

Joss sat back and held his hand out for the résumé. "No. Now is good." The sooner he figured out his Tim problem, the better.

He thumbed through the résumé. The Tim before him had worked at a couple of smaller airstrips. Had started taking flying lessons, though he had under ten total flight hours if the résumé were up to date.

But he didn't really care about the negligible flight hours. He wasn't trying to hire a pilot.

"Take a load off," Joss said, indicating the seat across from him. "I want to call your references."

Tim sat, and Joss went through each of the references one by one. All of them panned out. Apparently, Tim McIntyre was a hardworking, conscientious employee.

Well, fuck. If this was Tim McIntyre, then who the hell was the man he'd been fantasizing about all week?

"Hey boss, I put the groceries—" *His* Tim walked into the office and tossed the Jeep keys on the desk. "Oh, hey," he said when he saw the man sitting across from Joss. "I didn't know you were busy. I can come back."

"No," Joss said, "I've got someone I want you to meet."

The Tim sitting in the chair stood and held out his hand. "I'm Tim McIntyre. Nice to meet you."

Joss's Tim stopped offering his hand mid-extension. His face turned a shade of white Joss had only seen on the cold, dead, underbelly of a shark.

His Tim dropped his hand and turned to Joss. "I can explain."

It wasn't the anger on Joss's face that hit Milo the hardest. It was the hurt. Whatever fragile trust they'd developed had taken a brutal, possibly deadly, hit.

Milo glanced between Joss and Tim. "I can explain."

But could he really? In only a few short days, Milo had gone from wanting to meet Dan's family to wondering if knowing Milo existed would be the best thing for Joss. Clearly, Joss was still working through some things with Dan's death. Who was Milo to push?

Maybe the OPO had it right. He shouldn't have tried to circumvent the system. But he couldn't take that back now.

Unless he turned around and walked out that door.

But he didn't want to do that either.

Milo opened his mouth to speak, having no clue what would come out. Joss held up a hand, silencing him.

"Tim," Joss said, "if I could get back with you tomorrow, that would be great."

The confusion on Tim's face as he tried to read the tension in the room would have been comical if Milo weren't about to lose his job, and if Milo hadn't hurt a man he'd had no intention of hurting.

You should have listened to Derek.

Yeah, well, too late now.

"Yeah, sure," Tim said. Milo shifted away from the doorway and allowed Tim to pass. "My number's on my résumé."

"Got it."

When Tim was out of earshot, Joss turned to Milo, his hands on his hips. "What's your real name?"

"Milo. Milo Malone."

"You hungry, Milo?"

Wait. What? "Um... yeah?" Where was Joss going with this?

"Follow me."

Milo followed Joss into his kitchen. Milo had put away the cold groceries but hadn't put away the dry goods yet, not knowing where Joss wanted him to put everything.

"Sit."

Milo sat while Joss rummaged through the bags of groceries, pulling out the bread, then going into the fridge for mayo, mustard, and the lunch meat.

"Roast beef or turkey?" Joss's words came out muffled because his head was in the fridge.

"I can make my own sandwich." Why hadn't Joss fired him yet and sent him packing? Why was he making him a fucking sandwich? His *Last Supper*, so to speak?

Joss straightened and stared at Milo over the refrigerator door. "That's not what I asked." The undercurrent of anger seemed mitigated by frustration, or was that exasperation?

"Both. And I bought fresh tomatoes to put on it, too."

Joss glanced at the wall of pictures then back at Milo. "Are you fucking with me?"

"About the sandwich?"

"Yeah."

"Why—"

"Never mind." Joss's glanced at the photos again. "It's..."

The sentence trailed off, and the tension in the room shifted. Instead of slapping the sandwiches together the way Milo thought he would, Joss did it with care and an attention to detail he hadn't expected.

"Want a beer?"

Milo nodded, even though he could probably use something stiffer.

"It's what?" Milo prompted as Joss brought the food and the drinks to the table, the sandwiches cut on the diagonal the way he liked it, even though Joss had no way of knowing that. Joss looked like he ate a sandwich whole without cutting it.

Joss sat heavily, twisted off the top of his beer and took a long swallow before he said, "Dan liked his sandwiches that way. Roast beef, turkey, and thin slices of tomato." He shrugged. "But I guess that's not that unusual."

Despite the queasiness in Milo's stomach about the upcoming conversation, Milo took his sandwich in his hands.

Joss had piled Milo's sandwich high with roast beef and turkey, the fresh Roma tomatoes sliced extra thin, the way Milo liked it.

And Dan had liked his that way, too?

The hairs stood up on Milo's arms, and his saliva dried up. He had to take a sip of beer before the bite of the sandwich would go down.

It's a coincidence.

Coincidence? Or cellular memory?

Milo wasn't even certain cellular memory was something he

believed in. But he'd been down a number of internet rabbit holes and read a lot of anecdotal evidence supporting the notion that the recipient of donor organs took on some of their donor's traits as if the piece of the other person lived on inside them.

If it were true, it might explain a lot. Like Milo's taste in men changing, his weird obsession with flying that hadn't been there before his transplant. His fear of heights gone.

The subtle changes in his preferences in food and drink.

"How did Dan die?" Milo asked, the question coming out before he could stop himself. From Dan's social media page, he'd inferred Dan had died in an accident, but of course, there were no details about how it had happened.

Joss stopped mid-chew, his gaze landing hard. Moments ticked by, and Joss's eyes went back to the photo wall before they softened.

"A skydiving accident."

Derek had conveniently left that information out of his report. Milo sucked in a breath, his hand going to the tattoo on his ribs.

Was Foster right about his tattoo? Was it a skydiver and not an umbrella blowing in the wind?

That would make so much more sense as to why Milo had woken from surgery with that picture in his head. Why he hadn't been able to rest until he'd drawn it out and then eventually had it tattooed on his side.

Is that why he felt like he could fly?

"What's wrong," Joss said. "Why are you so pale? You look like you've seen a ghost."

"I—" No way could Milo tell Joss the truth about what he'd realized. "I didn't know that's how he'd died."

"How would you have known?"

He couldn't have. "I wouldn't have. I'm sorry for your loss. It's obvious he meant a lot to you."

"I loved—*fuck*. Why am I even telling you this?"

"Because you need someone willing to listen?"

Something shifted, and Joss's expression hardened. His jaw clenched. His lips went flat. Had Milo's comment hit too close to home?

"I didn't bring you in here to talk about Dan."

Here it comes. "I know that."

"You wanted to explain," Joss said as he took another bite of his sandwich. "Explain."

Milo made a split-second decision. He wasn't going to tell Joss the real reason he'd showed up on his doorstep. He couldn't see a way that that information would make things better for Joss.

And Milo could now see that his wanting to meet his donor's family was all about *his* wishes, and he really hadn't taken the family's wishes into full consideration.

While he hadn't meant any harm, searching Joss out had been selfish and short-sighted of him. He understood that now.

"I'd seen your job ad, and I was desperate to find something. When you thought I was someone else and you seemed happy to have me here, I—"

You sound like a blithering idiot.

"I jumped at the chance to be someone you... wanted." *Wanted? Seriously. A Freudian slip?* "I mean *wanted to hire*."

After sucking down most of his beer, Joss said, "I really want to be mad at you right now."

"I get that."

"I don't like being lied to."

Fuck. Is lying to protect Joss for the better? Is not telling Joss the real reason he'd showed up at his door even lying? He *had* needed a job. That part wasn't a lie. "Yeah. I get that, too."

"I like you, Milo." The way Joss said it, it sounded like he was surprised by the admission.

Could Joss like him more than as just a hardworking employee? Or was that dickful, wishful thinking?

At least Joss hadn't fired him on the spot. Milo totally would have deserved that. However... there had been an expected 'but' hidden in Joss's tone.

"But?"

"But I need to think about this. You learn fast. You have a good work ethic. You're great on the phone with the clients. All things Kincaid Air needs right now. But after that stunt, I'm not sure this is going to work out. I've got some thinking to do."

Milo pushed his plate away, his appetite gone, the second half of his sandwich uneaten. "Understood."

"Why don't you knock off for the afternoon. I'll catch up with you later."

Milo stood, taking his plate in hand to clean up after himself.

"Leave it."

Milo set the plate back down and left the apartment with a sinking feeling in his stomach. He returned to his room. Not long after, he heard the grumble of Joss's Harley starting up then gradually disappear.

Where'd he go?

He obviously didn't see Milo as a threat to his property if he left without so much as closing the hangar doors or kicking Milo out of the building.

But that doesn't mean he trusts you in any other way.

Even though Joss had told him to take the afternoon off, without a vehicle—and he didn't consider the Jeep as something he had a right to drive unless it was with Joss's consent—he couldn't go anywhere.

And he sure as hell couldn't sit in his room with nothing to do but dwell on his massive mistake. He needed to keep busy.

He poured all his anxiety and guilt and uncertainty into work.

Milo read the directions for the self-propelled walk-behind floor sweeper and started at one end of the hangar and worked his way to the other, careful to avoid the area near the Cessna where Joss still had parts laid out under the nose.

By the time he'd finished, sweat dripped down his torso. He pulled his T-shirt out of the back pocket of his shorts and used it as a rag to dry his face and chest.

He returned the sweeper to the storage room and went into Joss's air-conditioned office to finish filing some of the more organized piles he'd created. He wouldn't have time to finish filing all of Joss's paperwork in a few hours, but he could make a healthy dent.

Between filing, he took a few calls and made some reservations, including one on Monday for a freight haul up the coast.

A haul that Milo doubted he'd be there to help load.

He finished with the biggest stack of filing, then turned off the lights and closed the office door. It had been several hours since Joss had ridden off. The longer he remained gone, the more certain Milo became that he wouldn't have a job when Joss returned.

Maybe the right thing—the unselfish thing—to do would be to make the decision easy for Joss and leave.

9

Joss rode up higher into the San Gabriels, downshifting and leaning into the curves and accelerating into the straight-aways, needing to feel the freedom of the wind against his body.

At some point, he turned around and headed back toward the valley. He flew by the hangar, and since Milo hadn't set it on fire, he didn't bother pulling in.

When he finally stopped, he found himself in the parking lot of Derek's PI firm. Derek's Roadster was there, but so was another car. He was with a client.

Joss sat in the parking lot and debated leaving, his feet on the ground holding up his bike as the vibrations of his engine settled into his bones.

He didn't really know why he was there. It wasn't like he needed Derek's permission to fire Milo. Something he should have done on the spot.

Then why was he there?

Fuck it. He'd go back to the hangar and do what he should have done a few hours before.

The heart of rush hour had started, and traffic on the street in front of him slowed to a mind-numbing crawl. If he left now, he'd be lucky to make it home in under an hour.

But he didn't want to leave Milo hanging. That wasn't right, either.

He started walking his bike backward when the door to Derek's office opened. Derek walked out with a woman. She wiped her eyes and shook his hand, ducking her head and hiding her face behind a cascade of long black hair as she headed for her car.

Was that Porché Carlile? The porn star? Not that Joss watched a lot of straight porn, but you couldn't live near the valley and not recognize some of the more prominent players.

Derek caught Joss's eye and waved him into his office, heading in and leaving the door open for Joss to follow.

Joss almost took off down the road, but there had to have been a reason his subconscious had led him there. Derek would listen, and he wouldn't bullshit him.

And if he tells you you need to fire Milo, you're going to listen, right?

Yeah.

Most likely.

Probably.

Joss killed his engine, pulled off his helmet, and walked through Derek's open door, wiping the sweat off his forehead with his shirt sleeves.

Derek held out a glass with only a half-finger of whiskey since Joss had ridden in on his bike. Joss accepted it and tossed it to the back of his throat.

"Another?"

Joss almost shook his head, but for some weird reason, he had a Saturday with no flights scheduled for the next day, and the temptation awaited.

"If you want more, you can pull your bike into the office, come get it tomorrow, and we can both catch a rideshare home."

"Deal." Joss handed over his glass for Derek to refill. He made himself comfortable on the couch, and Derek brought over the two glasses and the bottle of whiskey and set them on the coffee table between them.

One of the best things about Derek was he didn't scrimp when it came to the hard stuff.

Kicking out of his shoes, Derek rolled his desk chair over, picked up his drink, and sat.

He didn't push Joss to talk. Instead, he stretched his socked feet out onto the coffee table and sipped at his drink.

Joss slouched on the couch, his legs stretched out, boots crossed at the ankles. Through the open blinds, the traffic passed by outside, with honks and beeps and revved engines.

Inside, the clock on the wall ticked, and the mini refrigerator hummed.

"I had a guy come to the hangar today," Joss said at last, his voice sounding overly loud in the quiet space.

Derek had his head leaned back, his eyes closed, and his drink clasped in his hands on his belly. He made a noise in the back of his throat, indicating he was listening and hadn't fallen asleep.

"His name was Tim McIntyre."

Derek sat up, his feet hitting the floor with a thunk, suddenly wide awake. His color blanched—unusual for an even-keeled guy like Derek—but not nearly as much as Milo's had. "The fuck?"

Joss chuckled even though it wasn't funny. "Yeah, that was my take on it, too."

"And?"

"And he was the real deal. Checked his ID and his references."

Derek set his glass down with care, his forearms on his knees. "And the other Tim?"

"His name's Milo Malone. He took advantage of an opportunity to get a job that he needed. Kicker of it is, he's hands down the best employee I've had from a work ethic standpoint, and he's sharp, observant, and—"

"He's got a killer ass?"

Joss shot him a look. "That has nothing to do with it."

"*Okaaay*," Derek said, as if knowing he'd been spoon-fed a lie. "Then why are you wincing about running this guy off? I've never known you to be shy about getting rid of someone who needed firing."

"I don't know." Joss was at a loss for why he couldn't do what he knew he should. "That's how I ended up on your doorstep, drinking your booze."

"What are you going to do about it?" The question came out casually. *Too* casually.

Joss stared at the man across from him. The entire time he'd known Derek, he'd never given Joss a reason to distrust him. Joss shook it off, refusing to allow Milo's deception to color his perception of his best friend.

Indecision ate at him. "I thought talking about it would help. I know what I should do, I just don't fucking want to do it."

"Then don't."

Joss eyed him. "He deserves to be fired."

"He does. But..." Derek didn't put up with a lot of bullshit, but he did have a compassionate streak in him that sometimes clouded his better judgment. "Take it from someone with first-hand experience, everyone fucks up. You could give Milo a second chance. Good employees are damn hard to find."

"Truth, right there." Joss tipped his glass in salute and sipped his drink, letting the alcohol mellow his rough edges.

He should have stopped at two glasses but didn't refuse a

third, the silence companionable and drawn out. "You don't think it would be a mistake keeping Milo around?"

"I think what would be a mistake would be not following what's in your heart and your gut. Logic may be the voice of reason, but it can also lead you astray."

Joss sent his friend a wry grin. "Sounds like another voice of experience."

"Mmm," Derek said as he swallowed another sip. "I've screwed up enough times in my life. A lot of hard lessons learned. In fact, I have a Ph-fucking-D in the life of hard knocks. Listen to those lessons. They'll keep you from making those dumb mistakes again."

Joss finished his drink, set it on the coffee table, and stood. "Thanks for the ear and the booze." He clicked through his phone to his rideshare app and ordered a car. "I'm gonna push my bike in here and get out of your hair so you can get home or...?"

"Meet up with my date."

"Why the fuck didn't you say something?"

Derek stood as well. "Because I'm here for you, and I don't get to see you as much as I used to."

The rest of it Derek left unsaid, the part where he hadn't seen as much of Joss since Dan had died. And even though Derek was his best friend, Dan had been the man who held the three of them together, the one who insisted they go out for drinks, or go on double dates, or have small dinner parties.

Without that drive, and with Joss up in the hills, most of the time it was easier for Joss to stay up there by himself than come down and be social. Besides, socializing without Dan wasn't the same.

Derek moved the chair and coffee table to make room for Joss's bike and held the door open. Joss's ride showed up as he lowered the kickstand.

"Thanks again."

"Anytime. Oh, and Joss?"

Joss turned in the doorway. "Yeah?"

"I know I said people deserve a second chance, but... be careful."

He didn't quite understand what Derek meant. It might have had something to do with the amount of alcohol he'd consumed, but most likely not. "Sure," he said, not knowing what else to say.

Most of the drive up to the hangar, Joss dozed in the car. It smelled of wet dog and sunscreen, but the blond woman with the deep tan and over-sized shades took his closed eyes as a clue and left him alone.

At the hangar, he thanked her and climbed out of the car. The world did a quick lap, and he caught his balance on the door before closing it, way more buzzed than he'd expected he'd be.

Then again, all that good whiskey on an empty stomach would do a number on anybody.

Darkness had fallen. Moths and other insects buzzed the security light in front of the hangar's now-closed doors.

Was Milo even still there?

Instead of entering his apartment, he went through the unlocked man-door. The main overhead lights were off, but in the glow of the inside security lights, he noticed the floor had been swept. He walked by his office with the shorter pile of papers that needed filing and headed for Milo's open door.

Who continued to work when they were on the verge of getting fired?

Someone who needed their job.

Someone who isn't afraid to put in the hard work.

Joss knocked on the open door and leaned his shoulder against the jamb, his heart doing that stupid loopity-loop in his chest when he caught sight of Milo laying propped up in bed, his shirt off, an arm above his head as he read... the Cessna engine repair book. Huh.

Milo glanced up, relief washing over his face. He set the manual down and stood. "I was worried. You were gone a long time."

Because that conversation was sounding more like something he would have with a boyfriend, not an employee, Joss pivoted. "Do you normally read Cessna repair manuals for entertainment?"

Milo huffed out a laugh. "I hated school but always loved learning. Engines are something I know nothing about. And I didn't know what else to do or when you'd be back so..." Milo shrugged.

"Sorry I kept you waiting. That wasn't fair of me."

"Neither was me pretending to be someone I wasn't."

Milo hovered a few feet out of Joss's reach. Probably the wisest thing the man had ever done, especially when all Joss could think about when he looked at him was the number of times he'd taken himself in his hand while thinking about Milo. "To be honest, *Milo* suits you much better than *Tim*."

Milo smiled that shy smile. "Yeah. That was really stupid."

Joss nodded, then spotted Milo's packed duffel on the floor by the bed. "You leaving?"

Why the thought of Milo leaving made his chest tight, Joss couldn't comprehend, especially with a healthy buzz working. Yes, he found Milo attractive and had enjoyed his company the past week, but that tightness in his chest was wholly unexpected and greatly disproportionate to the time he'd known him.

"I wasn't sure I would have a job when you came back. I wanted to be ready, you know... in case."

"I don't want you to leave." His voice dropped and went all soft. And fuck, if it didn't sound like he was talking to a boyfriend again and not his damn employee. "What I mean is you're good at your job, and I can use someone like you."

"What about Tim?"

"I have a friend I can recommend him to. He might need the help."

"Or *I* could work for your friend, and Tim could—"

"No."

Why are you so quick to dismiss that idea? It would work. Milo would have a job, and Tim would get the one he'd moved across two states to possibly take? Win-win.

Yeah, but—

But you want Milo.

Yeah. He could admit that, but only to himself.

Milo shifted, and Joss caught a glimpse of a tattoo on the left side of his ribcage. How had he missed that before? He wanted a closer look but now wasn't the time.

"Keep your job, Milo. Let me worry about Tim."

Milo sucked in a lungful of air, and color started to return to his body. "Thank—"

Joss shook his head. "Don't thank me. And don't lie to me again."

"I won't."

"Anything else you need to tell me before we put this behind us?" A second chance was a second chance. Joss wouldn't give a third.

"No." The answer came fast enough to be believable, but instead of maintaining eye contact, Milo reached for his duffel and set it on the bed.

Joss straightened and caught Milo's arm, turning him around. "You sure there's nothing else?"

Milo met his gaze. "Positive." Joss released his arm and Milo unzipped his duffel. "I'll unpack and—"

"What's that?" Joss pointed at the toy in the duffel bag, knowing damn well what it was.

"Oh." Milo pulled it out of his bag and unwrapped the white plastic parachute from around the toy soldier. He threw it up in the air. The parachute unfurled, and the man floated down and landed on the concrete. "I found it while Foster and I were hiking."

Joss picked up the little man and found the letter 'D' in black sharpie on the bottom of the tiny army boots.

The same 'D' Joss had scribbled on there for 'Dan.'

"You can have it if you want."

Joss had never met anyone who'd found one of his parachute men, and it meant something to him that Milo had found it. More importantly, it had meant enough to Milo for some reason for him to carry it with him.

"You keep it."

Joss handed it back, and Milo set it on top of his dresser, laying the parachute out and propping the man against the wall, completely ignorant of the toy's significance.

And Joss planned on keeping it that way.

10

O_N S_{ATURDAY}, J_{OSS} _{AND} M_{ILO} _{POWERED} _{THROUGH} _{THE} awkwardness left in the wake of the lie and the almost-getting-fired bit and tried to concentrate on work when there wasn't much work to do.

At least not of the taking clients up and letting them jump out of planes part. Milo continued organizing the hangar while Joss grunted and cussed his way through removing some part from around the Cessna's engine.

As a company that did most of its business on weekends when people were off work, it seemed weird to not have reservations. Milo searched back through Kincaid Air's reservation calendar. It highlighted the rarity of having a Saturday when Joss wasn't taking people up, jump after jump.

The next day they had four jumps scheduled. Not bad for a Sunday, but it didn't make up for the lack of business on Saturday.

Milo woke Sunday morning to find the hangar doors laid open and Joss out jogging the airstrip. A nice breeze blew through as the sun rose.

In the office early, Milo made coffee, ready to start pulling release forms and equipment for the first jump.

The phone rang, and though it was before official business hours, instead of letting the call roll to voicemail, Milo answered with his usual, "Kincaid Air, Milo speaking, can I help you?"

"This is Riggs," the caller said. "I had a party of five going up this morning. I need to cancel."

"Sure. Would you like to reschedule? We have a slot available next Sunday and some openings during the week if that—"

"That won't be necessary," the man said.

"Well, we—"

The phone clicked, leaving Milo listening to a dial tone. The guy had hung up on him. What the hell?

In the next twenty minutes, he handled two more similar calls, each canceling their jump, and each not wanting to reschedule. Meaning the people who had made their reservation had lost their deposits. And in the short time Milo had been working there, he'd learned quickly how much people hated to lose their deposits.

Although cancellations had happened, most eagerly rescheduled on the spot.

At least the second two callers hadn't hung up on him.

He sat back in Joss's chair, deep in thought when Joss strode in, sweaty and breathing hard, and headed straight for the coffee pot.

He turned as he poured. "Fuck, have you seen how beautiful it is out there today? Not a cloud in the sky. It's going to be a great day to fly. You ready for a busy day?"

"About that."

The excitement in Joss's eyes dimmed, and Milo hated to be the cause of that, if only indirectly.

"The first three jumps you had for the day canceled."

"When did they reschedule?"

"They didn't."

"Why not?" Joss came around to his side of the desk.

Milo rolled out of the way to allow Joss access to the scheduling program. Not that it would tell him anything that Milo already hadn't.

Clicking through the program didn't bring Joss any answers. He stood at last. "That's really weird. That, like, never happens."

"If you need to hold off on paying me on Friday, I understand."

Milo didn't really need much money since his job offered room and board. Well, the board part was only until Milo got paid and could afford his own groceries, but still, he had no bills and a roof over his head, so the money was secondary to his basic needs.

The priority was making it up to Joss after that lie and ensuring that Joss never regretted keeping Milo on.

What about the omission? Are you really not going to tell him what brought you to his door?

Nope. Right then, Milo didn't see how that would do either of them any good.

"Moneywise, one bad weekend won't put me in a dire situation. I still have freight flights to keep the lights on. Worse case, I can put the Otter's original seats back in and take up sightseers. I appreciate the offer, though."

"What do we do now?"

"We go about our day. We can't stop people from canceling if they want to."

"I certainly have plenty to do. And don't forget you still haven't packed those last two chutes from Friday."

Joss grunted as he took a sip of coffee. "You want to learn how to pack a chute?"

Milo grinned. "Definitely."

"Give me five to catch a shower, and we'll get started."

When Joss returned to the hangar in athletic shorts and a Kincaid Air branded tank, Milo tried to school his gaze so it wasn't blatantly apparent that he'd checked out Joss's pecs and package.

A pair of aviators might help. Wearing them inside the hangar wouldn't be obvious. Right?

He helped Joss lay out the first parachute on the long folding table on the other side of the hangar.

Joss demonstrated with the first chute, showing Milo how to straighten all the control and suspension lines to keep them from getting tangled, then how to fold the chute to open properly, then how to gather all the lines and fold them back and forth and tuck them into their keepers until you made a neat pack that fit into the container.

Joss double and triple-checked his own work as he went. When he'd finished, he labeled and initialed the pack and put the rig in the rack with all the others.

"Your turn," Joss said. "I'll have to do the final packing, but you can use this chute to practice."

With care, Milo laid out the parachute the way Joss had shown him, conscious of how close Joss stood as he watched Milo work. Light and breezy, Joss's cologne mixed well with the scent of scrub brush drifting in with the wind.

And that mild undercurrent of musk that was all Joss's, drifting about as the sun heated the hangar and sweat licked their skin, made Milo want to bury his face in Joss armpit and never come up for air.

But that might not be appropriate.

Might not?

Okay. It wasn't. But Milo couldn't help it if his thoughts kept drifting to sex when Joss walked around the hangar all day, most every day, in a muscle shirt with the Kincaid Air logo on his chest, showing off all of his hard work with the weights.

And don't get Milo started on the times when Joss walked around in only a pair of sweaty athletic shorts after working out or coming in from the airstrip after a run.

If nothing else, the cold-water faucet in Milo's bathroom was getting a workout.

About as much of a workout as your right hand.

Yeah, well, fuck... could anyone blame him?

"What's that grin about?" Joss bobbed his chin toward Milo.

"Umm. Nothing. I think I'm finally getting this chute packing thing down."

"Yeah, but don't get too cocky, that's how people end up getting killed."

Oh, fuckfuckfuck.

"No, sorry. I didn't mean—" Milo closed his eyes and took in a steadying breath. When he opened them again, Joss closed the short distance between them until Milo's back pressed against the packing table.

"I know you didn't mean anything by that. You're a sweet guy, Milo. You don't have a malicious bone in your body."

"Is that bad?" From the way Joss's brows furrowed, Milo couldn't be sure.

"It's... refreshing."

Joss's eyes flicked down to Milo's smiling lips and let them linger. *HolyfuckmeJesus*, was Joss going to kiss him?

"*You're* refreshing," Joss said.

"Yeah?"

Even if Milo could take a step back, he didn't want to, even though he knew he should. It somehow felt wrong—not because Joss was his boss, because that employee/employer taboo thing didn't mean much to Milo when it was only the two of them working at Kincaid Air.

Maybe it wouldn't feel quite so wrong if Joss knew the real reason you showed up on his doorstep.

If Milo had a muzzle, he'd slip it on his inner voice. He didn't need all that negativity in his head.

They were two consenting adults. If Joss wanted to kiss him, Milo would damn well let him.

Joss brushed a work-roughened fingertip along Milo's jawline.

Bet you can think of somewhere else you'd like to have Joss's hands.

Milo immediately went hard at the thought of Joss taking him in his big, strong fist. Almost every night, Milo had lain in bed listening to the sounds of the hangar around him. Hearing Joss occasionally open or close a door or flip on one of the hangar lights made Milo wonder if one of those times Joss would open *his* door and turn on his light in the middle of the night.

When it looked like Joss would step back, Milo rose on his tiptoes and kissed him.

A part of him expected Joss to pull away with an exclaimed, 'What the fuck?' Milo hadn't anticipated the grunt of surprise that rumbled up the back of Joss's throat or the firm grip of Joss's hand on Milo's jaw as Joss held him in place and took the kiss deeper.

Joss pressed against Milo, a hungry groan escaping one of them. Milo couldn't tell from whom. But then again, it was nearly impossible to think clearly with Joss's erection pressed against Milo's abdomen and his tongue sweeping the seam of Milo's lips.

Milo opened for him. He could taste the coffee on Joss's tongue. Wanting more, Milo tilted his head, his heart kicking in his chest.

Joss's lips on his felt like... it felt like a homecoming.

Milo's hands went to Joss's waistband, not caring that they were in an open hangar. That sturdy parachute table would make one hell of a fuck bench.

But Joss broke the kiss, an enigmatic expression on his face. Joss chuckled. The warm and rich sound made Milo's stomach do flips. "Well... *that* happened."

Milo sucked in a deep breath and blew it out. The hangar still spun, and he couldn't shake that muddy head in the clouds feeling. "Yeah. That did."

Joss nodded as if taking it all in. The ramifications, the attraction, the imprudence. He picked up one of Milo's hands and rubbed the tip of his thumb over the fresh black nail polish on Milo's index finger.

"Gay, not goth, then."

Milo laughed. With his own erection pressing against Joss thigh, Milo couldn't deny his statement. "Definitely gay."

Stepping back, Joss said, "Good to know."

IN THE TIME BETWEEN THE KISS AND THE ONLY FLIGHT OF THE DAY, Joss worked on the Cessna while Milo busied himself by practicing repacking the chute three or four times, before continuing with his hangar organizing. There was a rack of storage shelves that was a jumble of spare plane and parachute pack parts piled together with no account for order.

Milo went through the items one by one, separating them and labeling the shelves so Joss could grab what he needed with ease instead of digging through the piles and making an even bigger, jumbled mess.

The few times Milo walked over to have Joss identify a plane part, it wasn't as if Joss acted as if the kiss hadn't happened, but there were no lingering looks either. Milo found that surprisingly disappointing.

What did you expect? For him to drag you to his bed and not let you come up for air until the next group of skydivers came?

To say that enticing thought hadn't entered Milo's mind would be a lie. And he was trying to keep the lies to a minimum these days.

Thirty minutes before the skydivers' scheduled arrival, Joss went inside for another shower to scrub off the grease and grime. Milo laid out the rental equipment as well as the liability releases.

The men arrived together. Ten of them had piled into a couple of SUVs. A loud, boisterous group of guys that reminded Milo of a bunch of frat boys, only these guys were getting gray around the temples, and their bodies had expanded enough that Milo had to let out the belly straps on a few of the parachute harnesses.

Even though all the men were experienced enough to have their USPA 'A' licenses that allowed them to jump solo, Joss went over a safety briefing before they all loaded up and lifted into the air.

The quiet in the hangar after all the raucous laughs and the roar of the Otter's engines as it accelerated down the airstrip and lifted off made Milo's ears ring. He did a little filing before driving the multi-passenger golf cart up to the grassy drop zone a couple of hundred yards up the hillside to pick up the skydivers and bring them back down to the hangar.

He arrived at the landing area in time to watch the men land with whoops and hollers. As soon as the last man landed, Joss circled the Otter overhead and lined up for a landing.

"How was it?" Milo asked as he walked up to the first couple of men. He helped them out of their harnesses and started pulling in the chutes to put in the open trailer attached to the back of the cart.

"Oh, man." A tall guy named John, if Milo remembered

correctly, said, "Couldn't have picked a more beautiful day." He thumped his friend on the chest. "See, I told you you wouldn't die today."

His friend had his graying hair pulled back into a tiny ponytail. "Just because we survived doesn't mean we should trust this outfit."

"Excuse me?" Milo must not have heard him right. What was wrong with Kincaid Air?

"Nothing," John butted in, giving his friend a *shut the hell up* glare.

But Ponytail didn't shut up as the rest of the guys gathered their equipment and started returning it to the trailer. Ponytail thumbed toward Milo, and to John said, "This guy has no idea, does he?"

"Don't be an asshole." John shouldered by his friend and dumped his spent pack and chute into the trailer. Ponytail followed. "I've been flying with Kincaid for a long time. You saw for yourself, Joss does it right."

"This time."

"If there's a problem we need to know about—"

One of the guys who'd already climbed into the cart turned around and said, "Would one of you pussies show him the goddamn article already?"

"Show me what?"

John pulled out his phone and clicked over to an article from the *San Fernando Post's* online news feed. Milo climbed into the driver's seat next to John. The headline of the story read: *Accident or Safety Concern? Who's to Judge?*

Milo skimmed the article as the group of guys behind him grew impatient to get back to the hangar. The article sited Dan's death and a short string of incidents at Kincaid Air as a reason to question the safety of the entire operation.

"Are we going or are we sitting out here in the sun all day?"

Someone in the back of the cart muttered, his passive-aggressive skills on-point.

"Give the kid a minute. One minute more isn't going to kill you. I know for a fact you don't have a hot date waiting for you."

A rumble of chuckles rolled through the vehicle. With a thank you, Milo handed the phone back to John. Releasing the parking brake, Milo drove to the hangar deep in thought while the guys behind him bullshitted each other about the jump.

The article coming out at least explained why they'd had the last-minute cancellations.

The question was, was it true? Were Joss and Kincaid Air unsafe?

By the time Joss landed, shut down the Otter, and refueled it for the freight flight first thing the next morning, all the skydivers had left.

Even though he'd had the cancellations that morning, flying on such a beautiful day had left him energized.

You sure it was the flight? Maybe it had something to do with that scorching kiss and having Milo's dick pressed against your thigh that put that spring in your step and that stupid, goofy smile on your face.

Joss was man enough to admit it could be both. It didn't have to be an either/or situation.

He turned into the office to find Milo at his desk, hunched over the keyboard as he squinted at the words on the screen. He barely glanced up when Joss entered.

Joss sat in the chair across from him. "What gives?"

"I think I know why we had those cancellations this morning." By the concern on Milo's face, the reason had to be troubling. "One of the guys showed me this article that came out this morning."

Milo turned the computer screen around, and Joss read through the article, the anger seeping in at the mention of the anniversary of Dan's death. About Joss's possible culpability in Dan's death.

What a fucking fiasco.

"There's more."

Joss scrubbed a hand through his short stubble. "Of course, there is."

Milo turned the screen back around and started typing. Joss stood and came around to his side of the desk and looked over his shoulder. The laugh that escaped Joss was equal parts defeat and fight.

Milo had pulled up Ross Dixon's—of Dixon Skydive—business social media feed from the day before, calling out Joss and Kincaid Air for unsafe practices. Which probably accounted for the short article in the *Post* which hadn't delved any deeper than a paper cut.

"Dixon. That blowhard. I should have known he would be behind all this. Bastard was even too chickenshit to *at* me." At least if he'd had, Joss wouldn't feel so blindsided.

"Can you make him take it down? Libel and all that?"

"There's no libel when what he says is true." That only pissed Joss off even more. "But the leading words and the reporter refusing to look any deeper into the story made it seem like there's something more to Dixon's accusations when there isn't."

Milo looked like he wanted to ask more questions, but Joss didn't feel like defending himself in his own damn hangar. He crossed his arms. The scowl on his face was probably easy for Milo to read.

"Who is this guy anyway?"

"My chief competitor. His ass has been chapped for years. Ever since Dan and I bought this land. He'd had his eye on it for a while, but we were able to put a better offer together than he was at the time. He's been bitter ever since. Social media gives him a platform to spread his version of things."

"You could post on Kincaid Air's social media. Get your version of the story out."

"It will blow over." At least it had in the past. Though Dixon's reach and following seemed to be growing.

And the thought of putting the worst day of his life out there for everyone to read and judge seemed about as fun as jumping out of his Otter without a parachute. The first part might be exhilarating, freeing even, but the landing would be impossible to stick.

"It has a few thousand shares already."

Or Dixon could end Kincaid Air as he knew it.

There were other ways to make money as a small plane pilot, but none of them kept him as close to Dan it seemed than taking the skydivers up.

The phone rang, and Milo answered it, his 'answering voice' becoming all too familiar. It had a sweetness, a friendliness—a *genuineness*—to it that was all Milo. It made his clients want to hang on the phone and talk to Milo even after they'd finished making their inquiry or reservation. Joss couldn't explain it, but it drew him in as easily as it did others.

Except those others aren't sticking their tongues down Milo's throat.

And they wouldn't be. Not with Milo stuck up on the hill with Joss. That was one advantage to his employee not having his own transportation.

You know you can't keep him locked up here in the hangar like some sort of modern-day Rapunzel, right?

Milo wasn't locked up. Except for the Jeep—the Jeep Milo refused to use unless he was on official Kincaid Air business— he just didn't have a way of getting anywhere.

Big difference.

Joss's inner voice had turned into a sarcastic bastard over the years.

Milo held up the phone. "Some reporter from *The Valley Examiner*. She wants to talk to you."

Enough reporters had called him after Dan's accident. If he never talked to another reporter in his life, it would be way too soon. Still, he picked it up if only for the reporter to hear from him that he didn't have a comment.

"Joss Kincaid," his words said, but his tone had a fuck-off quality to it that he'd had a hard time tamping down.

"I'm Jacee Avila from *The Valley Examiner*. I wanted to ask you some questions about the recent article in the *Post*."

"No comment, Ms. Avila. I would appreciate it if—"

"I've read the FAA report."

That got Joss's attention. At least the woman had done some of her homework. He was impressed that she'd taken the time to dig into the Federal Aviation Administration's reports. Didn't change Joss's 'no comment,' though. "Then you know everything you need to know. Good day, Ms. Avila."

Joss hit end before the reporter could respond. He went to throw the receiver across the room, but Milo stripped it out of his hand.

"A hole in the wall isn't going to solve anything."

"I'd feel better."

"Would you?"

Probably not. "I'm going for a run. You can knock off for the day."

"You ran this morning."

"One kiss, and now you're my keeper?"

He did not just go there. But by the stunned expression on Milo's face, he certainly had. Lashing out at Milo wouldn't delete all the bad press or get Kincaid Air any more jumps scheduled.

Scrubbing a hand down his face, Joss peeked out over the top of his fingers and said, "That was uncalled for."

"I get it. It's been a rough day."

"That's no excuse."

Milo closed Dixon's social media page and stood. "About that kiss."

"What about it?" Joss expected to hear something to the effect of 'It was a mistake,' or 'It won't happen again.' Even though he didn't want to hear it, he braced for the hit.

"One kiss doesn't make me your keeper. It only makes me want more."

Milo walked out of the office, leaving Joss in a stupor of disbelief. The boldness shouldn't have surprised him, considering Milo had brazenly impersonated another person. The admission that Milo wanted more was information Joss didn't quite know how to process.

Should he be glad? Because fuck, if Joss didn't want more, too. Should he be concerned? Cautious? Or say fuck it and see where another kiss would take them?

His mind and body screamed for the release a run would give him. He needed a clear mind if he didn't want to screw things up with Milo. Having Dixon and the reporter all up in his head didn't put him in the headspace to think too clearly where his dick was concerned.

But it's not only your dick you have to be concerned about. It's your heart, too.

Which didn't make much sense considering he'd only known Milo less than a week.

Joss didn't fall hard and fast. It wasn't in .

But that didn't mean the thought of having Milo beneath him didn't intrigue him.

And make him hard.

11

AROUND THE AIRSTRIP, JOSS SET A BRUISING, BALL-BUSTING PACE he hadn't hit since that time Dan had convinced him to train and run the New York marathon with him. Joss's jagged, ragged breath sawed in and out of his lungs as sweat streamed down his forehead and into his eyes. They stung and watered, and he kept on running.

He ran until he could no longer think about Dixon.

Until his quads and calves burned with the liquid fire of lactic acid.

Until his dick deflated, and he pushed all thoughts of Milo out of his mind.

Until his stomach churned and threatened to make him vomit from the exertion.

Until he heard Dan's voice in his head telling him to stop beating himself up.

Joss collapsed on a patch of grass at the back of the hangar, the sun starting to set over the Pacific in the distance. He coughed and spat as he tried to catch his breath, the whir of blood rushing past his ears almost drowned out the buzz of a jet starting its approach into LAX.

Milo walked out, a cold bottle of water in his hand. He squatted down and twisted off the cap and handed it to Joss.

Joss rolled onto an elbow and sucked the bottle down in five or six long swallows. "You worried about me?" he panted, trying for a little levity.

"You were out there for over an hour. You practically ran a trench around the airstrip. You tell me."

"I'm fine if that's what you're asking." Joss sat up and leaned forward, stretching out his hamstrings.

"Fine enough to speak with a visitor?"

What now? "Who's here?"

Milo glanced behind him, and Joss followed his gaze. A young woman in a pair of no-nonsense khakis and a blue blouse walked out of the hangar with a notebook in her hand.

"Ms. Avila," Joss said, knowing full well who this woman was even though he'd never seen her before. "You don't give up easily."

"Persistence pays off in my experience." She held out her hand, and Joss wiped the blades of grass off his damp palm and shook hers. "I'd really like to talk to you if you'll give me a few minutes of your time."

"I've had my fair share of experience with reporters. I'd rather my words not get twisted around and cut up so badly that they do more damage than good."

"I'm not the enemy here, Mr. Kincaid. All I want is the truth."

The truth. "*In my experience,*" Joss pitched her words back at her, "the truth doesn't sell. Sensation sells."

"And sex," she said with a sly grin. "But we're not here to talk about that."

Joss huffed out a laugh. She had some balls. He stood and bumped his chin toward the weathered picnic table. "Have a seat. You've got five minutes."

They sat across from each other and, Milo being Milo,

brought out more water for them both before turning on one of the rear lights and disappearing into the hangar.

"Mind if I record this?" the reporter asked, pulling a mini recorder out of her shoulder bag. "I'll send you the unedited file to keep for your records."

He nodded his agreement. "Ms. Avila, why—"

"Call me Jacee."

When she pressed record on her mini recorder, he said, "Why are you here? Why do you care what some asshole competitor of mine says online, or what some reporter writes about me?"

"The guy who wrote that article in the *Post* is a piece of shit as a human being, and he's even worse as a reporter. He'll write whatever someone pays him to write. He doesn't care about the truth as long as he gets paid to report it. I've made it my mission to find the truth behind his stories and set the record straight."

"You seem to know him well."

"Mmhmm," Jacee muttered. "I should. He's my brother."

Joss barked out a laugh, then quickly sobered. "Sorry. That's not funny."

Jacee offered a wry grin. "But sometimes you gotta laugh to keep from crying. You know what I mean?"

"I hear you." He understood that sentiment as well as anybody. That Jacee allowed herself to be vulnerable spoke volumes to Joss. "Ask your questions."

She flicked her long, black hair over her shoulders, her smile wide. Her big, brown, intelligent eyes softened. "I've read the FAA's report, but I'd like to start by hearing the story from your point of view as the sole pilot on the flight when Dan Devine's accident occurred. Start from the moment you began preflight to the second you landed."

Joss had been ready to field a couple of soft-tossed questions. He hadn't expected her to start with a screwball straight to the ribs. He grunted when it hit. "You come out swinging for the fences, don't you?"

"I find it's the fastest way to the truth."

By the time he'd finished retelling the story, way more than five minutes had passed, and he and Jacee had to swipe at the moisture in their eyes. She cut off the recorder and packed her things into her shoulder bag and offered her hand again.

"Thank you for your time. And thank you for your candor. I'll email you the recording file when I get home tonight."

"When will you have the story finished?"

"A week. Could be a little longer. I'm at the start of my investigation, and I want to read some other reports. I don't want to rush this. I want to do this right."

"I appreciate that."

She started backing away. "Thanks again for agreeing to speak with me."

Joss found a smile when he said, "You didn't give me much choice."

"You had a choice. You want the truth out there more than I do."

She disappeared inside the hangar. Instead of following her inside, Joss walked to the end of the airstrip, his chest still tight and his emotions raw. He sat down on a large flat rock on the very edge of the airstrip above a ten-foot drop. Below, the hillside ran down toward the valley, the road twisting and turning until it disappeared into the darkness.

Behind him, he heard the grinding of metal wheels as Milo closed the hangar doors. Then the rear light kicked off. His eyes adjusted to the darkness, and a few of the brighter stars appeared up above. This view from the end of the airstrip was what had sold Dan on the property. A place where you could sit on the ground and still feel like you were flying.

He didn't know how long he sat there. Long enough for the

long ribbon of headlights and taillights on the I-5 way below him to thin, and long enough for him to hear the crunch of Milo's footsteps as he approached.

Beside him, Milo sat down, a grocery bag looped over his arm. "I brought you a sandwich to eat and an ear to listen if you want them."

"You didn't have to do that." Joss unpacked the sandwich and tore off a mouthful.

"It wasn't a problem." And it had been the only way Milo could think of that would allow him to check on Joss without it looking like that was what he was doing.

It didn't take a psychology degree for him to see that from the punishing pace Joss had set for himself on his run around the airstrip, the day had been a roller coaster of emotions for him.

All that on top of dealing with the recent anniversary of Dan's death, it couldn't be easy.

"Do you think Ms. Avila's story is going to help shut the critics up?"

Joss tucked a bite into his cheek. "I don't know. She genuinely seemed like she wanted to help, but Dixon's sensational posts and the first article are going to be what sticks in people's heads. It's like the newspaper printing a retraction in fine print. No one sees it."

He dropped the last half of his sandwich back into the bag as if he'd lost his appetite. "The hell of it is, stories like these grow legs. It's like a hyper-rapid game of telephone tag until, at the end, what people think happened isn't anywhere close to the truth."

"What is the truth?"

"That Dan died from a parachute accident. His main chute malfunctioned, and his reserve chute got caught up as the main chute released. He'd jumped along the coast. Something he'd done many times before. Only this time, he hit hard on the beach. Broke both his legs. But it probably would have been survivable if he hadn't slammed his head into some rocks. His helmet shattered. The brain damage, catastrophic."

"And the FAA report?"

"Yeah, fuck." Joss stared off into the valley, but Milo couldn't tell if he had turned his thoughts inward or if he was watching the display of city lights beneath them. "Officially, I was cleared of any wrongdoing. Dan had even packed his own chute that morning."

"And unofficially?"

Joss tucked up his legs and wrapped his arms around his knees, curling in on himself. "Unofficially, Dan had no business being up there that day. Technically, the winds were within the limits of safety. But barely. And he was using a new pack and a new type of chute that he hadn't used before. But he'd insisted we go up ahead of a front before the predicted bad weather grounded us for the next week."

"I don't get why Dixon is saying this is your fault."

"Because it's easy to blame the pilot. And it fits Dixon's narrative that I don't fly safe." Joss shook his head. "I don't know. Maybe Dixon's right. I've relived that morning a million times and I—"

Joss sniffed and blew out a heavy, shaking breath. Milo reached over and took his hand, half expecting Joss to pull away, but instead, his fierce grip clamped down on Milo's fingers. Joss tore his gaze away from the valley and focused on him. Milo saw the shine in Joss's eyes from the unshed tears.

He wanted to hold Joss's hand to his chest and let him feel

the strong beat of Dan's heart beneath his sternum. Let him feel that a little bit of the man he loved still lived.

"I want to relive that day. I want to make him spend the day in bed with me the way that we'd planned. I want to refuse to let his sexy, mischievous, cock-sure smile cajole me into doing what I knew I shouldn't. If only I'd said no, he'd be alive, and everything would be better."

Except then, Milo might not be sitting there, alive, and breathing the same air as Joss. Milo's blood type was one of the rarest, making it profoundly difficult and much less likely for the OPO to find a heart for him.

But right then, sitting on the end of the runway, with a man shattering beside him, Milo found it hard to wish Joss hadn't given in to Dan's smile.

Milo put his arm around Joss's wide shoulders and pulled him into his chest. Joss threaded an arm around Milo's waist, and it soon became unclear who held who.

Fuck.

Milo counted himself so damn lucky to be alive.

But one thing Janet at his OPO hadn't warned him about when he started writing those letters to Joss was how guilty being alive would make him feel, especially now that he knew the hole Dan had left in Joss's life.

For the first time since Milo put that first card in the mail, he wondered if breaching protocol and making contact had been the biggest mistake of his life.

After a few minutes, Joss straightened and rubbed at his eyes with the heels of his hands. He let out a self-deprecating laugh. "I'm usually not such a mess. But this time of year is always hard. Sorry, you got dragged into this."

Milo was well versed in the ups and downs of grief. He'd lost friends who'd been on the transplant list with him whose bodies had given out before a heart had been found. He knew how you could be going about your day until something catches you unaware. A sight. A sound. A smell. A memory that triggered you, and suddenly, it felt like no time had passed since the loss.

"It's not a problem. Though I must have glossed over the 'emotional support' duties listed on the job description."

"Pretty sure the job description needs updating. You can add that to your list of things that need to be done."

"Move 'updating job descriptions' to the top of the 'To Do' list. Noted."

Milo liked that Joss's humor had kicked back in. He stood and offered Joss his hand. "We should head in. You've got that freight run first thing in the morning."

Locking wrists, Milo pulled Joss to his feet, and they walked back to the hangar, each lost in their own thoughts. Joss might have cracked that joke, but the hunch of his shoulders and the way he hung his head as he walked told Milo he was still in a bad headspace.

Milo wanted to make it better, but he had no clue how. It wasn't like they were lovers, or hell, even good friends. Joss was his boss. He had to keep that in mind.

The way you kept that in mind when you stood on your toes and kissed him?

They parted ways at Milo's door, and he watched until Joss disappeared inside his apartment without a backward glance.

Heart heavy, Joss showered off the caked-on dried sweat, his muscles already tightening up, but his body and his emotions were too drained to do anything about it besides let the hot water streaming out of his showerhead ease his aching muscles.

Instead of walking around his house naked the way he had

before Milo had moved in, Joss dried off and pulled on a clean pair of athletic shorts to get a glass of ice water from the kitchen. He'd rather walk around his kitchen and den clothed in case Milo walked by than close the blinds on the window overlooking the hangar. He loved waking up in the morning to see Ol' Betts out his window.

Even in pieces, she was a sight to see.

He sucked down two glasses of water in quick succession, trying to replace what he'd lost while circling the airstrip. One of the things he hadn't gotten used to even after seven years was the silence, the stillness, in his apartment at night. Even if he and Dan hadn't been talking or had been in separate rooms, the apartment had had a vitality to it that it had lacked since.

Friends had told him he should move, that there were too many memories of Dan there. But besides it being his place of business, of it being his and Dan's dream, he wondered if he left, would his memories disappear with it?

He lay down on top of the covers, his hands clasped behind his head as he watched the lazy turn of the ceiling fan as it went around and around and around, sleep not even a thought in his head.

He sat up, remembering a parts order he'd asked Milo to place. If the parts didn't come in that week, it would put a huge kink in his timetable for getting the Cessna up and running.

Padding through the apartment, he opened his door to the hangar.

Don't wake him up. You can ask him about the order in the morning.

But he didn't want to wait. As he closed the door behind him, he promised himself he'd only peek in on Milo. If he were asleep, he wouldn't disturb him.

A glow came from Milo's window. The window Joss had

neglected to get a blind for. He'd have Milo put that on the list for their next trip into the valley.

He stopped at the open door, taking in the sight of Milo propped up in bed, the Cessna engine repair manual opened on his chest. He was sound asleep.

Leave before he wakes up and finds you staring at him like a creeper.

Excellent advice that he should take. But his knuckles rapped on the door anyway. Milo snorted as he came awake, the manual falling to the ground with a heavy thump when he sat up.

"What—" Milo rubbed at his bloodshot eyes. "Is something wrong?"

"I was wondering if you remembered to order those head-cover gaskets for the Cessna."

"Gaskets. For the Cessna." Milo leaned over and glanced at the time on his phone. "At one in the morning?"

"It was... I mean..." What the hell are you doing? "Forget it. It can wait until morning. Sorry, I woke you."

He started to leave, then Milo said, "It's not about the gaskets, is it? Why you're here?"

Joss leaned against the open door and shook his head, the words refusing to come.

"You don't want to be alone."

He shook his head again, feeling like the five-year-old who'd had a bad dream and wanted to climb into bed with his mommy and daddy. "It's so fucking quiet in there." His voice came out as little more than a gruff whisper.

Milo glanced at his bed. A twin. Joss hadn't fit on a twin bed since he was in middle school.

Joss waved him off. "Forget it."

"I could come with you... if you'd like."

Which was insane.

Joss definitely *wasn't* inviting his employee back to his bed. But apparently different parts of his brain weren't in agreement because what came out of his mouth was, "I'd like that."

"Okay." Milo stood and pulled on a pair of cut-off sweats over his boxer briefs.

"I promise to keep my hands to myself. This isn't a power play on my employee or a clumsy move to try to get you in my bed. I..." Joss blew out a breath, feeling nothing like the stoic, six-foot-something gym-rat that he looked like.

"Don't want to be alone," Milo finished for him. "I get it."

Milo held out his hand and damn if Joss didn't reach out and take it. Through the dark hangar, Milo towed him along, slapping off the lights in the den and kitchen as he made his way down the back hall. He stopped when the hall ended with two doors. One on the left and one on the right.

"Left," Joss said.

Like everywhere else in the apartment, the window in his bedroom didn't have a covering. It faced the hill behind the airstrip, catching the first rays of light in the morning. Besides, he had no near neighbors he had to worry about seeing into his bedroom.

The high sliver of moon provided enough light to keep them from tripping over the bed or the trail of clothes he'd stripped off on his way to the shower. Milo sat on the edge of the bed and scooted over, not bothering to get beneath the covers.

Joss hesitated, their hands dropping.

"Second thoughts?" Milo asked. He seemed to have no difficulty reading Joss's thoughts.

"And third and fourth and—"

"Get in." Milo's voice had an unexpected tone of authority that clicked with Joss. Sometimes he was so fucking tired of being the one in charge. "Stop overthinking it."

Joss climbed into bed and groaned as the mattress sank

beneath his weight.

"Roll this way." Again, that voice that left little room for argument. Not that Joss had planned to argue.

Joss rolled, and Milo pulled him into his chest, draping Joss's arm over his waist. Milo's arm came around Joss's shoulder. It took a little jostling before Milo shifted, and Joss's leg fell into the space between Milo's.

"This okay?" Milo asked.

"Yeah."

Milo's hand rested on Joss's back, his fingers absently tracing light circles between Joss's shoulder blades. The tension eased from Joss's neck and back as he allowed himself to accept the comfort Milo offered.

Fuck he needed to give the guy a raise.

"Why are you chuckling?" Milo asked.

That was supposed to have been in his head. "I was thinking that I needed to give you a raise. I know for a fact that cuddling isn't in the job description."

Joss had been joking, but the hand on his back stilled, and Milo leaned away. "Look at me." When Joss did, Milo said, "I'm not doing this for a raise, or because I think it will give me job security. I'm doing it because I want to."

"Why?" Joss had to ask. Why couldn't he shut up and leave it at that?

"I've never lost someone I loved the way you loved Dan, but in some way," Milo said cryptically, "I understand."

Joss almost pushed for more answers, but then Milo pressed a chaste kiss to the top of his head and said, "Get some sleep."

Snuggling in closer, Joss took Milo at his word as the exhaustion caught up with him and came crashing down. He settled his head on Milo's chest, the steady *thump-bump* of his heart echoing in Joss's ear, that feeling as if he'd come home, pulling him under.

Joss came awake in stages as the first rays of light filtered into the bedroom. Milo recognized that because he'd been awake for a while, listening to Joss's steady breathing. Milo's arm had fallen asleep long ago, but he hadn't wanted to move and wake Joss.

Joss raised up on one elbow, effectively pressing his morning wood into Milo's hip.

"Sorry." Joss twisted so that his erection no longer made contact, almost making Milo cry.

Not *cry* cry, but Jesus, what Milo wouldn't do to get his hands on Joss. His lips. His mouth. His tongue. "Don't be sorry."

Joss stilled, catching the undertones of Milo's words, but instead of shifting back, he said, "I promised not to lay a hand on you."

Milo grinned as he stared up at a sleep-tousled Joss. "That wasn't your hand."

Joss chuckled, dropping his forehead to Milo's chest and shaking his head. He raised it again. "I'm not sure how I should take that."

"You're confused?"

"A little," he admitted.

"Let me see if I can clear things up for you." Milo didn't know where his bravado came from, but he caught the back of Joss's neck and pulled him closer. Their lips touched. Joss groaned.

Apparently, that was all the clarification Joss needed because he rolled until Milo was partially beneath him. Joss braced himself on his arms and took the kiss deeper. Milo could still smell the scent of grass on Joss and the unique earthy scent of the scrub brush that grew all over the San Gabriels.

Joss nipped and nibbled, his tongue sweeping into Milo's open mouth. Their tongues tasting and exploring each other.

Milo let his hand drift down, his fingertip tracing the waistband of Joss's shorts. Joss ground against him, that thick dick pressing into Milo's pelvis. Joss broke the kiss, that deep, sexy voice grumbling in Milo's ear. "Put your hand on me."

The demand caught Milo off guard, and when he hesitated, Joss loosely took his hand and guided it down the front of his shorts. He wasn't wearing any underwear. "Touch me."

Gladly.

Milo took Joss's cock in his hand, already having a good idea of his length and girth from having it pressed up against him half the night. But touching him after thinking of little else for the past week or so seemed like an altered reality.

But this big hunk of man in front of him was all too real. Joss's steely warmth lay in Milo's hand. He drew his fingers up the silky skin, his thumb gliding through the precum gathering at the tip and swirling it around the crown.

Joss dropped his head to Milo's shoulder, his breath sucking in on a strangled hiss. "Stroke it."

Milo slid his hand down, but if Joss thought he would be calling all the shots, directing all the action, he had a few things to learn about Milo.

Milo might be smaller. He might paint his nails and be more femme, but he could never pass on a chance to be in control.

At least not since his transplant.

But Milo didn't want to think about that now.

Milo must have caught Joss unbalanced and unaware because when he pushed against the center of Joss's chest, he fell back. Milo scrambled on top of him, Joss's throaty, gruff chuckle made Milo's heart kick at his sternum.

"You want my hands on you?" Milo asked.

Joss's put a hand behind his head as his sexy, enthralled grin widened. "For a start."

Milo loved the way Joss went with it. Loved that Joss wasn't saying that they shouldn't, that he was Milo's boss, and that this was all wrong.

After all, they were two consenting adults.

Milo ducked his head and nipped and licked at the soft flesh near Joss's pit where Joss's raised arm connected to his chest. Milo breathed him in. Joss's scent could be bottled and sold as an aphrodisiac. At least for Milo.

Joss's shorts tented with his hard-on, and he settled back on his haunches and ran his hands down Joss's chest. Milo wanted to grind against him but denied himself. There would be plenty of time for that.

His fingers skimmed through the thin mat of hair on Joss's chest. Then they bumped down Joss's abdominals until his fingers hooked into the waistband of Joss's shorts.

Joss's free hand moved to Milo's thigh, not to stop him, but to give him an encouraging squeeze. Milo glanced up. "You haven't changed your mind, have you?"

"No." The answer came quick. Unequivocal.

After the emotional night before, Joss looked like he could use the release. Milo could, too. Nothing wrong with helping each other out, was there?

It's more than that to you already. You like him. Engineer whatever excuse you want, but in your heart, you know the truth.

Joss lifted his hips, and Milo slid the shorts down his legs. Joss kicked them off.

That massive cock jutted out from Joss's body, and Milo had to tell himself he wasn't there to sit on it, he was there to bring Joss pleasure.

I bet being buried deep in your ass would bring him a lot *of pleasure.*

Milo stifled the groan. Did he want to fuck Joss? No question. But he didn't want to jump straight to the fucking. He liked the tease and control and building anticipation, whether that lasted minutes, hours, days, or weeks.

Starting at the base, Milo ran a finger along the underside of Joss's cock, the vein underneath a thick rope, the engorged head a deep shade. Precum leaked out. Milo's own dick did the same, making a damp spot on his underwear.

That hand Joss had on Milo's thigh reached around and kneaded his ass cheek. Milo didn't waste time working Joss with his hands. He headed straight for the gold.

Leaning over, Milo licked Joss's slit, sucking the fat tip into his mouth and making sure he got every delicious, salty drop. Milo groaned at the taste. Joss's hand went to the back of Milo's head, his hiss of pleasure all the encouragement Milo needed.

Not that he needed encouragement.

He loved how Joss's body tightened with sexual tension, how his hips pumped as if on their own, how Joss's hand on the back of Milo's head guided and fisted in his hair.

Opening wide, he took Joss to the back of his throat, Milo's lips not even coming close the base.

"Don't try to take it all," Joss said. But that only made Milo try harder, but there was only so much even an eager man could take.

He added a hand at the root and used his hands and mouth and lips and tongue to tease and stroke and suck. Milo brought Joss to the edge of the abyss and pulled off.

"*Mother fucker,*" Joss chuckled. He brought his own hand down, chasing the climax.

Milo sat back, watching the show, his hand sliding down and freeing his own dick. They locked eyes.

"You like watching me jack myself?" Joss asked as he stroked his cock, concentrating more on the sensitive head.

Taking note, Milo nodded. Joss's eyes closed as his head fell back, his hand working harder and faster. He grunted, the cords in his neck drawing tight. By the way Joss's hips pumps and his lungs worked, blowing out harsh breaths and pants, Milo knew Joss was close.

Reaching down, Milo cupped Joss's balls, drawing a mumbled, "*fuuuck*" from Joss's throat.

"I'm so fucking close." Joss groaned, his hand slowing. "Finish me off."

Milo's hand replaced Joss's, his mouth sucking on the head and upper shaft while his hand worked the rest. In a few short seconds, Milo felt the first pulses of Joss's impending orgasm at the base of Joss's cock. He swirled his tongue around the ridge one final time before the hot pulses of Joss's load emptied into the back of Milo's mouth.

He swallowed as much as he could, but Joss was above average on more than length and girth. What little escaped, Milo carefully lapped up with a self-satisfied grin. As Joss came back down and his breathing slowed, Milo ran light fingers along the underside of Joss's cock.

Joss scrubbed his hands down his face, then glanced down at Milo. "You fucking slayed me."

Milo grinned, straddling the top of Joss's muscular thighs. Their cocks aligned, and he worked his hips, enjoying the friction on his super-heated dick. Milo wasn't best known for his stamina, and it wouldn't take much for him to lose it.

"Come here." Joss palmed the back of Milo's neck and pulled him in for a kiss, not one that devoured, but one that savored. When he broke the kiss, his soft eyes hardened. "Lose the clothes."

"I'm already about to come," Milo said. At that point, he'd be lucky if the thought of Joss touching him didn't set him off like an over-fueled rocket.

"Do it." Apparently, Joss didn't listen to reason.

Milo slipped off the bed and stripped out of his shorts, his hard-on slapping his belly. Joss slid away from the wall. "Come up here and turn around."

Milo straddled Joss face and stared down the length of Joss's torso and softening erection. In Milo's opinion, a soft Joss was as impressive as the hard one. But Milo didn't have much time to think. Joss's hands squeezed Milo's ass as his thumbs traced the line where his legs joined his body.

"Aw, fuck," Milo groaned as one of those thumbs grazed his taint.

His forehead fell to Joss's abdomen, and his whole body broke out in a rolling wave of goosebumps, sweeping his entire body in sensation. All that from one light touch.

Then Joss took Milo in his hand. "Mmmm. I love me an intact cock."

Exposing the head, Joss flicked his tongue over the sensitive flesh. Milo's breath caught in his chest, and all the blood in his body raced to his groin until his dick and balls grew impossibly heavy.

Joss didn't hesitate to put his mouth on Milo. He looped his arms around Milo's thighs and pulled him down until Milo bottomed out in all that amazing, warm, wet heat at the back of Joss's throat. Milo didn't have the kind of dick that would choke anyone. He was average-sized, but he got the job done, and he'd never heard any complaints.

Milo caught on quickly when Joss pulled him in and released. Pulled and released. He wanted Milo to fuck his face. Milo worked his hips, his cock sliding in and out of Joss's mouth. Joss's nose buried in his taint, his hot breath setting off sparks that threatened to incinerate him.

The tingling at the base of Milo's spine came quick, his climax even quicker. All he got out was a grunt of warning before he blew his load down the back of Joss's throat.

Spasms wracked his body as the orgasm rolled along his nerve endings. When he finished, Joss pulled free, and Milo shifted to his side, his breath an elusive phantom he tried hard to catch.

"Jesus Christ," Joss muttered, his hand gently stroking down Milo's thigh.

Joss rolled onto his side, squeezed Milo's ass, and gave it a light slap. "I love the way the morning light is shining on that ass."

Milo only had the energy to grunt. With a playful bite to one of Milo's ass cheeks, Joss climbed out of bed, his dick mostly soft but still more than a mouthful. "We'd better get cleaned up. We still need to load the cargo into the Otter."

"Sure," Milo sat up and turned to watch Joss's backside as he disappeared into his bathroom.

The quick way Joss transitioned from pleasure mode to work mode made Milo wonder if he was invited to join Joss in his shower, or if he was expected to use his own. In the end, he gathered up his clothes and padded back to his room and showered alone, telling himself what happened was a one-off.

They'd both needed to blow off some steam. It wasn't like they were suddenly dating or boyfriends or some silly shit like that.

Milo knew the score. He was still the employee.

And, even if Joss didn't seem too concerned about violating that boundary, it was best that Milo remembered that.

JOSS TOOK ONE OF THE ROLLING CARTS STACKED WITH CHIPTECH'S computer equipment while Milo took the other. The Simi Valley tech firms always hired him to ship their sensitive equipment to one of their business partners in San José, a little south of San Francisco, instead of using a commercial carrier where they had less control over who came into contact with their proprietary equipment.

He had no idea what the equipment did, only that he'd had to sign an NDA to get the gig. One by one, they loaded the boxes onto the Otter, setting them between the benches and strapping them down to the anchors on the floor so the load wouldn't shift in flight. By the time they were done, sweat slicked Joss's body for the second time that morning.

Though the first time had been much more pleasurable than the second.

Joss should have told Milo their encounter had been a mistake, but fuck if it felt like one. But he'd kept everything business as usual while he packed and prepped his plane for the flight. It was better that way, right? A clear demarcation between the personal and the professional?

Milo took his cart and started pushing it toward the hangar. Joss called out. "Hey, you ever been up?"

Milo turned. "Commercially. Not in anything smaller."

"Wanna come with me?" And yeah, that invitation didn't exactly keep work and pleasure separate, but Jesus, if nothing else, Dan's death had taught him that life was too fucking short to not do what you really wanted to do.

"I've got work and—"

"It's a beautiful day to fly. I can call your boss. Tell him I need your help."

Milo walked back to him, cupping a hand to his brow to block out the rising sun, his hair still damp from his shower. "I don't know. I don't want this to get weird."

"It's a flight. It's not weird." Why was he trying to talk Milo into it? "I can separate work and play."

Milo cocked his head. "Can you? Ever since I climbed out of your bed, you've pretended nothing happened."

Joss took a step closer and lowered his voice. He didn't know why. It wasn't like anyone would overhear. "I know something happened. You want to stand here and talk about it, or do you want to lock up the hangar and come with me?"

"Basically, you're going to pay me to fuck off for the day?"

Joss wanted to grin and say Milo had earned it, but he didn't want what had happened between them to be a string tied to Milo's job. In Joss's mind, the two were distinct and separate. "You my accountant now?"

"No."

"Then put those carts up while I finish preflight and get your ass on that plane." Maybe boss mode would get Milo in the cockpit beside him. It was a longish flight up to San José, and the company would be appreciated.

Admit it. You want to spend the day with him.

"Yes, sir," Milo snapped out, turning on his heel and taking Joss's cart with him. *Smart ass.*

Even after coming less than an hour before, that didn't keep Joss from getting a semi from that snapped 'yes, sir.'

Joss was playing with fire, but he didn't change his mind or tell Milo to stay behind. He finished his preflight checklist as Milo climbed into the cockpit beside him.

Once Milo buckled in, he handed Milo a headset so they could talk during the flight. "You hear me okay?"

"Check," Milo said. It sounded a little smart-assy, but that only brought a smile to Joss's face.

The sky was clear and blue, and the weather forecast in Northern California called for more of the same. Joss started his engines, increased his throttle speed, and taxied to the end of the runway.

"Don't touch anything unless I tell you to. Got it?"

"Got it," Milo parroted.

Milo was still in a mood. Joss watched as Milo's excitement built as they accelerated down the runway, gaining speed.

With his grin growing wider, Milo whooped when the wheels left the ground and cried out, "Time to fly!"

Goosebumps skittered across Joss's flesh, standing the hairs on the back of his neck. The yoke bucked in Joss's hands as Dan's words ripped through him. He quickly climbed, keeping a visual out for incoming flights into LAX more by rote than because he was paying as close attention as he should.

"What did you say?" The words fell out of Joss's mouth, and even with the headset, Joss wasn't sure Milo could have heard the breathless words over the drone of the Otter's twin engines.

Milo glanced over and blinked at him. "What?"

'Nothing' sat at the tip of Joss's tongue, but he couldn't let this go, even though he'd clearly heard Milo the first time. "That thing you said when we lifted off. What was it?"

"Time to fly?" Confusion knit Milo's brows together. "Is there a problem?"

Continuing to climb, Joss didn't quite know how to answer the question. Milo had no way of knowing that was one of Dan's sayings. A heaviness landed in his chest.

Joss stared out his windshield at the cloudless sky as he

leveled off on his charted course. He set his autopilot and tried to pull himself together.

Milo's eyes stared a hole into the side of his head. "Did I say something wrong?"

Yes, Joss wanted to scream in one of those tones that said, 'of course, you idiot,' but Milo was innocent. He'd been enjoying what Joss and Dan had always loved about flying. Joss couldn't fault him there.

When the tightness in his chest eased, he said, "Dan used to say that all the time, is all. No big. The words caught me off guard."

Milo's head snapped back to stare out his own windshield, the flash of guilt he saw in Milo's eyes he must have imagined. "Sorry. I didn't know."

Fuck. Now he'd made Milo feel bad. He reached across and took Milo's chin in his fingers and turned his head. When their eyes met, Joss said, "No harm, no foul, right?"

"Right."

The air traffic controller from one of the municipal airports along the way hailed him as he neared their airspace and cleared him to travel through. They continued north, the silence so heavy Joss wondered how they were able to remain aloft.

Then somewhere over the Los Padres National Forrest, Milo finally asked, "Tell me more about Dan?"

13

Joss took the yoke back in his hands and disengaged the autopilot, his movements stiff and robotic as if it took everything he had to force his body to do what he wanted it to do.

"I take that back," Milo said, not wanting to bring Joss any more pain. "You don't owe me anything. I'm your employee, not—"

"You're more than my damn employee." Joss's growl of frustration startled Milo.

Okay. Milo didn't think right then was the time to press for a definition of what he was to Joss. Not when his jaw was still tight from sucking Joss off.

Joss shifted in his seat and worked his head from side to side. He pulled his aviators to the end of his nose and leveled his gaze at Milo over the top of them. "You get that, right?"

The sincerity in Joss's eyes flashed bright, but Milo didn't know quite what to say to that. "I don't normally make it a habit of sleeping with my boss."

"That's good to hear." A smile teased the corners of Joss's lips.

"But to be fair," Milo said, "my last boss was a straight

woman who channeled Jabba the Hut personality-wise, so the temptation wasn't quite the same."

"And I've never had an employee sit on my face, for what it's worth." Joss groaned with a laugh and had to reach down and readjust himself. But then his smile waned, and he quickly sobered. "I want to thank you, though."

"For sitting on your face?" Milo tried to keep it light, not knowing where Joss was headed with this.

"That was amazing. But I'm talking about last night. Sometimes the feelings are overwhelming even after Dan's been gone for so long. And you were there for me. I want you to know I appreciate that."

Milo's throat tightened, and he only managed to squeak his words out. "You're welcome."

Below, Milo watched the traffic on what he assumed to be the 101 heading north. All the tiny cars and the wide-open spaces. A jet crossed their path high above them, belching a white, fluffy contrail.

"Sometimes," Joss said, his expression stoic as he scratched at the couple days of scruff on his jaw, "it's nice to sleep with someone in your arms. To have someone hold you back. To feel their warmth. To hear that steady heartbeat beneath your ear reminding you you're not alone. It gave me a sense of peace. That everything was okay, even when I know it will never be the same. I really needed that."

Milo's heart kicked his sternum, and he had to sit on his hands to keep from rubbing the center of his chest. Many weird things had happened in his life since the transplant, and he knew his heart, *Dan's heart*, couldn't respond to Joss. But fuck if it didn't feel like it had.

They came into contact with another tower, got diverted around a nearby airfield, and continued north again.

Words failed Milo, so he didn't say anything. Finally, Joss said, "Do you really want to hear more about Dan?"

The vulnerability in Joss's voice made Milo's throat tight again. He swallowed hard and said, "Yeah. I do."

"Dan was one of those guys who was bigger than life. Everyone wanted to be around him, have a piece of him because that *joie de vivre* couldn't be contained. It was like glitter. It got on you and infected you, and it was near impossible to wash off."

Milo smiled along with Joss. Even after Dan had been gone so long, Milo felt the love Joss had for Dan. That was something else that couldn't be contained.

"He loved to fly. Loved jumping even more. If he'd known what was coming, I don't think he could have given up skydiving. Not him. Flying. Falling. It lived in his bones."

"Sounds like an incredible person."

"He wasn't perfect. But he was mine. And I loved the way he loved me. He could take me in his arms when I'm being a total ass and love me and accept me for all my imperfections."

"I've lost friends. But I can't imagine loving someone like that and losing them. How do you not dissolve? How do you get out of bed? How do you—"

"How do you live with a black hole in the middle of your heart?"

"Yeah."

"Honestly," Joss said, "I don't know. The first year was the worst. Living in a mental fog. I almost lost the business and everything we'd built together.

"But I couldn't lose Kincaid Air." An enigmatic smile ghosted across Joss's lips. "Dan would have kicked my ass if he'd been there to see the utter destruction I'd made of the company. Eventually, I dragged my ass out of bed and forced myself to start flying again and start taking skydivers up."

"Was it harder to fly?"

"It was easier, somehow. Like up here, I was closer to him. Sometimes, I can feel him when I fly. I know that sounds stupid or all 'woo-woo' shit, but—"

"No. I totally get what you mean."

Especially when there had been times when Milo hadn't been sure if something he did, or something he ate, or something he said, had come from *him*, or Dan.

The only thing that kept Milo from thinking his imagination had been running wild with him was that other transplant recipients had had similar experiences. They couldn't all be imagining it, right?

On the horizon, the southern end of San Francisco Bay came into view. Joss reached up, adjusted their airspeed, and contacted the tower at the municipal airport where they were scheduled to land.

Turns out, the airport sat on the edge of the bay. After refueling and offloading the computer components and watching them drive away in ChipTech's van, Joss turned to Milo and said, "You ready to get something to eat?"

"I'm starved, but where are we going to find food around here that isn't in a vending machine?" Milo turned in a circle by one of the hangars. Lonergan Municipal Airport was nothing more than a double strip airport with a short tower with a bunch of hangars and small cargo and private planes.

"The airport has a small restaurant overlooking the bay. Their burgers are thick and juicy, and the view's amazing."

"Lead the way."

Milo followed Joss. They passed the tower and ended up at the building past the end of the runway. Joss held the door open for him, pushing his aviators to the top of his head as they entered the restaurant.

An older blond woman in shorts and a T-shirt that said *Pilots do it in the air* grabbed a couple of menus, and with a huge, welcoming grin on her face said, "Look what the wind blew in."

"Hey, Marla." Joss kissed her cheek. "Good to see you again."

She eyed Milo up and down. "Fresh meat?"

Joss shook his head but smiled. "This is Milo Malone. He works for me."

"Mmmhmm." Marla drew the sound out, a flirtatious smile on her face. "He *works* for me, too."

Milo waited for Joss to say it wasn't like that, but he didn't, and Milo didn't know what to think about that. Before he could figure that out, Marla picked up Milo's hand and examined the black nail polish he'd reapplied and that had already started to chip again. Who would have thought working at the hangar would be so hard on his nails?

"Honey, I've got what you need for those nails. "It's a glossy clear coat, and you'll practically need a jackhammer to get the color off."

"Really? I tried *Paint No More* and some others, but it doesn't seem to really help and then—" Milo glanced up at Joss. Milo had forgotten he was standing there.

"This is fascinating," Joss said, like a straight guy who couldn't give a shit.

Marla laughed. "You wanna eat inside or out?"

"Out," Joss and Milo said in unison.

She led them out to the back deck, the bay and Freemont in the distance. With the cover overhead, a comfortable breeze, and the fans spinning at a moderate rate, the temperature remained pleasant. There was only one other person eating outside. A mechanic, if the greasy coveralls were an indication. He didn't even bother looking up from his phone when Milo and Joss sat.

Marla had pen and pad in hand. "What can I get you boys to drink?"

"Ice water is fine for me," Joss said.

"Do you mind if I have a beer?" Milo asked Joss.

"Fine with me. Unless you'd planned on flying back?"

Milo chucked. Yeah. They'd never make it off the runway with him at the controls, even without the beer. "I'll have a Preacher Peach."

Joss turned as white as an Italian statue and settled his sunglasses over his eyes again.

The floor fell from beneath Milo's stomach. "What's wrong?"

IF JOSS HADN'T SPENT THE FLIGHT UP TALKING ABOUT DAN, MILO'S order might have only raised Joss's brow instead of lodging a boulder in his throat.

Fuck, he hated this time of year when all his feelings welled to the surface and bobbed along, waiting for the tiniest wave to roll him under and pummel him against the sand and rocks until he was abraded and bloodied.

"Nothing's wrong." He turned his attention to Marla, not sure how his words had slipped by the lump in his throat and had come out only sounding a bit put out. "I'll have the blue-cheese burger and fries."

"Oh. You're ready to order your food, too." Marla scribbled his order down and turned to Milo. "Are you ready to order as well?"

"I'll have what he's having."

Marla collected the menus and went to place their order.

"You could have told her to come back," Joss said. "You didn't even get a chance to look at the menu."

"I don't care about the food. I care about what happened when I ordered the beer."

Joss tossed his sunglasses on the table and dug the heels of his hands into his eye sockets. Drawing his hands down his face, he admitted, "Preacher Peach was Dan's favorite beer."

Milo swallowed hard. His eyes dropped to the table and stayed there. When he glanced back up, he'd gone ashen. "I can cancel the order."

"*Jesusfuckingchrist*," Joss stood abruptly, his plastic chair tipping over. "Canceling your order won't bring Dan back."

"You know what? Maybe I should wait by the plane."

The guy with his face in his phone stared at the two of them. Apparently, they were more entertaining than anything the guy had been scrolling through. But fuck it. What did Joss care?

Milo headed for the porch steps that would take him back to the plane without having to go through the restaurant. Joss wanted to let him go, but something stopped him.

"*Milo.*" He didn't raise his voice, but he had one of those voices that carried.

Milo stopped at the top of the stairs, not turning back, but not leaving either.

"I was out of line. Don't go."

Milo hesitated, and when Joss thought Milo would leave anyway, Joss held out his hand, "Please."

Milo turned, his gaze going to Joss's hand then back up to Joss's face. Those few seconds while Milo decided what he'd do tick, tick, ticked by.

Joss's heart stalled in his chest, and his stomach had that weightless feeling you get when your engine fails, and your plane is about to drop out of the sky.

Milo took a step toward him, and Joss's heart caught, then leveled out, the blood rushing past his eardrums with a steady hum.

He'd made a complete ass of himself.

He held out Milo's chair and scooted him back in before taking his own. Before he could apologize, Marla swept through the double doors with their beverages and food order and set them on the table.

Despite the lingering queasiness in his stomach, Joss dug into his burger while Milo took a tentative sip of his IPA.

Red crept up Milo's cheeks and settled in the tips of his ears. "You're staring."

Was he?

Joss set his burger down and wiped his hands and mouth. Hard to deny it when he'd been caught. "I didn't mean to make you self-conscious about the beer."

Milo dunked a fry into a container of ketchup and shrugged. "It still tastes good."

It wasn't exactly forgiveness. Then again, Joss hadn't exactly apologized. They finished their meal in silence. Each watching the windsurfers as they zigged and zagged around the bay.

The silence ate at Joss. He'd blown up at Milo for no damn reason. *The guy had placed an innocent order, and you jumped his ass.*

And not in the good, fun kind of way.

When Marla brought the ticket, Joss paid and said, "You want to go down and stick your feet in?"

"Isn't it cold?"

Joss grinned and nodded. "Yep."

"Sure. Why not?"

They left using the porch stairs and picked their way over thick bands of seaweed that had found its way to the pebbly beach. Nearby, seagulls flew above screeching as the little small shorebirds scuttled around in the shallows pecking at bits and bobs beneath the surface.

Joss and Milo removed their shoes and waded in. That far back in the bay, the only waves that made it to shore were from the wakes caused by the powerboats that occasionally passed by.

Milo stumbled and hissed in a breath, muttering a curse. Joss caught his hand to stabilize him. "You okay?"

"Yeah." Milo stood on one foot, his other in the air. "I stepped on a shell or something."

Joss glanced behind Milo at his upturned foot. "You're bleeding. Put your hand on my shoulder."

"What are you doing?"

"Just do it."

When Milo did, Joss lifted Milo in his arms. Milo let out a surprised squeak, his arms tightening around Joss's neck. It was stupid how much he liked having Milo in his arms, tucked against his chest.

They were only fifteen or twenty feet from shore, so he didn't have long to enjoy the contact. He sat Milo down and took the foot Milo held up. A thin trail of blood trickled from the cut on Milo's heel.

Joss pressed the clean top part of his sock to the cut and put pressure on it. It wouldn't bleed long, but it would be sore to walk on.

Milo leaned back on his elbows, his eyes closed against the sun. "You going to kiss it and make it better?"

Milo's tone teased, but tell that to Joss's dick.

"I could start there," Joss said, the pitch dropping out of his voice until it became little more than a grumble. Milo squinted up at him. "And then I'd like to work my way up."

"A little exploration?"

"Like Magellan, I'm always up for discovering new territory."

Jesus. Milo shouldn't look at him like that, or else he'd be tempted to take him right there on the beach in front of everyone.

As thrilling as that might be—right up until the police were called—Joss preferred a little more privacy when he had sex.

Besides, thorough scientific exploration took time.

Joss broke Milo's heavy-lidded gaze and pulled the balled-up sock off Milo's cut. He kept his eye on it for a few moments. "Looks like the bleeding stopped. You about ready to go?"

"Toss me my socks and shoes."

Joss put his shoes on minus one bloody sock. Milo left his sore foot bare and stuffed Joss's bloody sock into his pocket. Joss held out his hand and pulled Milo to his feet.

He rested his sore foot on his toes, but it was a bit of a hike back to the plane. It would take an hour to get back if Milo hobbled the whole way, and Joss wanted to get home and still have some daylight left to get some work done around the hangar.

Joss turned his back to Milo. "Hop on."

Milo laughed. "No way."

"I'm the boss."

"What is everybody going to think if they see you hauling my ass across the tarmac on your back?"

Joss glanced at him over his shoulder. "I don't care. Do you?"

Milo glanced around at the nearly deserted restaurant and the Cessna 182 taking off at the end of the runway. Joss didn't have to look to know what kind of plane it was. He'd recognized it from the pitch of the engine as it sped down the runway. "No. I guess not."

Joss turned around again. Milo hopped onto Joss's back, locking his arms around Joss's neck. Joss wrapped his hands under Milo's knees and hiked back to the plane.

By the time he'd made it back, sweat dripped down his back. His lungs labored, but not enough that he hadn't caught his breath by the time he'd finished his external preflight.

He handed Milo up into the cockpit and walked around the nose and climbed in.

After buckling in and finishing his preflight, he turned to Milo. "Hey."

Milo gave him his attention. "You need me to do something before taking off?"

"No. I need to say something."

"Okaaay," Milo said, clearly confused and a little gun shy.

"I'm sorry for being an asshole back there. You were doing your best to make the situation better, and I was... I was..."

"A dick?"

Joss chuckled. "Yeah. Big dick. Little reason."

"The reason's more than *little*. I get it."

"Still no excuse to take it out on you. You did nothing wrong."

Milo shrugged as if it had already been forgotten. "Don't be so hard on yourself. All those stages of grief. They're not linear. And anger is a hell of a lot easier to express than some of the other emotions."

"And still..." Joss caught Milo's chin between his thumb and forefinger and leaned in for a kiss. Not much more than the brushing of lips, but he'd needed the intimate contact, and by the way Milo's expression softened, maybe he had, too. "I'm sorry."

Milo cupped the back of Joss's neck and brought him back in for another light and lingering kiss.

Though this one made his shorts snug.

"Apology accepted."

14

Even though their number of skydiving reservations were down, the week passed by with a lot of work... and zero dick.

Probably for the best. Nothing good could come from fucking your boss.

Fucking your boss? What about fucking your donor's partner? What about that mindfuck? Especially when he has no clue who the hell you really are to him.

And Dan.

The Big Ass Fan turned above them in the hangar. The hangar bay doors stood wide open, and the Friday evening sun started to set over the valley. From his vantage point on the short scaffold Joss had set up next to his Cessna, the buildings in the valley caught fire in the sun, the glass from the buildings sparking and sparkling as a ribbon of cars headed down the I-5 down below.

"Hand me that pin wrench, will you?" Joss lay on the scaffolding beside Milo, dirt and grime and a light sheen of sweat marring his bare chest as he worked to loosen a collar.

Milo's father hadn't been the fixer type. To him, there were two kinds of men in the world. Those who could fix things and those who made enough money to pay others to fix things for them.

But Joss landed in the middle. He had a successful skydiving operation, and he seemed to have the ability to fix whatever was broken. Milo glanced at the tools lined up on the magnetic tray and plucked the pin wrench up and slapped it into Joss's hand like a well-trained surgical tech.

They worked that way for more than an hour. Joss cussing and removing stubborn parts while Milo handed him whatever tool he called for.

Milo didn't know how he knew what tools were what. He chalked it up to Dan's influence. One might think that would be creepy as hell, but Milo found comforting.

What would Joss say if he knew his partner's heart beat a couple of feet away?

Milo shook the thought away. The longer he knew Joss, the more he learned about Dan, the less Milo thought telling Joss would help either of them. For now, Milo kept that potentially explosive tidbit to himself.

Technically, it was past quitting time, but when you lived where you worked, that fine line blurred.

But it wasn't like Milo had anywhere he needed to be. Foster had complained about not seeing him in forever yet wasn't willing to drive out to the hangar to see him, not when all the fun things happened in the valley.

Milo couldn't blame him and didn't hold it against him. Besides, staring at Joss's broad chest wasn't a chore.

Joss's phone rang in his pocket. Both of his hands were occupied, so it kept ringing.

"Get that would you? That's Derek's ring tone."

Milo dug into Joss's front pocket, trying to ignore Joss's

muffled *ooof* when his finger accidentally brushed against Joss's dick.

"Put him on speaker. If I let go now, there's a spring I might lose and never find again."

Milo answered the call and held it close to Joss.

"Derek, you're on speaker," Joss said with a grunt as he continued working on whatever it was he was working on.

"Don't tell me," Derek said, "you're working on that fucking plane, aren't you?"

"What if I am?"

"Fixing that plane won't bring Dan back, you know that right?"

Joss jerked at the words, bumping his head on a solid hunk of metal. "Ow, fuck. What part of 'you're on speaker' do you not understand, asshole?"

"Glad to see you're in a good mood this evening. Should make having drinks a real pleasure."

"Damn it." Joss's head fell back on the scaffold. "I totally forgot about tonight. Look can we—"

"No, you can't put me off. You put me off last week. You can't stay up on that hill and hibernate."

"Jesus Christ." Joss let go of whatever he'd been holding onto. Milo heard the ping, ping of nuts or screws—and probably that sacred spring—hit the concrete below. Joss grabbed the phone out of Milo's hand and clicked it off speaker. "I'm not hibernating. I'm working."

Milo stood trapped on the scaffold, Joss's body taking up most of the real estate, his legs hanging down over the steps on the other side.

Milo couldn't quite hear all of Derek's words, but between the ones he caught and Joss's end of the conversation, he got the gist of it.

"Yeah, okay," Joss said at last, the defeat lacing through his tone. "I'll get cleaned up and see you in an hour."

He stuffed his phone back in his pocket and sat up. "We're done here."

"I figured."

"You want to come with me?"

Milo caught the immediate 'yes' from leaping from his throat. A chance to spend time out on the town with Joss? Yes, please. Managing his excitement, he asked, "Where we going?"

"Oh, well, um. I'm having drinks with Derek. I thought maybe you'd want to go see your friend or something? I can drop you off."

So... not the invite Milo had imagined. *Fool.* He should have known better. After all, they hadn't touched or kissed or done anything quasi inappropriate since they'd landed Monday evening after their San José flight.

The only thing that made Milo think that maybe things hadn't reverted back to pre dick-sucking day was the way Joss would check on him each evening before he shut off the hangar lights and headed in for the night.

When Joss checked on him, Joss would lean against Milo's door jamb—sometimes fully clothed, sometimes bare-chested and sweaty after a run or a workout—and talk about mundane work-related things. Things Joss really knew the answer to, but they gave him an excuse to put off saying goodnight.

At least that's how Milo had read it.

But maybe it was better this way. Joss was a good boss and an even better human being. Milo had no business getting all caught up in that complication when he couldn't imagine bringing up the fact he was Dan's heart recipient.

Not now that he'd gotten to know Joss more.

Know Dan more.

And fuck if that didn't mess with Milo's head. There had

been times before meeting Joss when Milo felt guilty that he was alive and his donor was dead. Getting to know your donor and who your donor loved and who loved him? *Christ*, it nearly rips a hole right through your freshly donated heart.

And he had to wonder again about the wisdom of seeking out his donor's family.

Since the Preacher Peach beer incident, Joss hadn't called Milo out on noticing him doing something that Dan had done or liking something Dan had liked, but he looked at Milo sometimes with that same confused devastation on his face that he'd had back under the lazy fans of the airport restaurant.

Maybe distance and time apart would be better.

"Milo?" Joss tilted his head. "You okay?"

"Yeah. And a trip into town sounds good. I'll give Foster a call and see if he's free."

They met at Joss's Jeep thirty minutes later. Milo had caught Foster on his way to Exeter, one of the gay clubs in town, so Milo had spiked his hair, shadowed his eyes, put on his tightest pair of jeans, added shirt cropped midway down his torso, and called it good.

Joss looked Milo up and down when he climbed into the Jeep. Joss had lowered the top and Milo would be lucky if his hair were still in place by the time Joss dropped him at the club.

"What? You act like you've never been to a club before. You're not so old you don't remember the clubs, are you?"

That brought an amused smile to Joss's clean-shaven face. Damn. Milo liked the three days of scruff Joss usually sported.

But a baby-faced Joss wasn't a letdown.

"I remember. I just hadn't expected you to get all dolled up." He took one of Milo's hands and held it up to the interior light. "And paint your nails purple."

"I'm gay. In case you hadn't noticed."

"That wasn't a complaint or a criticism." He fired up the Jeep and backed out of the space. "And I got the *gay* part when you sucked my dick."

———

"YOU DIDN'T HAVE TO PAY FOR DINNER," JOSS SAID AS HE AND Derek settled in at a two-top table at the back of Sneaky Pete's for drinks after dinner. He sat with his back to the wall. He enjoyed watching the crowd while not being in the thick of it.

Especially when he wanted time to unwind with his friend, and he wasn't out looking to get laid.

Well, at least not by anyone here...

He cut that thought off before his mind drifted to other things like the way Milo felt in his arms or the way Joss's balls drew up and he got a semi every time he thought about Milo's lips stretched around his cock.

Joss came back to himself to find Derek waving his hand in front of his face.

"Where did you go?" Derek asked.

"Nowhere. I'm here."

"You weren't here during dinner. Not mentally, at least. And you're certainly not *here* now. Get out of your head and join the rest of the world for a bit."

A waiter came over. He had a bare chest, wide leather cuffs on his wrists, and a fuck-me grin on his young face. "Hello, boys." He popped a hip out suggestively. "What can I get you two?"

The waiter's eyes flicked behind Joss to the pitch-black back-room patrons frequented for anonymous sex.

"Yeah," Derek said with a gleam in his eyes that even the dim-lit interior of Sneaky Pete's couldn't hide. "What can he get you?"

"Double whiskey," Joss said, ignoring the mild disappointment on the waiter's face.

After Derek placed his order and the waiter left to get their drinks, he turned to Joss and said, "You broke his heart."

Joss rolled his eyes. "I'm sure there are plenty of guys in here who will help him mend it."

"Right. Who needs a random blowjob from a cute waiter when you've got Milo sitting back at the hangar?"

"Fuck you," Joss said, without any bite.

One side of Derek's lips raised in a half-smile. "You know I'm busting your balls, right? Whatever you do or don't do with Milo—"

Joss held up his hand. "I never should have told you about the blowjob. Nothing else has happened. I don't need a well-intentioned caution, my friend."

"Playing devil's advocate, and ignoring my own reservations here..." Derek leaned back as the waiter dropped off their drinks. When they were alone again, he continued. "Why the hell not?"

Joss took a sip of his whiskey. It was smooth as it warmed a trail down to his stomach. He thought about giving the standard reason, the employer/employee thing, about not wanting to take advantage of his position or to be a fucking cliché. But there were other things. Things that he hadn't been willing to admit.

Even to himself.

"I could get lost in him so fucking easy. And I don't know if it's because I crave that kind of attention, or if it's him, or..."

"Or what?"

Now here came the real fucked up part. "Or if it's because of Dan."

"Dan?" Derek mopped up the condensation dripping onto the table from the beer he'd barely touched. "I don't follow."

Joss's throat tightened, and he had no idea why. His

emotions had been more manic than they'd ever been since that first year after Dan's death. Why wasn't this shit getting any easier? "Sometimes... he reminds me of Dan. Not physically. It's the little things. And I can't help but wonder if that's part of the attraction. That I'm hunting that thread, that glimmer of what used to be."

Derek sat forward, his voice low when he said, "Now I know you've lost it. Milo is nothing like Dan."

"Not on the outside," Joss could freely admit. "But I don't know. It's something on the inside."

"Like what?" Derek didn't hide his skepticism. Joss would have been more surprised if he'd had.

Derek finally drank some of his beer, and Joss tossed the whiskey to the back of his throat, caught the eye of their waiter, and pointed to his glass for another. Derek raised a brow. "Hitting it kind of hard tonight, aren't you?"

"You're not my mother or my keeper," Joss all but growled. That brow of Derek's went higher. "Fuck. Sorry. But not that sorry. It was your fucking idea to drag me off the hill. Not mine."

"Fair enough." Another man might have been put off by Joss's emotional whiplash, but Derek was the kind of friend who could see below the surface and find the person beneath. Probably what made him such a cool-headed investigator. "You were telling me how Milo was like Dan."

"You really going to make me do this?"

Derek leaned back in his chair and propped his elbow on the table, his back turned more toward the wall so he could watch the people in the bar as well. But you also couldn't convince Joss that Derek hadn't made that subtle move so that Joss didn't feel like he was in an interrogation. Derek let the silence drift on, his thumb swiping through the condensation on his glass, waiting for Joss to fill the void.

Joss knew it was an investigative technique Derek had honed back when he'd been a detective, but fuck if it didn't work.

The waiter dropped off his new drink and Joss took a fortifying sip. "Some of the things he says, could be direct quotes. When we took off for our flight to San José, he said, 'Time to fly.'" Something subtle shifted in Derek's eyes, but nothing concrete enough for Joss to read. "He likes his sandwiches the same way Dan did. He orders fucking Preacher Peaches for fuck's sake."

"It's a popular beer, especially in the gay bars in the valley. You're bound to run into someone else who drinks it. You know that, right?"

"Yeah, sure. It's not just that, though. He was helping me with the Cessna the way Dan would. Handing me tools and talking about nothing important. Dan used to joke he liked to help me because it was the only time he could get me to sit still for more than a minute and listen."

He went to take another sip of his whiskey, but with the sudden tightness in his throat, there was no way in hell it would go down. Christ, what he wouldn't give to hear Dan's stories again.

When his throat loosened, Joss continued. "And when Milo came to my bed. The next morning, he flipped me on my back and kind of took over. He couldn't overpower me, we both knew that, but his dominant energy... it flows through that kid like—"

"Kid? Why are you distancing yourself from him like that?"

"Now you're my therapist?" Joss thumped his head on the wall behind him but hardly felt a thing. Could be the alcohol or the fact that the hurt in the center of his chest overwhelmed his system and he couldn't feel any more pain.

"That energy flowed through Milo the way it flowed through Dan. I know you don't have to be as big as me to be dominant. I know all those other things I mentioned, other people can like and say and do. But putting them all together, it makes me wonder if what I'm attracted to are the things that remind me of Dan. And Milo's a nice kid—fuck, guy. *Man*." Joss took a breath and collected his thoughts. "I don't want to lead him on or hurt him."

"Hurt *him*? Or hurt yourself?"

"Maybe both. It's not like I don't know Milo's not Dan. He's his own person. I get that. It's just hard not to forget that sometimes."

Derek nodded but uncharacteristically didn't have much to add. They drank in companionable silence and watched the goings-on in the bar. One of the things he loved about Sneaky Pete's was that it was the kind of gay bar that catered to a diverse crowd. There were the conservative types, the leather guys, the twinks. Most fully clothed. Others danced in leather harnesses and jockstraps.

A man walked up to their table, his eyes lasered in on Derek the entire way. He would have looked like your everyday joe, except for the suspenders holding up his jeans, a *CockSure* leather jockstrap over his junk behind an open fly.

"Wanna dance?" He had kind eyes and a mischievous grin, the kind of grin that Derek had never been able to resist as long as Joss had known him.

Sneaky Pete's had little in the way of a dance floor. What they had was a postage-stamp-sized corner of the bar where the tables had been pushed aside. But when you were bumping and grinding against your dance partner, how much room did you really need?

Derek's head bobbed to the beat coming through the speakers, and Joss knew he'd decline even though he wanted to say yes.

"Go," Joss said, "I'll be here when you get back."

Derek took the outstretched hand and let the man pull him

to his feet. They disappeared with matching grins into the crowd in a matter of a few seconds. Joss thought about leaving, but knowing Derek, if he found him gone, he'd drive up to the hangar and not let him hear the end of it. Instead, Joss sat there and drank.

And wished he were back at the hangar, sharing a quiet beer with Milo at the end of the airstrip as they watched the lights of the planes as they approached LAX.

15

A sweaty Milo leaned into Foster as he polished off his beer, though it did little to quench his thirst after all the dancing and bumping and grinding. He'd been groped and kissed and fondled more in the last hour or so than he had in a long time, and he was... *over it.* "Let's get out of here."

He had to yell to be heard over the thump of the bass and the hoots and hollers of the dancing crowd. His head throbbed to the beat, and all he wanted was a little quiet and maybe an aspirin.

And Joss?

"What's gotten into you? You used to love the clubs. That old-man heart of yours is a real drag."

Milo had told Foster about the stuff he'd read about the cellular memory thing. About the things he'd said and done and ate and drank that wasn't normal. At least not normal for him pre-transplant. And really, he wasn't sure Foster wasn't wrong.

"I can catch a rideshare to the hangar if you want to stay. And you should. I don't want to be blamed for you not getting laid."

"No, it's okay. I'll come with you."

They pushed through Exeter's doors and spilled out onto the sidewalk. Moderate traffic passed by. It was still early enough that the valley had a good vibe, and as much as Milo didn't want to be in the club anymore, he also wasn't ready to go back to the hangar. He didn't want to have to hang around, waiting for Joss to come home or come home with another guy.

He didn't want to think about that even though he and Joss had no kind of agreement. Why would they when they'd only messed around that one time? They were both free to see other people. A good thing.

Right?

Maybe Milo should have taken that blond guy up on his offer to take him home. Maybe if he got his rocks off, Joss wouldn't be so appealing.

He turned right on the street instead of left toward the parking lot.

"Hey, where you going?" Foster jogged to catch up. He wore tight white jeans and a cropped top that barely covered his nips and showed off his trim waist and developing abs. His guyliner was on point, and he smelled sexy enough to fuck.

If he weren't Milo's best friend.

"Let's walk."

Foster groaned but fell into step. "I have a perfectly good vehicle. We could see all the sites in the comfort of my Vette."

"You're the one trying to work out more."

"Yeah. Work out. Like in a gym. With hot guys. And open showers. Not walking along the street at night."

"I promise you're not going to melt. I'll even buy you a drink later. My treat."

Foster held his hands out in a look-at-me kind of way. "I'm not going into just any bar in the valley dressed like this."

"We'll find someplace. Promise."

Foster indulged Milo. They walked the streets for over an hour. Got propositioned on a couple of corners while they waited to cross, got whistled at, and some asshole threw their drink at them out of their car window, narrowly missing Foster's white pants.

"Fucker!" Foster yelled out, both middle fingers raised. When the car turned the corner, Foster sank against the display window of a sex shop and said, "Hold up. My feet are killing me. And where is this drink you promised me?"

Milo glanced around. They'd kind of wandered into a seedier part of town. Maybe this walking on the streets wasn't such a good idea after all. He pulled out his phone to see where they were and if there were any gay bars nearby.

"There's a bar called Sneaky Pete's a couple of blocks over. Do you think you can make it, or do you want me to call your mother?"

Foster laughed and wrapped his arm around Milo's neck and gave it a teasing squeeze. "You're such an asshole."

"But an asshole who's going to buy you a drink."

They followed the map app on his phone. The streets got narrower. The traffic thinner. The lights dimmer.

"You sure you know where you're going?"

Milo did a three-sixty, looking around. "This place is supposed to be around here somewhere. Look." He held his phone out for Foster to see. "We're right on top of the dot."

"I can hear music," Foster said. He glanced up and down the street, but there were no signs for a bar. He pointed up the street. "I think it's coming from up there."

The music got louder as they walked, though nothing like Exeter, where your car windows vibrated with the bass when you pulled into the parking lot. A door up ahead of them opened, disgorging out two guys holding hands as they walked up the street.

Foster caught the door before it could close, the music spilling out into the air. "I think this is the place."

There were no signs above the single door with a dark reflective coating. But it had to be the place. There was nowhere else on the street that looked open. Milo filed in with Foster on his heels. Even though it was dark outside, his eyes still had to adjust to the dim, crowded bar.

"Oh, yeah," Foster said as he glanced around. "I think this is my kind of place."

There were men of all ages. And Foster being Foster, even in a crowded room, he drew immediate attention. A man walked over to Foster and leaned in, his words only slurring slightly when he asked, "Can I buy you a drink?"

Foster hesitated, and Milo knew it was only because he was with him. "It's okay," Milo said. "I think I'm going to dance."

He made his way to the dance floor by himself. He had to squeeze in, but it wasn't long before a guy came up behind him and put his hands on Milo's hips and whispered near his ear, "Shake that sexy ass."

Milo still had enough of a buzz to do what the man asked. The guy had jet-black hair, soft, inebriated eyes, and an intoxicating smile. They danced together for a while before he turned Milo around, locked his arms loosely around Milo's neck, and said, "I'm Teagan. What's your name?"

"Milo."

"You move like sin, Milo. And fuck if that's not the sexiest thing."

Milo smiled at him. Teagan didn't have that sexy growl that Joss had or that lumberjack body, and probably didn't have that monster cock, but he seemed sweet, and genuine, and didn't push too hard on Milo's boundaries.

Then those big brown eyes of Teagan's got big and bright with an idea, and his smile held a secret that drew Milo in.

"Come with me." Teagan took Milo's hands in his and started backing off the dance floor.

Milo tugged back. "Where to?"

"Do you trust me?"

Milo had absolutely no reason to trust a stranger, besides the booze, so he said, "Yeah."

"Follow me then." That time when Teagan pulled, Milo followed.

"What are you staring at?" Derek asked, still sweating from his time on the dance floor as he tried to see what Joss had seen. But as crowded as the bar was, Joss doubted Derek would spot him.

And even if Derek had, he wouldn't have had the gut-punch reaction Joss had had when he'd seen Milo walk through Sneaky Pete's door with his friend trailing behind him.

Sneaky Pete's was no place for a guy like Milo. It would chew him up and spit him out and squish him like a wad of gum on a hot sidewalk.

Joss didn't glance away from the dance floor when he said, "I thought I saw someone I knew."

"Half these guys in here are people you know. What makes this guy so special?" Derek grumbled when Milo hit the edge of the dance floor, his hands in some other guy's. "I should have fucking known. Joss, let it go."

"I don't know what you're talking about."

"You look like you're about to storm across the bar and rip that poor, unsuspecting sap limb by limb. I'm telling you the assault charges wouldn't be worth it."

"I'm not tearing anyone apart."

"Coulda fooled me."

Milo didn't see him and Derek in the corner, his eyes focused on the man in front of him and not the rest of the bar. Did Milo even know the guy was leading him to the backroom? If Milo wanted to go there, then Joss would have to live with that. Milo's sex life wasn't his business, except...

At the last second, Joss's hand shot out and snagged Milo's arm before he could be dragged past the black curtain. Milo let out a squeak of surprise and froze on the spot. The guy whose hand Milo had been holding was brought up short as well.

"What the hell?" the guy said. "Let go of him."

Instead of letting go like a normal, reasonable, rational person, Joss stood to his full height and said, "I don't think so." Being the size he was, Joss was usually careful not to use his body to crowd or intimidate people, knowing how he could come across, but right at that moment, he leaned into his size and used his scowl to ramp up the pucker factor.

A baffled Milo said, "What are you doing?"

"You know this asshole?" the other man asked.

"Teagan, this is Joss, my boss."

Joss didn't let go of Milo to shake Teagan's hand. Teagan didn't either.

"Great." Teagan slathered on the sarcasm. "Leave these old geezers, and let's go have some fun."

"Is that what you want, Milo? Groping. Sucking. *Fucking?* In a dark backroom in a derelict gay bar? With *him?*"

Joss added the *with him* part at the last second when he realized he wouldn't mind dragging Milo in that dark room and seeing what they might discover. *Together.*

Milo shook Teagan's hand free and peered around the curtain into the dark room as three men staggered out, zipping up their pants and raking back their hair. "Is that where you were taking me?"

"Where did you think we were going?"

"I don't know." Milo shrugged. "Out the back to talk?"

Was Milo that naïve?

Teagan leaned in as if he were going to whisper in Milo's ear, but his voice was loud enough for everyone to hear. "I'm not interested in talking."

Joss chanced a glance over at Derek who hadn't moved from his spot. The expression on Derek's face didn't rise to the level of judgmental but came damn close. Joss pushed his friend out of his mind and concentrated on the debacle unfolding in front of him.

"Why don't you run along," Joss said to Teagan.

Milo shook off Joss's hand, and by the stormy expression on Milo's face, Joss expected Milo to tell him to fuck the fuck off. "You've been drinking," Milo said instead.

Teagan laughed. "It's a bar, genius."

The light in Milo's eyes dimmed. "I think you should go, Teagan."

"You're kidding me, right? I could make it so good for you." Teagan tugged on Milo's hand. "Come on. Don't be a tease."

"You heard him," Joss said. "Now let go of him and back the fuck off before I break your fingers."

"Classy," Teagan said, though he dropped Milo's hand. "Call me if you get tired of shriveled dick, yeah?"

Joss let Teagan think whatever the hell he wanted to. If the guy left without Milo, he'd be happy. Teagan didn't even wait around for Milo to answer.

Milo gave Derek a small wave. Derek nodded back. "Join us?"

Hitching a thumb over his shoulder, Milo said, "I should go find Foster." Before he left, instead of thanking Joss for intervening, he said, "What the hell was that all about?"

Annoyance flashed in Milo's eyes, and Joss shoved his hands

into his pockets, thinking for the first time that maybe he'd done something wrong.

"I didn't want you getting in over your head?"

"Is that the truth? Or is that the first thing that popped into your head that didn't make you look like a possessive asshole? I'm not a kid. That's not your place."

Derek shook his head at the mess Joss had made. Joss raised his hands in surrender. "My bad." He pulled his chair out for Milo to take. "Let me buy you a drink."

"You know," Milo said, the disappointment clear in his voice. "I think I'm going to go home. I'll see you in the morning, yeah?"

Before Joss could tell him that his scheduling program had notified him that their one and only jump the next day had canceled and that they had nothing on the books and therefore a free day the next day, a booming voice rose above the general din of voices and beat of the music.

"Well, well, if it isn't Joss Kincaid." Ross Dixon swaggered up to the table, his beer gut straining the extra-long capacity of his belt. "Kill anyone lately?"

16

MILO DIDN'T EVEN HAVE MUCH OF A CHANCE TO BE ANNOYED AT Joss for overstepping before Joss shrank in front of his eyes, even though he hadn't moved a muscle. Milo knew the man who'd walked up to the table had to be Ross Dixon, asshole extraordinaire, and the reason Kincaid Air had been struggling to book clients ever since he'd started his news and social media blitz against Joss.

Spinning on his heel, Milo got in Dixon's face even though Dixon had a few inches and about fifty pounds of fat on him. "What the fuck did you say?"

Dixon rocked back on his heels, an infuriating, smug smirk on his face. "You heard me."

Joss still hadn't said anything. Derek stood. "You should go before it gets ugly for you, *friend*."

Derek said the word *friend* the way most people spit out the word *asshole*.

"All I'm saying is someone needs to take this guy's pilot's license from him before someone else dies."

"The FAA cleared him. Dan's death wasn't his fault." Milo knew he should let it go. He wasn't telling this guy anything he didn't already know. Besides, Milo knew Dixon was only trying to get a rise out of Joss. But to do that by throwing Dan's death in Joss's face was a whole other level of complete assholery.

"If anyone should have their license taken away, it's you. Dixon Skydive has been written up on how many safety violations so far? I think the last count was six. Or have there been more?"

That's right. Milo didn't have a whole lot to do with his downtime other than research the man who was single-handedly trying to run Joss out of business.

Milo's words must have hit home because the smirk slid from Dixon's face. "Who the fuck are you?"

"An employee." The pride in those words couldn't be helped. From the short time Milo had been at Kincaid Air, he'd seen how Joss ran things. How safety conscious he was. His attention to detail when it came to his plane or the skydiving equipment. How he took great care of what clients they did have. And Milo was proud to be a part of it.

Dixon looked between Milo and Joss and back again. "An *employee*? Is that what they're calling fuck boys these days?"

Milo reared back to take a swing at Dixon, but he found Joss's strong arms wrapped around his chest, pinning his arms to his sides. Derek stepped between Milo and Dixon. "Back the fuck off before Joss lets him go, and Milo kicks your ass."

"I'm okay," Joss muttered in Milo's ear. "He's not worth getting slapped with an assault charge, I promise."

"Hey, Dixon," a beefy, tattooed bartender hollered out. If Dixon had more hair, the bartender could easily mop the floor with him. "Beat it. I don't need any trouble."

Dixon slowly backed away and finally turned and headed for the door with a raised middle finger at the bartender. Joss's grip loosened, and he spun Milo around, catching Milo's jaw in his strong, steady hand. "It's been a long time since someone defended me like that. That was fucking fierce."

Without warning, Joss mouth came down on Milo's. Milo tasted the whiskey on his tongue and felt Joss's loosely leashed intensity. It would be so easy to slip under that spell. And so Milo let himself fall. He didn't know who moved, but one of Joss's muscular thighs ended up between Milo's legs, his quad brushing up against Milo's hard dick.

Before they could take the kiss any deeper, Derek cleared his throat and reclaimed his seat. "Maybe you two should take advantage of the backroom after all."

Joss broke the kiss and tucked Milo under his arm and pulled him into his side. He slugged back the last of his whiskey and said, "I think we're going home."

Milo nodded when Joss glanced down at him for confirmation. Even with the disturbance they'd caused, Foster was nowhere to be found. A feat in that small of a bar. "Can you tell Foster I left?" he asked Derek. And maybe make sure he gets back to his car? We left it at Exeter."

"Yeah," Derek said. If he was put out by the favor, Milo couldn't tell. Though Derek did look as if he wanted to say a lot more. Maybe warn Joss about Milo. But for reason's Milo didn't understand, instead of that warning, Derek said, "You two get out of here."

Joss adjusted himself, dug into his front pocket, and dropped his keys in Milo's hand. "Take me home."

Those three little words Joss growled held so much promise, it was all Milo could do not to run out of Sneaky Pete's dragging an inebriated Joss behind him.

"You drunk?" Milo asked as they crawled into the Jeep.

"Not drunk. Just lubricated enough that Dixon's words could hit, but they couldn't stick. *Fucking prick.*"

It was late enough that the trek back up the hill to the

hangar took almost no time by valley traffic standards. And with Joss's hand resting lightly on Milo's thigh, his thumb lazily stroking Milo's leg, Milo was still hard when they got there.

Since Milo had the keys, there wasn't any fumbling with the keys in the lock. Only the light over the sink had been left on, but it was enough to keep them from bumping into the couch or the table.

The awkwardness started to settle in Milo's gut. He was always bad at the transition from coming home to getting it on. He went to the kitchen as if it were his apartment and not Joss's. "Do you need coffee or water or something, I don't know, to help flush your system. You've got a flight in..." Milo glanced at his phone. "Eight hours and—"

Joss caught Milo's wrist and backed him against the wall, bracing a forearm above Milo's head as his lower body pinned him. "Our schedule is open tomorrow. Our one reservation canceled. We've got all night. And all day. If you want."

"You're drunk."

"We've been through this. I'm not drunk. I'm pleasantly buzzed. You worried I'm too far gone to give consent?" The low rumble of Joss's chuckle reverberated in Milo's chest. Joss nuzzled Milo's ear, nibbling his sensitive lobe. And Milo forgot all the reasons why they shouldn't. "You afraid I'm going to accuse you of taking advantage of me?"

JOSS'S BODY BLOCKING MOST OF THE LIGHT FROM THE FIXTURE over the kitchen sink, throwing Milo's face into the shadows, but not enough that Joss didn't catch the twinkle in Milo's eyes as he waited for Milo's answer.

He licked and nibbled along Milo's jawline. His hand went to the waistband of Milo's pants and slowly slid over Milo's bulge.

"You think I'm too drunk to know what I'm doing when I cup your junk?" Joss grumbled in his ear.

He pressed his hard-on against Milo's hip. "You think this is the whiskey making me hard?"

Milo swallowed audibly but didn't answer. The pulse in his neck thumped, and Joss ducked his head and kissed his way from that lifeline up the length of Milo's neck until he was back at his ear again. "You think I'm too drunk to see and feel and smell what I'm doing to you?"

He quit rubbing his hand down Milo's clothed dick long enough to take Milo's hand and press it in the center of his chest. "You feel that thump? The way my body responds to you? The way it wants you?"

Milo nodded, a strangled "yeah" falling from his lips.

Joss pressed his forehead against Milo's, their joined hands pressed against his chest. "God, I want you. What do you say?"

"Hell, yeah." Milo's voice squeaked with the strain, and fuck if that didn't make Joss even harder. He couldn't figure out what it was about Milo that turned his crank. The nail polish and eye shadow on a distinctly male form. The way Milo responded to his touch. The way he could calm Joss just by being in the room.

And the way Milo had rushed to his defense in a snap...

Joss took Milo's jaw and held him in place as he brought his mouth down on his in a scorching kiss that sparked and blazed down his nerves, quick as det cord, setting fire to his groin.

Breaking the kiss, Joss said, "Watching you stick up for me was hot as fuck."

Milo's heavy-lidded eyes opened wide, the lust clearing from his gaze. "Has no one ever fought for you?"

"Not since D—" Joss cut himself off. He didn't want to make this about Dan. Or to bring Dan between the two of them. This. Right here, right now. Had nothing to do with his partner and everything to do with the sweetly complicated man in front of him. No matter how Milo played things, there was something he was hiding. Joss just hadn't determined what that was.

And damn if he totally didn't care right then what that might be either. He'd worry about that later.

"Not in a very long time," Joss amended.

Taking the hem of Milo's shirt, Joss raised it up and pulled it over Milo's head. Then he reached for the button on Milo's jeans. "This okay?"

Milo looked a little green around the gills as he put a staying hand on Joss's forearm. "There's something I need to tell you."

"Unless you're about to tell me you have an STI," Joss teased, "or you don't want to do this, can it wait?"

A beat, two. Joss waited. Milo ducked his gaze, and when he looked back up, his color had returned to normal, and a smile tugged at his lips. "My last STI screening was clear, and I'm definitely not withdrawing consent. And yeah, I guess it can wait."

Milo let go of Joss, and he unbuttoned Milo's top button and carefully pulled down the zipper. Milo shoved his pants to his ankles, kicked off his clothes, and stood there in front of Joss in nothing but a deep purple jockstrap and a cocky grin.

Jesus, fuck. Milo was going to kill him.

Joss's heart did a header in his chest, and his dick grew three sizes. He'd bust the zipper on his jeans if he weren't careful. Joss palmed Milo's bare ass cheeks and lifted him. Milo wrapped his long legs around his waist, his strong arms around his neck, and his stunning smile around his heart.

Joss strode down the hall, but before he could dump Milo on his bed and have his way with him, Milo said, "Can you put me down a sec?"

As much as Joss loved to have Milo's ass in his hands and Milo's dick pressed against his stomach, he put Milo down, and turned on the bedside lamp. Milo detoured into the bathroom.

Joss followed him in. Milo balled up a wad of toilet paper, wet it in the sink, and went to swipe at his lightly frosted lids.

"What are you doing?"

"I'm taking off my makeup. I didn't think you'd want to fuck if—"

Joss clamped a hand on Milo's wrist , took the toilet paper from his hand, and tossed it in the trash. Milo had subtly blended shades of purple and brown on his upper lid and brow. It wasn't garish.

It was... *him.*

Joss had never been with a guy who wore makeup, but he found he kinda dug it.

"Leave it," Joss said. "I like that you're brave enough to wear it. I like that you are comfortable being you. I like what that says about the man that you are. Take it off if you're taking it off for you, but don't take it off on my account."

Milo cocked his head. "You mean that, don't you?"

Why was that so hard for Milo to believe? "I wouldn't have said it if I didn't."

He picked Milo up again. When he'd locked his ankles around Joss's waist, he carried him into the bedroom. At the last second, when Joss would have dropped Milo onto his back, Milo shifted, and Joss tumbled onto the bed. He let out a loud *oof,* when Milo landed on top of him.

"I'm in charge now," Milo said as he straddled Joss's hips and stripped the shirt off Joss's back.

Joss didn't argue. He settled on his elbows and watched as Milo stripped Joss's pants off his legs. It wasn't a slow seduction. It was quick, utilitarian, and perfectly fine with Joss. The quicker they got naked, the quicker they got to the good stuff.

Milo straddled Joss's hips again, sitting on the tops of Joss's thighs and taking Joss's cock in his hands. *"Jesus."* Milo used two hands to gently stroke up Joss's cock. "This is a meaty monster."

"It's big, but it's not *that* big. Black Stallion isn't going to be calling any time soon and offering me a huge contract."

Milo slid his thumb through the precum at Joss's slit, and Joss's head fell back, his eyes almost rolling closed at the sweet sensation.

When Joss could form a coherent thought again, he said, "You think you can take it?"

Milo's saucy grin returned, and he dropped down on all fours, his hands by Joss's head. "Oh, I can take it." Leaning down, Milo kissed him, his tongue sweeping into Joss's mouth, the gentleness of the touch at odds with his cockiness. He broke the kiss, held Joss's gaze and said, "But I want to fuck you first. You good with that?"

Joss reached up and fisted his hands in the short strands of hair at the back of Milo's head and pulled him in for another mind-altering taste. Milo never did what Joss predicted, and he loved that sense of unbalance, somehow intuitively knowing Milo wouldn't let him crash and burn.

As big as Joss was, most men expected him to take charge, to be the top, to drive the narrative. And usually, Joss didn't have a problem with that, but sometimes, he loved being dominated, and more importantly, loved being fucked.

He reached into his bedside table and handed Milo the lube. "I'm so fucking good with that."

17

"Condoms?" Milo asked as he shimmied off Joss long enough to *adios* his jock.

"If you want," Joss said, "but my last test was clear as well. If you hand me my phone, I can show you my results."

"I'll take your word. But I do have one rule. If we're doing this," Milo waved a hand between the two of them. "Then I at least expect a heads up if you're going to be fucking someone else. Someone like me—" Milo cut himself off before he spilled more of the truth than he wanted to.

And yeah, there had been a moment in the hall where he'd almost told Joss everything, but he'd chickened out after reminding himself that he could have this with Joss and not tell him about the transplant.

Yes, he'd come to Kincaid Air to find Dan's family. But things had shifted. Changed. Milo wasn't there because of Dan anymore. He shook those thoughts off and filed them under 'maybe examine another day.'

And with his compromised immune system from the anti-rejection medication, it was much easier for him to catch an infection than most people. "*I* can't take the chance that—"

Joss caught Milo's hand and pulled him on top of him. "I'm not planning on letting anyone else fuck me. You got that? I know some people like to keep things open, especially at the early stages, but that's never been me."

Milo leaned in for a quick kiss. "Good to know. I'm glad we're on the same page, then."

Linking fingers, Milo positioned Joss's hands on the mattress by his head, loving the way it opened up Joss's pecs and hollowed out his abdomen. Milo had no illusion that Joss couldn't overpower him with ease if he wanted, but he loved that Joss was game to let Milo take control.

On the journey to Joss's dick, Milo kissed and licked his way down Joss's torso. The way Joss hissed in a breath and muttered a curse when Milo's tongue flicked his nipple made Milo's cock strain for relief. And as much as he wanted in Joss's amazing ass, he refused to rush.

As he worked his way down Joss's body, Joss's dick trailed a line of precum up Milo's torso. Milo ran a finger through the slickness and sucked his finger clean. Joss had a unique taste, beneath the saltiness. A taste Milo craved. Unable to hold off any longer, Milo took Joss in his hand and sucked him into his mouth.

With his free hand, Joss held the back of Milo's head and pumped his hips. But Joss was slow and careful not to choke him. Milo appreciated that. But he wanted to feel Joss at the back of his throat.

He took Joss deep. Stealing Joss's breath, and from the unintelligible sounds coming from Joss's throat, Milo had absconded with Joss's reasoning as well. That Milo could bring such a big man metaphorically to his knees fed Milo's sense of power.

Power that he'd never had when he'd been lying in that hospital bed waiting for a heart to become available.

The blood whooshed in Milo's ears. His head became light

as he stuffed Joss to the back of his throat, briefly cutting off his air. When Milo felt the first pulse of Joss's impending orgasm, Joss pulled Milo off and held him steady while Joss caught his breath. He stared down the length of his body at Milo, his eyes heavy-lidded and half-gone. "I want you inside me when I blow."

Milo kissed the tender flesh on the inside of Joss's leg, giving him a teasing nip as he sat up and reached for the lube. He ran a slick finger down Joss's crack and lubed his hole, working his fingers around the tight muscle. Joss worked his hips, pressing against Milo's fingers, begging to be fucked.

Milo slid a finger into his hole, drawing a low, guttural groan out of Joss as his legs fell open to give Milo better access. Joss took one finger to the knuckle and then a second. Milo worked him until Joss's breath came quick, and his cock leaked precum like Old Faithful before the big eruption.

There was so much more Milo wanted to do to Joss, but neither of them was going to last much longer. And with their schedule cleared for the next day, they'd have plenty of time later that night, or even tomorrow, to continue exploring and driving each other mad.

"Fuck," Joss said on a strangled chuckle when Milo pulled his fingers free and lubed up his own dick. "I was so close."

"I'm not going to last long," Milo said.

He almost felt guilty about that until Joss said, "Me either."

Settling between his legs, Milo lined his cock up to Joss's hole and pressed. Between the lube, and the prep, and the fact that Milo didn't have a monster dick, he eased inside Joss and buried himself to his balls.

He stilled, trying to stave off the inevitable for a few precious seconds longer. "You feel so fucking good," Milo groaned. "You're tight and—"

Joss worked his hips, taking Milo out to his tip before taking him all the way back in again. "Drive. I need it hard. Fast. Whatever you can bring, I can take."

Milo rose to his knees, wrapping his arms around Joss's thighs for leverage and did what Joss asked.

No, *commanded.*

Milo slammed into Joss again and again, the tight ring of muscle clamping down around Milo's dick as Joss's cock slapped against his stomach. Joss's breath came short and quick, and his hand went to his cock. Milo wanted Joss in his hand when Joss came, but he also didn't want to break his rhythm.

Precum slicked Joss's dick as his hand worked the head and shaft in a near frenzy. Milo dropped Joss's legs and fell to his hands, his balls slapping against Joss's ass.

Joss stiffened, and a strangled roar ripped from his throat. Cum spurted across his abdomen and chest. Milo pumped twice more before lightning exploded across his nerves. He lost his load in Joss's ass, thoroughly convinced he would never get enough of this man.

Milo collapsed on Joss's chest, his lungs heaving along with Joss's. Milo pulled out—a damn shame—but Joss wrapped his arms around Milo and held on tight when he tried to move away. "Uh, huh. You're not going anywhere."

Milo nipped at Joss's chin. "We're going to stick together."

"I'm not in a rush to get rid of you."

Milo's cheeks pinked, and he ducked his gaze.

"Why did that embarrass you?" Joss asked. He shifted them to their sides so he could get a better look at Milo's face.

"I never expected a guy like you to be into a guy like me."

Joss's brow rose. "A guy like you?"

"I'm scarred and scrawny and—"

Joss covered Milo's mouth with his hand to shut him up. When he felt confident he'd made his point, he removed his hand and said, "You're one of the hardest-working, sweetest men I've ever met. Your scars only show me how strong you are. You're sexy as hell and..." Joss leaned in and took that mouth with a bruising, demanding kiss that made his spent dick stir again. "I love the way you fuck me."

"That was a highlight," Milo said, his soft eyes holding a salacious edge.

Milo covered his mouth and coughed, his lungs still working overtime though Joss's breathing had almost returned to normal.

"You okay?" Joss asked. "You're still breathing hard."

Something shuttered across Milo's eyes, and his smile faltered a fraction before he caught it again. "I'm fine. Maybe I need to run with you in the mornings if we're going to be doing a lot more of this."

Joss rolled on top of Milo, catching his weight on his forearms so he wouldn't crush him. "Better buy you a pair of running shoes then, because we're not stopping."

Controlling much? Fuck, that sounded bad, especially considering he was Milo's boss. "Unless you want to stop. Because if you do, we can, though—"

Milo shut him up with a kiss, a much more efficient and effective method than the hand Joss had used over Milo's mouth. Not only did it keep Joss from spewing all the insecurities rattling around in his head, it got him horny again. Milo broke the kiss too soon and said, "I like where this is. Where it's headed. Don't let the boss thing get in your head. You've made it perfectly clear that my job doesn't depend on me fucking you."

"It doesn't."

"But fucking you is a nice bonus."

Their skin peeled apart when Joss shifted. "As much as I'd

like to give you another *bonus*, I think we need a little cleanup first before we have to call in for a rescue and they have to chisel us apart."

Milo chuckled and patted Joss on the ass. "Lead the way."

The water was warm and welcomed. Giving in to Milo's sensual touch, the alcohol still swirling in Joss's system, and the dump of prolactin after coming, Joss leaned his palms against the tile in his shower, let his head fall between his shoulders, and closed his tired eyes.

Milo's hands soaped up Joss's back and worked their way to his ass before finally reached between Joss's legs to get all the nooks and crannies around his nuts and cock. "Mmmm. Feels good. I like your hands on me."

He grew half-hard, but Joss didn't know if he had the strength to do anything about it.

"You look like you're dead on your feet." Milo turned him under the showerhead until he was sufficiently rinsed and cut the water. "I think it's time to put you to bed."

Joss grunted. He didn't have the will or the energy to argue. Milo worked a towel up and down Joss's body, dried himself off, and steered Joss toward the bed.

Joss lay down, rolled onto his side facing Milo, and propped a pillow under his head. Milo stepped back, his towel draped low around his waist.

"Where do you think you're going?" Joss asked.

"To bed?" Milo's expression said *the old man has clearly lost his mind.*

Joss heaved himself onto his arm and grabbed Milo's wrist. "Stay with me."

A furrow formed between Milo's brows, concern and compassion etched in those thick lines. "You don't want to be alone again?"

"No," Joss said. "I want to be with you."

"Isn't that the same thing?" Milo asked, though he let Joss tug him onto the bed.

"No." Joss settled Milo next to him. Milo's back to Joss's chest. "It isn't the same thing at all."

Milo threaded his fingers through the hand Joss laid over Milo's belly and held it to his chest. His deep contented sigh had Joss snuggling closer as his eyes drifted closed.

The next thing Joss knew, a streak of sun shone through his bedroom window as it rose above the San Gabriels. He woke up to find himself half-laying on Milo, with a leg thrown over Milo's hip and his head on Milo's chest. He loved hearing the steady beat of Milo's heart beneath his ear.

Milo stirred, his fingers trailing up Joss's spine, sending an army of erotic goosebumps marching across his skin. Joss shifted and took Milo's flat nipple into his mouth, teasing the tip with his tongue.

"*Mmmphf*," Milo muttered unintelligibly, his hips bucking as he tried to find friction for his morning wood.

Joss tossed the sheet away and rolled between Milo's legs, loving the feel of Milo's hard-on trapped against their abdomens. He started low on Milo's sternum. Milo's fingers twined and tugged in Joss's hair, holding him in place as he kissed and licked his way up Milo's scar, loving and appreciating every divot, every imperfection marring his skin.

Milo's hand went to his chest and blocked Joss's advance.

Joss glanced up into Milo's cringing eyes. "What's the matter?"

"Can you kiss me somewhere else?"

"Why? I love your scar."

Milo's head fell back with a groan, his hand more firmly in place, as if the last thing he wanted to do was think or talk about his scar. Joss crawled up Milo's body until he could look down at Milo's face. Milo's eyes were glassy and rimmed with red. *Fuck.*

Joss had stumbled onto a land mine. And he had no clue how to step away without it all blowing up in his face.

"I have to see the reminder in the mirror every morning that I came this close..." Milo held his thumb and forefinger only millimeters apart, "to not surviving."

"But you did survive." Joss inched his finger up the scar, and this time, Milo removed his hand and let him continue the journey to the scar's apex unimpeded. "Without that perfectly imperfect line on your chest, you wouldn't be here. When I see it, it reminds me how fucking lucky I am that you're still here."

Instead of Milo's tears drying up, they fell from the corners of his eyes and rolled toward the pillow. Joss kissed them away, tasting the saltiness on his lips. "I didn't mean to make you cry."

Milo's chuckle came out with an embarrassed sniffle. "Most guys either actively avoid my scar or are so busy pretending like it isn't there that it's the proverbial elephant in the room. Only it's in the middle of my chest."

"Fuck those other guys," Joss said. "You're with me now, and we should celebrate your scar every goddamn day."

Milo's eyes went wide, and Joss had to think back on what he'd said that might make the man beneath him panic. *You're with me now.* Shit. The words fell from his lips as the truest truth he'd ever spoken.

And though it may be early in their relationship, he didn't want to take them back.

"I'm with you?"

Joss leaned in, brushing his lips against Milo's, hoping Milo would feel the tenderness Joss had in his heart for this incredible man. And fuck, Joss was falling for Milo, and he didn't even want to put his hands out to break his fall.

"For as long as you'll have me."

Milo wrapped his arms around Joss's neck and pulled him in for a hungry kiss. One that devoured instead of tasted, and Joss was there for it all, taking the kiss deeper, his tongue doing to Milo's mouth what the rest of him wanted to do.

He pinned Milo's arms above his head. Kissing his way across Milo's collarbone, breathing the scent of him in as he licked and nibbled his way around Milo's armpit, down his side, to Milo's ticklish ribs to the tattoo he found there.

He traced the lines of the tattoo with his finger. "What's this?"

"An umbrella."

Joss gave him a teasing, *no shit* glare. "I know that. What's it *mean*?"

1 8

Milo hesitated.

Joss asked you about your tattoo. Simple question. Don't make this weird.

"That life's blowing me in another direction?" Milo said, his fingers tracing a trail down Joss's side. He loved the play of muscle, the bump of Joss's ribs, and the sheer, leashed power contained there.

Joss rolled to his side and propped his head in his hand, an indulgent smile on his scruffy face. "You say that as if you're unsure."

Milo rolled to his side to face him, his hard-on begging for more than talk. "I am a little, I guess. When I woke up from my surgery, I had that image in my head, and I couldn't let it go until I got my tablet back a few days later and sketched it out. I thought it was significant, at least to my subconscious, so I had it tattooed on my side."

Joss traced it with his fingers again, going over each line and fine detail, the amusement in Joss's eyes shifting to more melancholy.

"Dan had a tattoo on his ribs."

A wash of goosebumps swept Milo's body that had zero to do with having Joss's hands on him. If Joss said Dan had an umbrella tattoo, Milo would... he would... hell, he didn't know what he'd do. But all the cellular memory stuff could stop any time before it completely freaked Milo out.

"It wasn't on his left side, though," Joss said, "It was on his right. A skydiver."

Heat rushed through Milo's veins as adrenaline seeped in, his heart doing the Cha-Cha in his chest. That's exactly what Foster had thought the tattoo was. And frankly, Milo had no idea what to think anymore. He let the revelation hit him and tried to roll with it instead of letting it take him under.

Joss looked like he had another question. Milo's phone rang in the other room. It was his mother. And while the last thing he wanted to do was talk to his mother while he lay naked in another man's bed, it beat having to answer whatever question Joss might think up. Because if Joss pushed too hard, Milo wouldn't be able to keep his secret to himself.

And he wasn't ready to destroy their budding relationship yet.

Milo sat up, and Joss fell back. "That's my mom. If I don't answer it, she's not going to stop calling until I do. I've learned it's best to pick up and get it over with."

He crawled out of bed and ran naked down the hall and picked up right before it rolled to voicemail. "Hey, Mom," he said, a little too out of breath for such little effort.

Maybe he *did* need to start running with Joss in the mornings. He returned to bed and reclaimed his spot.

"Hi, hon. Your father and I wanted to check in. We hadn't heard from you in a while. Is everything okay?"

"Ma—Mom." Milo mangled the word when Joss nipped at this inner thigh. Blood rushed back to his dick, and it felt so wrong for Joss to do that while he talked on the phone to his mother that Milo blushed. Joss grinned up at him and placed open mouth kisses in a slow, stroll up Milo's leg. Milo put his hand on Joss's shoulder, but instead of pushing him away, he splayed out his legs giving Joss better access. Joss's low rumble of a chuckle hit like an electric charge to Milo's dick, and he momentarily lost the ability to comprehend speech.

"I swear, Milo. Are you even listening?"

The irritation in his mother's voice registered, but so did the affection. As much as he wanted to hang up and concentrate on what Joss was doing to him, he'd missed her voice. He needed to do a better job at keeping in touch.

"Sorry, what did you say?"

"I asked how things are going. Do you need money? Or—"

"No, Mom. I don't need money. I have a job, remember?"

"But California is so expensive, and... you know how your father and I worry." As much as Milo tried to forget sometimes how close he'd been to death, his parents' constant worry wouldn't let him forget it for long.

He guessed he understood their concern, but he had his own life to live, and that didn't include being coddled by his parents, as well-intentioned as they were.

Joss licked a trail up the underside of Milo's dick, and Milo nearly swallowed his tongue. His breath caught, and he coughed and coughed until it turned into a coughing fit. He held the phone away from his face until the coughing subsided, and he caught his breath.

Joss glanced up at him, concern etched in the lines between his brows. He shook his head when Joss nearly spoke.

"Are you okay, hon? Do you need to call Dr. Marwati? I have her number right—"

"No, Mom. I'm fine. It's allergies."

"But—"

After the coughing fit, Joss had settled back between Milo's legs, his chin resting on his folded hands on Milo's chest, giving him the much-needed reprieve from his very welcomed advances. Milo didn't know if he would have ever been able to talk to his mother on the phone again if Joss had made him come while he talked to her.

To distract his mother, he offered something he knew he probably shouldn't. "Did I tell you I've met someone?"

"Awh, honey."

He heard the emotion in his mother's voice, and it made his chest tight. Fuck. He'd overheard his mother and father late one night when he lay in the hospital waiting for his transplant. They'd thought he was asleep. But he'd heard it all.

Their fears.

Their grief.

What stood out the most, though, was his mother's fear he'd die before he'd had a chance to fall in love.

Milo couldn't say he was in love now. It was way too early for that. But a crush sounded too infantile, and infatuation seemed too inconsequential. So, he didn't put a label on what Joss was to him.

"Tell me about him," his mother said, the hope and curiosity clear in her voice.

He couldn't tell her how they'd met. She'd only worry more. But he didn't need to go into those kinds of details.

"He's a good man, Mom," Milo said as he stared down at those sexy, inquisitive eyes staring back at him. Joss's expression softened, and he pressed a kiss to the protective scar over Milo's heart. "I think you and Dad would like him."

"Does he treat you well?"

Joss must have overheard because he made a motion for Milo to give him the phone. That conversation could go really bad knowing how much his mother liked to talk. Milo couldn't take the chance she'd accidentally spill the beans about his transplant, but he also couldn't figure out a good reason not to let Joss speak to his mother.

Joss raised a brow—a dare if you will—at Milo as he made the *give it here* motion again.

As a compromise, Milo hit the speaker button on his phone and said, "Joss wants to talk to you. You're on speaker."

"Hello, Mrs. Malone. I wanted to let you know Milo is in good hands." He gave Milo a salacious wink and ran one of those 'good' hands up Milo's thigh.

His mother blew out a breath, and even though she didn't know Joss from Adam, her relief came through. "I know he's a grown man, but we worry. Ever since his—"

"Mom, we don't need to get into all that. We're fine here. *I'm* fine here. And he makes me happy. Okay?"

Somehow, Milo managed to get his mother off the phone without her going into his life story the way she sometimes did. Talk about party-killer conversation.

When he hung up the phone, Joss placed it on the bedside table and rolled onto his back, taking Milo with him. "Allergies, huh? I haven't heard so much as a sniffle."

Milo over-exaggerated his eye roll for dramatic effect. "Not you, too. I get enough of that from my mother."

"I apologize." Joss ran his hands down the small of Milo's back and squeezed his ass cheeks, grinding their pelvises together. "Let me make it up to you."

SATURDAY MORNING, AFTER A LIGHT BREAKFAST, A HARD RUN, AND his second shower of the day, Joss walked into his office and dropped into the seat across the desk from Milo, his ass still deliciously sore from the pounding he'd taken from Milo earlier that morning.

But he wasn't complaining one damn bit.

In fact, he'd racked up a personal best on his lap time around the airstrip. Nothing like some good morning sex to put some extra fuel in your afterburners.

Milo glanced up. "Why are you scowling? I left you with a smile on your face."

"You're not supposed to be working. We're taking the day off, remember?"

"A forced day off. If we'd have had some reservations, we would have been busy today."

The furrow between Joss's bow deepened, and he felt the tinge of a headache starting to brew. "Don't remind me."

"Well, this social media shitstorm Dixon brought on isn't dying away like you thought it would. We need to take this guy on before all his lies destroy what you and Dan built."

Joss admired the way Milo didn't tiptoe around Dan or the fact that he'd existed, and Milo's fire and passion couldn't be hidden beneath his otherwise mild manner.

Mild manner. Unless you get him naked and in your bed. Then watch the fuck out.

Joss had to hold back his grin. He didn't want Milo to think he was laughing at him. "Why do you care so much what happens to this place?"

Milo glanced up, unable to hide the hint of *are you an idiot?* that flashed across his features. "Because it's my job. I work here." Then he lowered his voice, an indulgent smile on his face when he said, "The last twelve hours notwithstanding, I'm not just your boy toy."

"You keep looking at me like that, and you won't be getting any more work done today. Work that you shouldn't be doing on your day off."

"I was killing time. And I decided we're going to fight Dixon."

We. Joss had been alone for so long that he quite liked the sound of that word.

Leaning forward in his chair, Joss said, "How so?"

Milo held up a pale blue business card. The same business card that the reporter had given him before she'd left. Joss had almost forgotten about her. He hadn't seen any news stories since she'd left, and he'd thought if anything were going to come from the interview, it already would have.

"I called. Jacee said her piece is coming out in tomorrow's paper. In the feature section. She went ahead and emailed it to me early with the promise I wouldn't do anything with the information she gathered until the paper came out. After that, she said we were welcome to do whatever we wanted to with the information she found."

Joss pulled his chair around next to Milo and looked at the computer screen with him.

"Dixon shouldn't have started this shit," Milo said. "Jacee is a research beast. She got her hands on some of the FAA reports. Jesus Christ, how has this guy not lost his license?"

Joss read through the list of violations. Some minor. Others major. Some he knew about. Some he'd had no clue. Bottom line, Dixon Skydive was a liability to the sport, and it was only a matter of time before he got someone killed. Or a whole plane-load of innocent people killed.

"I have to hand it to Jacee," Milo said, "She knows how to dig up dirt."

"It's all public record, though I guess you have to know where to look. Most people won't make an effort to find out the facts for themselves. They'll just believe a blowhard like Dixon and take what he says at face value."

"Not anymore." Milo clicked through to another tab and pulled up Kincaid Air's Website. "I made this information page. It's not live yet. But if it's okay with you, I want to post it tomorrow after the article comes out and put a link to it on your business social media page."

Joss didn't have to click on the first document and its associated photos to know it was the FAA report on Dan's accident. He didn't know where Milo was going with the information, but he was willing to hear him out.

"What's that report going to do?"

"It's going to make it easy for people to find and read the truth for themselves. They'll be able to see you were cleared of any wrongdoing and see Dixon for the lying piece of shit he is." He scrolled further down the page. "And this shows your clean record before and after the accident."

Milo continued to scroll down. The next document, Joss didn't recognize. "And this is something else Jacee found. It's a class-action lawsuit against AirMaxx, the manufacturer of the parachute Dan had used. There have been a number of accidents and fatalities scarily like Dan's. Hopefully, the courts will hold the manufacturer accountable."

The parachute Dan had used had been a one-off. A new design Dan wanted to try that he'd thought might make a good addition to their equipment line. It had been the next best thing to come down the pike in parachute design and deployment, and like all the electronics geeks who had to get the newest and greatest phones and computers and televisions as soon as they came out, Dan couldn't pass up buying the new parachute.

A parachute that had become popular over the last five years.

"How have I not heard about these deaths or this lawsuit?"

"Nobody really has. The lawsuit has been working its way through the courts with little notice. Jacee said something about a gag order that might have helped keep it quiet, but she found a source within the company that was willing to talk to her under the promise of anonymity. I'm hoping that if the word gets out about all this, it will relieve people's hesitation about jumping with Kincaid Air."

"But how many people are going to read that article or page through to find this stuff on my website?"

"They're going to know because we're going use social media to our advantage."

Joss pulled a face. If there was anything he hated more than social media, he couldn't think what it was.

"I looked through Kincaid Air's social media page. Do you realize you haven't posted anything in over a year?"

"That was always Dan's thing."

"Well, it needs to be your thing, too. Surprisingly, you still have quite a few followers. I guess people are bad about deleting accounts they follow. Lucky for you. Anyway, I've made a series of posts. They'll automatically post over the next week. Some are photos you had on your computer of jumps. Others are about the information Jacee found, with hashtags—" Milo glanced at Joss. "Hashtags are—"

Joss laughed. "I know what hashtags are. I'm not that much of a dinosaur."

"Okay, well, the hashtags are used by some of the more popular skydiving groups in the area as well as popular hashtags they seem to follow. It should show up on their feeds. Maybe once the truth comes out, we'll get some of our business back."

Joss leaned over and kissed Milo. "You're brilliant. And thank you."

"You're welcome." Milo closed the internet browser, and the desktop screen saver caught Joss's eye.

It was a picture of Dan, all dirty and grease-stained from working on the Cessna with Hatchet the semi-tamed squirrel on his shoulder. He was feeding him a peanut. "Where did you get that?"

"Um..." Milo paled, or was that a shade of green? "I found a photo file. This is a much better background than the operating system's default. I thought it was an amazing picture of him. But I can change it back if—"

"No. It's fine. I like seeing him happy. That's how I like to picture him. That he's looking down and smiling like that."

"He seemed so perfect." Milo's voice came out wistful and reverent as if Dan were the pinnacle of the perfect person no one else could hope to achieve. "He's feeding a squirrel, and—"

Joss stood and took Milo's chin in his hand and made him look up at him. "Dan was a good man, Milo. But he was far from perfect. He had failings like you and me. I haven't forgotten that. And you shouldn't forget that either."

Joss pulled Milo to his feet. "I'm starved. How about I fix us some lunch." He leaned in, his voice a low gruff of a whisper when he said, "And then we can decide what we're going to do for dessert."

WHAT A DIFFERENCE A COUPLE OF WEEKS MADE. FRIDAY NIGHT, Milo held a hand over his mouth as he coughed and clicked print. It was getting harder and harder to hide his cough from Joss. But he felt fine. With all the new business since Jacee's piece came out in the paper, coupled with Milo's social media push, when did he have time to go to the doctor?

The printer spooled up and started spitting out liability release forms and equipment rental agreements to prep for the jumps for the next day. Joss would be taking up three different groups, the busiest Milo had seen it since he'd started.

He wanted to pat himself on the back for the social media campaign he'd launched for Kincaid Air, but the increase in business probably had more to do with the special discount Joss had running for new clients.

The slap of Joss's shoes on the concrete came moments before Joss cut the lights in the office.

"Hey," Milo said. "I'm still working here."

"Well, stop. It's after seven. I'm tired, and I'm hungry."

"Go fix dinner or order takeout if you don't want to cook. I can pick it up as soon as I'm done here."

Joss came into the office and pulled Milo's rolling chair away from the desk and brought him to his feet. "I'm not cooking, and we're not getting takeout."

"Cold cereal is fine, too. But I think the milk has gone bad."

Joss caught Milo's chin with a thumb and forefinger and pressed his lips to Milo's. Milo stepped into Joss's arms, deepening the kiss. Forget food. When Joss put his hands or his lips on Milo, he forgot all about the hunger in his belly and was driven by another, baser, hunger.

Taking a step back, Joss broke the kiss, their breath already coming fast. Deep down at the bottom of his lungs, Milo felt a scratchiness that concerned him. Come Monday he'd see about making that doctor's appointment. But until then, he had other plans.

"Uh, uh," Joss said as he took another step back when Milo advanced. "Keep your hands and lips to yourself. For now. I'm taking you to dinner. Get a shower and get dressed. If I let you keep kissing me, we won't ever leave."

"I don't see a problem here."

"We're going to celebrate not only the uptick in business but..." the diabolical gleam in his eye said he had some exciting news. "Also, that Jacee called and said that her article triggered an investigation and that Dixon Skydive now has the FAA crawling so far up his ass that he might never shit again."

Milo laughed. Couldn't have happened to a more deserving person. "Definitely a reason to celebrate."

"You coming inside to get ready?" Joss asked. "You're in my bed every night. I don't see why you won't move your stuff in. It's not like you have a house full of furniture to move. We could each take an armload, and you'd officially be moved in."

Joss had been bugging him for almost a week to move his stuff inside the apartment, but as much as Milo wanted that too, he didn't feel right moving in as if everything was copacetic when he had a big secret banging away in his chest. Until he found a way to come clean, he had to keep that sliver of separation.

"We'd better get cleaned up if we're going to make it to dinner," Milo said, avoiding the topic altogether.

Joss's brows furrowed. "Is it, you know... because of Dan? Is it too weird?"

"He's got a little something to do with it." Technically, it wasn't a lie.

Leaning against the wall, Joss pulled Milo between his legs and locked his wrists behind Milo's back. "I'm not still hung up on him if that's what you think. I still love him. I always will. But an old boyfriend taught me I could love again. There's plenty of room in my heart for more than one person."

"I get that. And I know I could never take Dan's place—"

Joss put a finger to Milo's lips. "Relationships aren't Lego pieces. They're all different. You can't exchange one for the other. There is no 'place.' There's only you and me and what we want. My invitation is open. When and if it feels right, let me know. Yeah?"

Milo nodded, feeling even more like he was leading Joss on. He should have listened to Derek in the beginning. But if he had, would he be standing in Joss's arms right then?

Did the *rightness* of the relationship outweigh the deception?

Joss swatted Milo on the ass. "Hit the shower. I'll meet you at the Jeep in twenty."

After his shower, Milo dressed in his room. He dug his stethoscope from beneath his clothes in the top drawer of his dresser and pressed it to his chest. He closed his eyes, the steady, eddy beat of his heart something he might never get used to hearing, not when before it had sounded like a washing machine with bad bearings and a frayed belt that wanted to break.

He took a couple of deep breaths and listened to his lungs, but he didn't have the knowledge and training to know what he heard.

Pulling the earpieces from his ears, he hid the stethoscope under his clothes again, Joss's, "Hey, are you ready?" catching him off guard.

Milo whipped his hand out of the drawer and shoved it closed. Joss cocked his head. *Smooth, Milo, real smooth.*

"What?" Joss asked.

"What, what?" Milo answered with as much innocence as he could muster.

"You look like you're ten, and I caught you looking at your father's porn stash."

Joss reached for the drawer, but Milo caught his hand and started for the door. "Don't be silly. There's nothing in my father's old Hustler magazines that I want to see."

Chuckling, Joss glanced over his shoulder at the dresser as they headed for the Jeep. "Fair enough. Not even a little bit of a *bi* side, huh?"

"Not even a fraction. I'm a grade-A, bona fide *homosexual*." Milo drew the word homosexual out and threw in some sass along with it. "Naked lady parts do nothing for me. I found the Cessna engine repair manual more stimulating."

"Oh, yeah? In that case, remind me to show you my manual on hydraulics sometime."

Milo laughed, his smile remaining as they drove across the valley. The drive took forever, but the view over the ocean from the deck of the restaurant made the travel time worth every second. The waiter delivered their drinks, a club soda with lime for Joss since he had flights in the morning, and Milo had gone with tea.

"You know it's okay if you want a drink. Just because I can't, doesn't mean you can't."

"You trying to get me drunk so you can have your wicked way with me?"

Joss leaned in, his eyes ablaze with unchecked mischief. "I don't need to get you drunk when you already can't keep your dick out of me when you're sober."

Near their table, a throat cleared, and Milo glanced up to see Derek standing there with a man near his age. They looked like they were on a date.

"Tell me you didn't hear that," Joss said, amusement now mixed with the mischief.

"Okay," Derek said, "if you want me to lie to you."

Milo lowered his eyes and felt the heat rush up his cheeks, more because of Derek's 'lie' comment than from Derek overhearing what Joss had said.

Oblivious to the undercurrent, Joss stood and pulled Derek in for a hug before extending his hand to the man beside him who was handsome in that slick Hollywood way a lot of the men —and used car salesmen—in the valley seemed to sport.

"Care to join us?" Joss asked.

"Thanks, but I only came by to say hello."

Derek's date nodded. Milo didn't catch his name. The two men sat at a table halfway across the room, and neither he nor Joss could keep from sneaking glances their way all through their meal.

Derek and his date had several drinks before ordering, so Joss and Milo were nearly finished with their meal when the two men were served.

"Do you think Derek's gonna get laid tonight?" Joss asked.

Milo cut his last bite of steak into two pieces to savor what little he had left. He glanced around the restaurant. The waves rolled into shore, the low-level roar of the water could be heard beneath the clinking of glasses and general chatter.

Even with the lights dimmed for evening dining, it couldn't

hide Derek's date's stiffness. His clunky movements, and what appeared to be clipped, one-word answers to Derek's questions.

"No," Milo said, feeling a little bad knowing that it was because of Derek that he'd been having the best sex of his life.

"Agreed," Joss said. "It doesn't look like it's going well."

The man across from Derek placed his napkin on the table, excused himself, and headed down the back hall towards the men's room. When Joss and Milo's cheesecakes arrived, and still no date, Derek went down the hall only to return to his table a minute later and raise a hand for his check.

"That doesn't look good," Joss said around a bite of the best graham cracker crust Milo had ever put in his mouth.

"Where the fuck did the guy go? Derek wasn't gone long enough to dispose of the body."

Joss laughed but sobered quickly. "I feel for him. He hasn't had much luck in the dating department for a while now."

After paying his check, Derek walked over, his hands deep in his pockets. "Pull up a chair," Joss said, more of a command than an invitation.

Derek blew out a breath but robbed an empty table of its fourth chair and sat at the end of their table. "He fucking ran out the back door. Can you believe that shit? Who does that?"

Milo pushed his half-eaten cheesecake toward Derek, and Derek took the fork out of his hand and dug in. "What the fuck is wrong with people. If you want to leave, fucking say so, you don't have to run out the back door like a fugitive."

"Well," Joss started, a hint of humor in his voice. "How many normal questions did you ask him before you started interrogating him?"

Derek glanced up from the dessert he was devouring long enough to say, "I don't interrogate my dates. I ask them questions to get to know them better."

"Sure, like how many felony arrests do you have? Do you

really make the kind of money to afford those suits or are you dealing on the side? You know, normal, everyday, date questions."

"You're a fucking asshole," Derek said, though the corners of his lips twitched up in a brief, reluctant smile. "And really, if they can't handle a few pointed questions without dissolving into a puddle of insecurity, they're not the fucking guy for me."

Derek scraped up the last of the raspberry topping with the edge of his fork, and before he could pick up the plate and lick it clean, Joss slid him the last few bites of his own dessert. Derek grunted his thanks. "Maybe I should become a monk. At this rate, it certainly wouldn't put a damper on my sex life."

"The right guy is going to come along the way Milo came along for me. Be patient." Joss squeezed Derek's shoulder and stood.

Derek cut Milo a look that Joss didn't see because he excused himself to go to the men's room as well. "You haven't fucking told him a thing, have you?"

The air whooshed out of Milo's chest, and he felt the scratchiness again at the bottom of his lungs. He almost coughed, but he took a sip of his watered-down tea and managed to suppress it.

Milo knew he wasn't proficient enough to lie his way out of it. "No," he said simply.

"He's gone for you, and he has no clue." Derek shoved the two plates away, and they almost knocked over the dregs of Joss's club soda. "I was afraid of this. You made a promise to me. You said you wouldn't fuck with his emotions."

"I haven't. I'm—I'm not. We're both still feeling this thing out."

Derek checked the hall. Joss was walking their way.

"You've got a day. Twenty-four hours. Tell him. Or I will."

"Now, who's going to hurt him?"

"Who's hurting who?" Joss asked as he reclaimed his seat.

"Nobody," Derek said. He stood and clapped Joss on the shoulder. "Thanks for the dessert." To Milo, he said, "Don't forget what I said."

Joss watched Derek walk away, a puzzled expression on his face. "What the hell was that all about?"

"I'm not quite sure," Milo lied, not liking how easy it came that time. "I think he's a little grumpy after his date ditched him in the middle of the meal."

The waiter came over, and Joss handed over his credit card. "I really feel bad for him. He's a good man. A little too intense for his own good sometimes, but there's no other person you'd want in your corner."

"I'm sure," Milo said, not knowing what else to add.

After Joss signed the bill, he led Milo out onto the deck overlooking the ocean. The moon was high and shined on the ocean's surface, leaving a streak of white cutting through the dark water. Joss put his arm around Milo, pulled him into his side, and whispered into Milo's ear. "I'm so thankful you walked into the hangar that day. Have I ever told you that?"

The way Joss looked into Milo's eyes made Milo think Joss had a whole lot more in his heart he wanted to say but, for some reason, didn't.

Milo's heart tripped in his chest. Or was that Dan's heart tripping? Fuck. Milo didn't even know for sure anymore.

Ducking his head, Joss kissed Milo's forehead. "You make my heart full, Milo. I'm not sure what that means, but I wanted you to know."

SUNDAY AFTERNOON, JOSS OPENED THE DRYER DOOR BEFORE THE wrinkle guard quit on him. The waft of hot air hit him in the face as he dug out the clothes and started folding them. Milo's purple jockstrap lay on top of the pile and damn if he didn't want to see Milo in it again.

Maybe when Milo got back from town, Joss could convince him to put on a bit of a show, not that the jock would stay on for long.

He folded the clothes, not even minding that it took him longer. Not when it meant that he had someone in his life again. Someone who had the ability to shine a light into all but the darkest corners of his heart.

For the first time in eons, Joss felt lighter. Dan's loss was still there. It always would be, but it wasn't as sharp or as shredding.

With the clean laundry basket full, he put away his clothes and almost put Milo's in the drawers he'd cleaned out for him in his dresser, but he wanted to respect Milo's decision about when he wanted to officially move in with Joss. He didn't want to push Milo's boundaries.

After all, they had all the time in the world.

Besides, Milo had been a little off ever since they'd gone out to dinner Friday night and had run into Derek.

He carried the basket to Milo's room and stuffed his shirts and shorts in the bottom and middle drawers. He opened the top drawer for his underwear and socks.

His hand bumped into something solid beneath Milo's socks. Joss almost closed the drawer. Snooping was wrong. *Way* wrong. But... He remembered back to Friday night when Milo had acted as if Joss had caught him doing something wrong, and Joss couldn't contain his curiosity.

Digging beneath the clothes, he grabbed a rubber tube and pulled it free. A stethoscope hung in his hand. Joss turned it over and over, confused. Did Milo have a medical fetish that he hadn't told Joss about? They'd had the *what are you into* talk a while ago, and though Milo had a couple of things he wanted to try that Joss hadn't considered before, the whole doctor patient thing had never came up.

He shoved it back into the drawer and closed it, not sure if he would bring it up or wait for Milo to mention it.

With the laundry done, Joss changed into a ratty pair of shorts and a grease-stained wife-beater and headed to the parking pad at the back of the hangar to clean out the Otter. He wanted to work on the Cessna but was stuck until Milo returned from his trip across the valley for some much-needed carburetor parts.

Cleaning the Otter wasn't a big job because he never let it go more than a day or so between cleanings. About fifteen minutes later, Joss was finishing up the last of the cleaning, sweeping his way to the back of the plane and flicking the dirt out the jump door.

"Hey. Watch it."

Joss stuck his head out the door. Derek stood on the tarmac, his hands stuffed in the pockets of his suit pants. "What are you doing here?"

Derek shrugged, and Joss narrowed his eyes at him. "Don't tell me you were in the neighborhood, because I know that would be a lie."

"What? I can't visit my friend if I want to?"

"Take this." Joss handed Derek the broom, the unused dustpan, and the leather cleaner he'd used on the front seats. "Make yourself useful."

Joss swung down and closed the roll-up jump door. Derek glanced around as they walked the cleaning supplies back to the hangar.

"Where's Milo?"

"Running an errand in town. Should be back any minute now."

Joss's lower spine ached from stooping over in the Otter

while he cleaned. Once inside the hanger, he gave Derek the rolling stool by his workbench, and he dropped down onto the top treads of a nearby two-step stepladder.

The only indication Joss had that Derek had finished work for the day was the loosened tie around his neck.

"You and Milo are good?"

Not exactly a seamless segue. Was that the real reason Derek had stopped by? And if it were, why did Derek care about his budding relationship?

Joss picked up some grimy bolts and half-heartedly started cleaning them. "You drove all the way out here to get the scoop on my love life? You saw us Friday night. It's all good."

"Yeah?"

"I said it was. Why are you all weird about this?"

"You're my friend. I worry about you."

"You weren't worried about me when Vin and I got together a few years ago. What makes this so different?"

Derek scooted his rolling stool closer, leveling Joss with an assessing gaze that made Joss feel more like a suspect than a friend. "Maybe the fact you're so defensive about it? Like you're afraid I'm going to poke holes in your perfect little romantic bubble."

"Milo's a great guy," Joss said, that defensiveness Derek accused him of now glaringly obvious, even to Joss.

Derek raised his hands, palms out. "Look, I never said he wasn't. And I can tell he makes you happy. Which makes me happy for you."

"But?"

"I don't even know if there is a 'but.' I saw the way you looked at him."

Joss scoffed but met Derek's hard gaze straight on. "And how was that?"

"Like you're all in." Derek didn't even soften the blow.

"You think I'm jumping without a chute."

"All I'm saying is you should double and triple-check your harness before you make that leap."

Setting aside the bolts, Joss started to clean the carburetor casing with an old toothbrush and parts cleaner. The acrid scent of the cleaner stung his nose and made his eyes want to water. That he had half a mind to tell Derek to go fuck himself told Joss that maybe Derek had a point about his defensiveness.

But, fuck, Joss had played it cautious before, and that hadn't kept his heart from breaking when he and Vin had called it off. Time and distance proved Vin had made the right decision, and Joss was glad they could still be friends. But at the time? It had hurt like hell. Like the outer layer of his heart had been filleted, leaving a raw mess bleeding in his chest.

But it was his relationship with Vin that had proved he could love again after Dan, so he had zero regrets.

Why not go all in now?

On the other hand, throughout his and Derek's years of friendship, Joss knew one thing to be true. Derek didn't jump to conclusions, or focus on insignificant details, or see problems where none existed. Derek's assessment made Joss think. He put the carburetor down and focused on Derek. "What do you know that I don't?"

"It's not about what I know," Derek said.

Joss let the cryptic nature of Derek's response slide as he thought back on some of his interactions with Milo.

"It's what's in here," Derek continued, his hand on his chest. "What has your head been ignoring because your heart is so full of that new relationship energy that it is taking all of your focus?"

Joss grunted but didn't voice any of the concerns or questions about Milo he'd pushed to the side. Maybe Derek had a point. And the fact that Derek had driven all the way out there for that discussion said too much.

"You want to stay for a beer?"

Checking his watch, Derek stood. "I should head back to the valley. I only have a couple of hours before I have to sit on some guy's house all night for a local defense attorney working a personal injury case."

"You can't keep working all day and all night, too. You're going to run yourself into the ground. Find help, Derek. There's got to be an investigator out there that's as meticulous and focused as you are."

"If there is, he or she is nowhere around here. At least not the caliber I need. I need someone who hasn't been an extra on *CSI* and now thinks they'd make a great investigator."

Joss chuckled. "This close to Hollywood, that would certainly narrow your options."

He walked Derek to his car and watched his friend's taillights recede, dreading that sometime soon, he and Milo needed to talk.

2 0

MILO STRODE INTO THE HANGAR AS TWILIGHT TURNED TO NIGHT. He found Joss working on the Cessna. No surprise there. He dropped the parts he'd picked up on the workbench and walked over to the scaffold.

"I'm back," Milo said.

Joss rolled to his side to face Milo, the socket wrench still in his hand. "Come closer."

Milo took another step until his chest almost brushed the platform he'd raised. Joss leaned over, a flicker of darkness in his eyes lightened. Before Milo could wonder much more about it, Joss kissed him. Joss's kisses always left Milo a little breathless and dazed, no matter how short-lived.

"Thanks for doing that. You've saved me so much time."

Milo caught Joss's wrist before he could roll over again. "Take a break with me. The night is beautiful, and the moon is almost full. You do know that the Cessna is going to be here tomorrow, right? And the next day? And the day after that? There's more to life than the planes."

"Yeah, but with business picking up again, thanks to you and your brilliance, I'll have less and less time to work on it."

Releasing him, Milo took a step back and propped up his faltering smile. "Yeah. Sure. I get it."

Joss muttered a curse. "Give me a minute. I need a shower, and I'll be out. Okay?"

He knew that Joss was humoring him and probably preferred to stay and work on the plane, but he appreciated that Joss spared the time for him. "I'll meet you out there."

With a grin Milo couldn't contain, he spun around and went to his room to change into some shorts and a muscle shirt. Not that he had a lot of muscles to show off, but the night was still warm, and if Joss found a nip slip impossible to resist, Milo was more than okay with that, too.

Knowing Joss wouldn't drink the night before flying, Milo grabbed a couple of bottles of water from the fridge, tossed some cheese and crackers into a plastic container, and threw it all in a plastic grocery bag. Next, he hunted down a blanket he'd seen in Joss's hall closet and headed for their favorite spot—the drop-off at the end of the runway.

It would be the perfect place to watch the moon rise.

Before he could make it outside, the framed photos on the wall near the kitchen drew Milo in the way they always seemed to do. He'd looked at them many times now, sucked in by the huge grin on Joss's face, the light in his eyes, the pure joy that radiated from him in all the photos of him and Dan.

The door to Joss's bedroom opened, and he came down the hall in nothing but a pair of athletic shorts, his hair damp and unbrushed, the spicy scent of his bodywash wafting off his water-warmed skin.

Milo wanted to sink into him, but they'd have time enough for that outside.

"What is it about these pictures? I catch you staring at them all the time."

The pain in Milo's chest seemed all too real. Sometimes he

worried he might be rejecting Dan's heart, but he had no other symptoms of organ rejection. And that pain only surfaced when he thought about Joss and Dan. About how sometimes he felt as if he'd come between them even though Dan's accident hadn't been his fault.

He knew that fact down to every last fiber of his being, but it didn't prevent his head from wondering into nonsense territory. Maybe he needed to talk to a therapist. All the survivor's guilt weighed on him.

Add in his appreciation for the gift Dan had given him, and his being alive to to live those moments Dan never would again, it kind of fucked with his head.

"I like seeing you when you were happy," Milo finally said.

The grove between Joss's brows deepened, and the corners of his lips turned down as he crossed his arms over his chest. "I'm happy now."

The man in front of him and the man in the pictures were not the same man. At least not on the inside. "Maybe. It's different, though."

"Nothing wrong with different, Milo. My heart took a beating. But I survived. Whatever this world threw at me, it brought you into my life. I'm not sorry about that."

He wrapped a big, beefy arm around Milo's neck and pulled him into his side. He pressed a kiss to Milo's temple, took the bag of food and drinks off Milo's arm, and started for the hangar door.

At the end of the runway, Joss dropped the grocery bag and took the blanket from Milo's arms. Milo walked to the edge of the rocky drop-off. Wind blew up from the valley floor, buffeting his shirt and ruffling his hair. He held his arms out to the side and leaned into the wind, not a full-on Kate Winslet standing on the rail at the bow of the Titanic, but it felt just as freeing.

Joss came up behind him, wrapping a protective arm around

his waist, his lips pressing against the nape of Milo's neck as the twinkling lights in the valley below danced and sparkled.

"At night, in the dark, you forget the ground is only ten feet below you, and you can look across the valley and imagine you can fly," Joss's low, gruff voice whispered in Milo's ear.

"It would feel amazing," Milo said.

"That's why Dan loved to skydive so much. He loved the world from far above. Loved being separate and in his own little world where everything is possible for those precious seconds. He would have tried cliff diving if I had let him. I was too afraid he'd get himself killed." And ironic chuckle escaped Joss. "Now I wish I'd said yes. I feel guilty that I deprived him of that experience."

Milo turned in Joss's embrace and wrapped his arms around Joss's neck. "You loved him. You wanted him safe. No one, not even Dan, can blame you for that."

Joss pulled him in and held on tight, his grip so fierce Milo didn't know if Joss would ever let him go. But there could be worse ways of going than being surrounded by Joss's strong arms.

Ending the embrace, Joss led Milo to the blanket with the cheese and crackers he'd unpacked. They lay out on their sides, propped up on one arm, facing each other while they ate. They changed the subject to the inconsequential, the mundane, and the hilarious.

Three questions into Twenty Questions, Milo asked, "Most embarrassing moment."

"That one's easy," Joss said as he layered a piece of sharp cheddar on a cracker. "It was back in my high school football days. Back when I still wanted people to think I was straight even though I knew I was gay as fuck."

"Let me guess. Your mom saw your browser history that you forgot to delete."

Joss laughed. "That was bad enough, but nowhere near the top of the list."

Milo covered his ears and, with a chuckle, said, "I'm almost afraid to hear this. What could be worse than your mother seeing your porn history?"

The moon rose higher, highlighting the spark in Joss's eyes. Somewhere on the road above the airstrip, headlights glowed as a car came down through the hills, but from what Joss had told him, with the way the road tilted and curved, the end of the runway lay in a blind spot to drivers on the road. Milo might have to take advantage of that. If he'd have given it a little thought, he would have snuck into Joss's room and brought the lube.

"How about the whole football team walking in on me and the student trainer sucking each other off on one of the benches in the locker room?"

Milo's hand flew to his mouth, but the laughter still escaped. "Oh, no."

"We were buck-ass naked, too. Seconds from blowing our loads. I don't know what the hell we were thinking. Eric was on his back on the bench, my cock in his mouth while I was over the top of him with his dick in mine. We both froze. A dozen or so pairs of eyes stared back at us, slack jawed. The coached shoved his way through all the sweaty bodies, trying to figure out why everyone had blocked the door."

Milo covered his eyes shut and peeked at Joss through the cracks between his fingers. "Oh, God."

"My dick instantly shriveled, and the coach..." Joss shook his head, the amusement written on his face. "The coach took one look at us and said, 'I think you boys need to put those away.' And then to the team said, 'The rest of you hit the showers.'"

"What? You've got to be kidding me?"

"Even for back then, Coach Clark was a cool, take-it-in-stride kind of guy. You had to work overtime to ruffle him."

"And two of his kids sucking cock in the locker room wasn't enough to do that?"

"Apparently, not."

"Did you catch hell from the rest of the team?"

"Some didn't like it. But fuck them. Some didn't care. One was sucking my cock by the end of the season."

"And the others?"

"I was a big kid, even back then. I wasn't someone they could tease and shove into a locker. I was the one that opposing coaches always double-teamed. No one dared say anything to my face. It pretty much became a known secret amongst the team. But I've got to hand it to those kids, what happened in that locker room never left it. The rest of the school never found out. My teammates were either too loyal or too scared to spread any rumors."

Milo felt the heat of embarrassment at the back of his neck, and he hadn't even been the one who'd been caught. "Did you learn your lesson?"

"Two, actually."

"Oooh." Milo rolled onto his stomach and rested his chin in his propped-up hands, ready to hear what Joss had to say. "Do tell."

"One, discretion has its place."

"And two?"

Joss leaned forward, catching Milo's chin in his hand and holding him still for a kiss that stirred Milo's dick—not that hearing about Joss sucking a guy off in the locker room hadn't already made him hard—and promised things to come. "That I really, really, like sucking cock."

"I think the telling part of show-and-tell is over. And I think it's time for the show part," Milo said. "You know what the kids are saying these days, 'video or it didn't happen.'"

The thought of sucking Milo's cock made Joss hard. He made a show of adjusting himself. "You want to see a video of me sucking Eric's cock?"

"Or, lacking that evidence, you could... you know... offer a full demonstration. I think I could take that as proof."

"You're so good to me." As those words spilled out in jest, a realization hit. Milo was not only good *to* him. He was good *for* him. For the first time in a very long time, he didn't feel like he was going through the motions to get from day to day and putting on a smile trying to convince everyone else—and maybe himself—that he was all right. "Of course, we'd have to be naked to make the recreation as close to real as possible."

One of the things he loved about Milo was he wasn't shy about his nudity, once he'd got past his self-consciousness of Joss seeing the scar on his chest. Milo shucked his clothes in a flash and tossed them aside.

"Your turn." Milo lay down, hard cock up, and leaned his head back to watch Joss. "Am I in the right position?"

"Perfect."

Joss lost his clothes as well and crawled on his hands and knees to hover over Milo, their kiss upside down. But that was where any similarities to that time in the locker room and the present ended. He hadn't had a knot of unvoiced feelings in his chest for Eric. Or had a simple craving for the boy's touch. For his approval.

Joss nibbled on Milo's bottom lip as Milo reached up and ran his hands down Joss's body, lighting an erotic trail from his chest to his abdomen. He glanced down the length of Milo's body, at the wet tip of his proud cock glistening in the moonlight.

Around them, insects buzzed, and the breeze blew enough to keep the mosquitoes at bay.

He worked his way down Milo's body, the cushion of grass beneath the soft blanket offering protection for his knees. But as soon as his lips latched onto Milo's nipple and that throaty groan escaped Milo's lips, he forgot about his knees and focused on the man laying bare beneath him.

Joss grunted, his forehead falling to Milo's chest when Milo wrapped his fingers around Joss's cock and gave him a long, slow stroke. "Fuck," Joss muttered. "I love it when you put your hands on me."

"Move down so it can be my mouth."

Joss forgot about his slow stroll down Milo's body and crawled forward until Milo could reach him with his mouth. One long lick of Milo's tongue against his precum-leaking slit and Joss's balls tightened, his hips flexing, craving more.

The best thing? He wasn't a kid anymore. He didn't have to worry about people walking in on them. Or what other people thought. Or if they approved. All that mattered was the man beneath him, wanting to give him pleasure.

Milo's cock bounced within reach, and Joss sucked him down to the root in one smooth move, the tip of Milo's dick hitting the back of his throat as Milo thrust. Milo's head fell back, his hand replacing his lips around Joss's dick, but Joss was good with that, because he was determined to do what hadn't been done in that locker room, and that was to suck the man beneath him to completion.

Joss set a demanding pace as Milo's hips worked. Collecting some of his saliva on his fingers, Joss trailed a finger down Milo's taint and slicked up his hole. Milo's hand fell away and gripped Joss's thighs for leverage.

Joss worked Milo's cock with his mouth as his finger breached Milo's hole. Milo groaned, grazing the inside of Joss's thigh with his teeth as he fucked Joss's face. From the moans and groans and erratic strokes from Milo, he wouldn't last much longer. Joss increased his suction, and Milo stiffened. Hot cum shot into Joss's throat. He swallowed and swallowed, getting every last bit of the salty goodness.

Milo trembled beneath him, and Joss let Milo's softening cock fall from his mouth. He kissed his way down Milo's inner thigh. Milo coughed as he caught his breath, but before Joss could question him about it, Milo rolled over and wiggled his ass.

Joss squeezed those sexy cheeks, unable to stop himself from biting one of them. He turned around and settled himself on top of Milo, his dick sliding into that perfect space between Milo's ass cheeks and the top of his thighs. He took his weight on his arms, so he didn't crush Milo, leaning down and kissing his way up Milo's neck.

Joss whispered in his ear, "You have an amazing ass."

Milo squeezed his thighs, making Joss grunt and start to thrust into that tight space. "Fuck me," Milo demanded.

Joss loved that demanding side of Milo, but as big as Joss was, there was no way that would work without lube. And he didn't want to break his contact to go get some.

"We can try that next time," Joss said. To Milo's sigh of disappointment, Joss added, "Promise. Besides, I'm not sure you can take me."

Milo twisted beneath him until their eyes met. "You're big. But you're not impossibly big. And I've never been the kind of man who backed down from a challenge."

"Something else I admire about you."

Joss stroked in and out of that gap, his dick rubbing across Milo's taint and balls. Milo arched his back, one hand reaching around to cup the back of Joss's head so he could sneak kisses.

"Harder," Milo commanded.

"Aw, fuck," Joss said. His head fell to Milo's shoulders as he pumped harder and faster. His balls drew up tight, and the first pulses of his impending orgasm hit. Milo reached between his legs, making a tighter spot for Joss's cock. That touch sent him over. He stiffened above Milo with a guttural groan that ripped from his throat, his cum filling the gap at the top of Milo's thighs.

He collapsed on top of Milo, hugging his arms around Milo's chest and kissed the sweaty spot between his shoulder blades before rolling to his side. Joss considered himself extremely lucky to have found love twice, but three times?

How did he deserve that?

You don't have to question it. Just don't take it for granted.

Milo shifted to face Joss, bringing his hand to the nape of Joss's neck and pulling him in for a tender kiss that sent aftershocks to Joss's dick.

The evening breeze dried the sheen of sweat on their skin, and Joss loved watching the moon as it rose higher and higher, this bright, silver ball in the sky. Was it the pull of the moon bringing him closer to Milo, like the pull of the moon on the ocean?

But his attraction didn't feel ephemeral. What he felt for Milo seemed all too real. Maybe it was time to put what was in his heart into words.

"I wanted to tell you—" they both started at the same time and laughed.

Milo coughed again, and it turned into a coughing fit that made his eyes water.

"When are you going to get that checked out?" Joss asked.

"You sound like my mother."

"Maybe that's because we both care about you."

Milo's tentative smile made Joss's heart hurt as if Milo couldn't believe Joss cared about him. "I can't stop thinking that if Dan were alive today, that I wouldn't be here."

"What do you mean?"

Milo closed his eyes and took a steadying breath. "Nothing. Forget I said anything. Sometimes I can't believe how lucky I am to have found you. I love waking up to you every day. I love our sex. I love having you in my life."

"What are you saying?"

"I... I've needed you in my life for a very long time. You were what I was missing."

Before Joss could tell Milo how he felt, how his infatuation had turned into so, so much more. How he looked forward to each day with Milo. Of waking up with Milo's leg thrown over his. Of feeling Milo's lips on his body, hearing his laugh in his ears, Derek's evasive words popped into his head.

It's not about what I know.

Now that Joss thought more about those words, it sounded as if Derek *did* know something.

What has your head been ignoring?

Fuck. Maybe he'd ignored more than he should have.

Milo snapped his fingers in front of Joss's face, an amused grin curling his lips. "Did I short circuit something in there? Does my having feelings for you make you want to run scared?"

His smile told Joss he was teasing, but instead of answering, Joss said, "Derek dropped by this evening. We had an interesting conversation about you."

21

Joss's words slammed into Milo. There had been no anger in them, but the tiny hairs on the back of Milo's neck stood straight up.

"You're as pale as the moon," Joss said. "What's going on?"

"What did Derek tell you?" Milo forced the words past his lips, his heart beating so fast he couldn't be certain he'd said them out loud.

Instead of answering Milo's question, Joss's eyes narrowed as he pulled his legs away until Milo's foot wasn't resting between them anymore. "What brought you to my hangar?"

"I needed a job and—"

"I don't doubt you needed a job, but I thought you were someone else, and you went with it."

"I've apologized for that."

"But you can't tell me you showed up here specifically looking for that job. I'm asking again. Why my hangar?" Joss's voice went soft, and his eyes closed for a fraction of a second as if he didn't want to hear the answer but needed to. "Why my door?"

The guilt weighed on Milo, crushing his chest until it became nearly impossible to breathe. His head got light, and the world seemed to tilt and twirl.

Tell him.

You need to fucking tell him.

Milo had thought he could build a life with Joss and not tell him about Dan's heart beating in his chest. But now he knew he couldn't go on another minute living that lie. It would eat at him day by day until there was little left of him. He knew that now.

Milo pushed himself to his feet and pulled on his shorts. He gathered Joss's clothes and dropped them in a pile in front of him. "Get dressed. Follow me."

Without waiting for Joss, he started the long walk back to his room. He kept telling himself that Joss would understand. That it would be okay—a little hiccup in their relationship that they might be able to laugh about someday.

But that was also a lie.

There was no coming back from this.

Deep down, Milo had known it from the start. Which explained why he'd kept the truth to himself. But Joss didn't deserve being fed the lie.

"What the hell, Milo?"

Milo kept walking. Joss's heavy footsteps closed in on him at the hangar, but Joss didn't stop Milo or ask any more questions. He followed silently, keeping his troubled thoughts to himself.

In his room, Milo opened his top drawer and reached for the stethoscope. He glanced up at Joss, Joss's expression stormy as he leaned a muscular shoulder against the door jamb.

"Maybe you should sit down for this," Milo said.

"I'm not sitting down. Stop with the theatrics and fucking tell me already. You're scaring me."

"It's not scary." Though Milo broke out into a cold sweat, his hands shaking, his knees weak for an entirely different reason than the orgasm Joss had just given him. He could be seconds away from blowing up his relationship.

And doing what he'd promised Derek he wouldn't do—hurt Joss.

But what kind of a relationship would he have if he built it on a profound lie?

Milo pulled the stethoscope from the drawer and walked toward Joss. He put the ear tips in Joss's ears and put the diaphragm on his chest over his heart.

The scowl on Joss's face turned to bewilderment as he listened to Dan's heartbeat. He listened for ten or fifteen seconds before pulling the ear tips out of his ears. "Yeah. I've listened to a heart before."

His chest tight, Milo's words came out a mere ghost of its normal, vital sound. "Not my heart. *Dan's* heart."

A lungful of hot air whooshed out of Joss. He lost all color to his complexion, looking a lot like those photos of Milo before his surgery.

Joss grabbed the door jamb to steady himself or to keep from wrapping his fingers around milo's neck. "Come again."

What little voice Milo had cracked. And Milo couldn't quite tell if Joss wanted Milo's words to be true, or if he hoped it was another one of Milo's lies.

Even though Milo had seven years—and not Joss's seven seconds—to come to terms with his transplant, and seven years to think about what he'd say to Dan's family if he ever met them, none of those eloquent words came to mind.

Instead, he indelicately blurted out the obvious. "Seven years ago, I got a heart transplant. That heart was Dan's."

Emotions flittered across Joss's face too quickly for Milo to recognize and categorize. Joss's eyes filled with unshed tears and red rimmed his eyes.

Milo put a hand on Joss's arm to help him to the bed before his legs gave out, but Joss shook him off and managed under his own steam. He didn't say anything for the longest time, and Milo stood there, knees knocking, waiting for... *something*.

Yelling.

Screaming.

A fist to the wall.

An accusatory finger to the middle of Milo's chest.

Anything would be better than the blank stare as Joss's brain processed the information.

They should have been laying naked out under the stars, basking in the afterglow of their orgasms. Not stuffed in Milo's tiny room, the musky smell of sex hanging in the air like an inescapable reminder of the lies Milo had told.

Joss fell back on the bed, his hands scrubbing down his face. "Those motherfuckers."

Milo had expected Joss to turn his emotions on him. "Who are you talking about?"

"The OPO. Second Life. That donation was supposed to be anonymous. That's why any correspondence has to go through them." Then the realization hit with a barely audible *oof.* He dried his eyes with the heels of his hands. "Those cards were from you."

Though Joss didn't need a response from Milo to know the words were true, Milo nodded. Dan's heart hammered erratically in Milo's chest. He leaned against the dresser for support. Joss nodded as well, though more to himself as his scattered mind fit all the pieces together.

"This isn't Second Life's fault. They didn't give me your address. After years of no response from you, I found it on my own."

Joss sat up. The color returned to his face with his visible anger. "All this is about you and what you wanted? You don't think there's a reason why the OPOs operate the way they do? That choice to have contact or not," Joss poked himself in the chest, "that was my goddamn choice. It wasn't for you to make for me."

"You're right." By the stormy expression on Joss's face, being right didn't make it any easier for Joss. Fuck. What had Milo been thinking?

You were thinking about you. And what you wanted. You weren't really thinking of him.

Joss stood and started pacing the small room. Milo didn't move from his position in front of the dresser because he didn't want to be trampled. Joss stopped abruptly, his gaze fixed on Milo's. "How did you find me?"

Milo stood taller, not shrinking away from Joss's question, but hedging, wanting to protect Derek from the fallout. "Obviously, I knew when Dan would have died. And I knew there was only a certain radius from the transplant center for me to be eligible for the heart. I worked with that information."

Joss shook his head while he paced, finding an obvious hole in Milo's explanation. Joss wasn't a stupid man. He'd piece it all together at any moment. Milo wanted to crawl away but told himself right then and there, he would not lie again. If Joss asked him a question, he would answer with nothing but the full truth.

Joss stopped pacing abruptly again, inches from the wall. His head fell back, and he stared up at the ceiling as if asking for strength from someone up above. God? Dan? His hands went to his hips, and he turned. "Derek."

One word.

But it was the only real answer that explained how Milo had found him. If he'd been able to find Joss on his own, it wouldn't have taken him seven years to show up on his doorstep. He would have shown up that first year. Again, highlighting Joss's assertion that he'd been only thinking of himself and not the loved ones Dan had left behind.

———

IF JOSS'S HEART TOOK ANY MORE BEATINGS THAT DAY, THEY'D HAVE to put *him* on the transplant list. He didn't have to wait for Milo's nod to know Derek had been involved, bringing on a whole other set of complicated emotions that he didn't have the bandwidth to deal with right then. Derek had tried to warn him in his own way, but Joss had expected more out of their years-long friendship. There'd come a time to deal with Derek, but he had to handle this situation with Milo first.

And handle it without breaking the fuck down.

"Fucking unbelievable," Joss muttered. He focused on his anger because it was an easy emotion to understand. And of course, the one person he had in his life that he could really talk to about these things had been an integral part of the deception. "Was this all some kind of game to you?"

Joss gestured between the two of them, not knowing where to hang his anger. On Milo? Derek? Dan?

Himself?

He should have known that a man randomly showing up at his door was too good to be true. And he should have known better than to let his defenses down so fast and so completely.

Being lonely isn't a crime.

Wanting a deep connection with another person is normal and valid.

"You lied to me." A statement, not a question, because there was no doubt about that.

"Yes." Though Milo's voice faltered, he didn't equivocate. Joss begrudgingly admired that.

"Even after the whole Tim fiasco. When I gave you the chance to come clean, was it just about the money?"

"A little maybe. But I could have found another job, so it was more than that. I had already developed a thing for you and—"

Joss held up a hand to silence him. He didn't want Milo's feelings for him getting mixed up with this. This wasn't about feelings. This was about deception. And Joss couldn't help feeling like a fool for falling for all the bullshit.

How could he know if any of it was real?

He couldn't even look at Milo. Not with tears building behind his eyes and threatening to fall. No way was he letting Milo see how badly he'd gutted him.

"You need to leave," Joss said, the one thing that he knew to be the absolute truth right then.

Milo didn't argue. He scooped up his wallet off his dresser and headed for the door, his bare feet padding on the concrete. He hesitated at the doorway, and Joss's eyes fell to the stethoscope on the floor near his feet.

"Wait," Joss said at the last second.

Milo hesitated, and Joss picked up the stethoscope and put it to his ears. If he never saw Milo again, he couldn't pass up his chance to hear Dan's heart one last time. Joss didn't even have the words. He made a vague motion that Milo instinctively understood.

Milo turned back toward the room and placed the diaphragm over Dan's heart.

In Joss's ears, Dan's heart beat fast, strong, and true. Joss put a hand on Milo's shoulder, holding him in place, though he'd made no move to leave.

Then Joss did the only thing he could do.

He rested his forehead on Milo's shoulder and broke the fuck down.

Joss didn't know how long they stood there with Dan's heart beating in his ears and the sobs wracking his body. They held onto each other. He didn't know who was holding who up at that point.

Finally, Joss pulled himself together, handed Milo the stethoscope, and dried his face with his hands. He didn't want to let Dan go.

Milo go.

Fuck. He didn't even know who he was letting go anymore. He just knew he needed space. Milo sniffed and took a shuddering breath, but Joss couldn't let himself focus on Milo's feelings too. Joss's were complicated enough as it were.

"You can stay with Foster, yeah?"

"Yeah." The word came shakily as Milo turned to leave. "I'll call for a car."

"Take the Jeep."

Milo turned back to him, and Joss glanced up and held his gaze. It was probably one of the more painful things he'd done, looking into Milo's eyes and seeing the regret and guilt swimming around in them. If Joss didn't hold strong, the swirl of powerful emotions in those eyes could sway him, he knew the power they had over him.

Over *his* heart.

"You won't get a car to come up here this late at night," Joss explained.

"I'll bring it ba—"

"I don't care about the fucking Jeep. Keep it for all I care. You just need to leave."

"But it's Dan's J—"

Joss held onto the anger to keep from breaking down again. "You don't think I fucking know that?"

Milo backed two steps away. Joss dropped his eyes to the floor, knowing he wouldn't be able to send Milo away if he watched those tears fall.

To Joss's relief, Milo finally left. Joss waited there, in the half-dark, the light from Milo's room spilling into the hangar until the Jeep's engine growled and the tires barked as Milo popped the clutch.

Joss stormed past the workbench, the light reflecting off the carburetor. He palmed it in his hand and heaved it into the darkness. He heard the crunch of thin metal as the big sliding hangar door shook with the impact and then the dull thud when the carburetor hit the solid concrete floor.

Between the door and the carb, he'd probably cost himself a few thousand dollars in damages, but he couldn't find a damn with both hands. He headed straight for the shower, needing to wash the musk—and Milo—off his skin. He'd never get Milo out of his head if he kept catching whiffs of cum and sweat as he moved around.

After his shower, Joss threw on his protective gear with the Kevlar material and strategically placed skid pads, knowing it was probably a mistake to climb onto his bike in his current fucked-up mental state. But he couldn't stay at the hangar a second longer with the walls closing in. Not when everything he looked at or touched either reminded him of Dan or Milo.

Maybe he should set a torch to the whole place and ride off into the hills and not stop until he hit the Atlantic.

The rumble of his Harley's engine soothed him as he pulled in the clutch and stomped the gear shift down to first. Instead of driving toward the valley, he turned right out of his drive and headed into the hills, taking the corners fast and aggressive. If he didn't lay the bike down, skid off the road, or swerve into the oncoming lane on a tight curve and hit a car or truck head-on, it would be a miracle.

But with all the thoughts and feeling filling his head and pushing him harder and faster, it left no room for caution.

22

FOSTER OPENED HIS DOOR WITH BLEARY EYES AND BEDHEAD. "What the fuck, Milo. Do you know what time it is?"

"I need a place to stay the night. Can I crash here?"

Foster must have rubbed enough sleep out of his eyes for it to register that Milo stood before him in nothing more than his athletic shorts, his chest and feet bare. Joss had wanted him out, and Milo hadn't wanted to take the time to get his clothes. There would be time enough to get his things the next day when he went to work.

Aw, fuuuck. Did he lose his job *and* Joss?

Joss had always said that their relationship wouldn't stand in the way of Milo's job, but this wasn't some minor tiff. The finality in Joss's voice still reverberated in Milo's head. He would be an idiot to think he wasn't fired.

Not that being fired even registered on his top ten list of fuckups for the night. On the drive down to Foster's, he'd almost called Derek, but it was so late, and really, what could Derek say besides he'd told him so? And while Joss hadn't taken a swing at him—something Milo totally would have deserved—after ignoring all of Derek's warnings, Milo didn't think he'd fare so well in Derek's company.

Foster took a step back, a silent invitation.

"I told him," was all Milo said as he stepped into Foster's apartment. He went to the couch and fell face-first, his feet kicked up behind him.

"You want to talk about it?"

"I royally fucked up." The couch muffled his words, but Milo didn't care. "What more is there to say?"

"Are you two over?"

Milo covered his head with his arms, his breath still coming harder than normal, but with the regret crushing his chest, he'd earned his breathlessness. "I don't know. I think so. I mean… he told me to go. So yeah, it's gotta be. Right?"

Foster sat on the coffee table in nothing but a pair of boxers, but neither one of them cared. "You're asking the wrong person. Give him the night. Maybe go see him tomorrow when everyone's emotions aren't so wrecked. He seemed like a reasonable guy. I'm sure you two can work it out."

Milo eyed Foster through the triangle of space between his forearm and bicep. "You're saying what you think I want to hear."

Foster swiped a hand through his hair. It only made the bedhead worse. "It's the middle of the night, Milo. I don't know what you want me to say."

Milo rolled to his side to face Foster. "The truth."

Foster blinked a few times, and Milo couldn't tell if he were thinking or if he hadn't heard. Then Foster rubbed his hands down his thighs and said, "If some guy pulled the same stunt on me that you pulled on Joss, yeah, it would be over. No question. You can't come back from a breach of trust like that. At least not in my book."

The center of Milo's chest stung, and the erratic beat of his heart didn't make it any better. Here Dan had given him the ultimate gift, and he'd taken it for granted. He'd fallen hard and fell fast, with no regard for the consequences. "I love him," Milo said.

"I think it's a little too late for that."

Milo didn't disagree.

"How does he feel about you?"

"There have been moments where I've thought, maybe, he might feel the same." Milo shook his head. "I don't know. I know he cares. But he's commented so many times how much things I did and said reminded him of Dan, that..."

Milo let his words trail off, not knowing how to put into words his greatest fear.

"That what, Milo?" The sleepiness laced Foster's words, and Milo knew Foster was trying his best to help. But if Foster's half-lidded eyes were any indication, the need for sleep was quickly pulling Foster under.

"That I wasn't sure if he was falling for me or falling for those parts of me that reminded him of Dan."

There. He'd said it. Like ripping off a Band-Aid, only instead of tugging out a few stray hairs and pulling on his skin, it left a hole in his chest that made it even harder to breathe. He hadn't wanted to face his concerns, so he'd buried them deep.

Foster winced. "Ouch."

"Tell me about it."

Foster's eyes drifted closed, and he caught himself as he nodded off. "Sorry. Long day. Did you say something?"

Patting Foster on the knee, Milo said, "Go to bed. My problems will still be here in the morning."

"Yeah, sure." Foster stood. "For what it's worth, I think beneath all this mess, you two were really good for each other. I've never seen you that happy before. But that doesn't mean I think you should go back to him."

Milo pasted on a semblance of a smile, one that a politician might use when he was trying to be polite but couldn't quite make it real. "I hear you."

Foster retreated to his bed. Milo lay on the couch in the dark. There were blankets and pillows in the hall closet, but fabric and fluff wouldn't make him any more comfortable.

A couple of coughs turned into another coughing fit that left him breathless and feeling every lungful of air as it sawed in and out of his lungs. He sat up, hoping it would bring relief, but it didn't help. He would have thought that After telling Joss the truth, the guilt of lying to him would have lifted that heavy weight on Milo's chest.

Or maybe the guilt of hurting Joss weighed even heavier than Milo's relief from coming clean.

Despite the quiet and the dark, sleep never came. His coughing and wheezing interrupted his fitful dozing as much as Joss's words, and anger, and sobs. At some point, Milo had stumbled into the hall bathroom, winded and lightheaded to take a piss, before falling back on the couch.

He stared out Foster's sliding glass door until the darkness turned to light, and Foster stirred in his bedroom. Foster came out in a fancy suit and fixed coffee. Before Foster left, he sat Milo up and wrapped his arm around Milo's neck and kissed the side of his head. "There's coffee for you. We'll talk more when I get home. Maybe we can figure a way out of this mess."

Milo's grunt must have been enough of a response because Foster stood, grabbed his keys, and headed out the door, leaving the silence to descend around Milo.

He couldn't sit there for the next nine hours waiting for Foster to get home. He had to fix this now.

If he still could.

Monday morning, early birds flitted across the road in front of Joss's motorcycle as he pulled into his drive, the morning sun on his back. He'd driven deep into the Mojave Desert and back, and he still didn't have any answers. Or felt any better.

The only thing he knew was he'd have to cancel his jumps that day. It would be bad enough for him to fly without any sleep, but without focus and clarity, there was no way he could pilot without putting everyone in danger.

The first thing he noticed as he put down the kickstand and removed his helmet was that the Jeep was still gone. Not that he'd expected to find Milo on his doorstep as the sun rose, but a part of him had wondered if he would.

He headed straight for the office and made the necessary calls and excuses. He thought about canceling flights for the next day as well, but he couldn't expect to regrow his business after Dixon's false accusations by canceling all of his reservations.

For now, he'd take it one day at a time.

He found the stethoscope on the floor near Milo's door. He walked into the room and sat on Milo's bed, turning the diaphragm over and over in his hands, the familiar *tha-thump* of Dan's heart now permanently etched into his brain. A part of him had known that Milo had held something back, but he would never have guessed the truth.

He left the stethoscope on the bed, retrieved the carburetor from the concrete floor, and made his way into his apartment. The stillness and silence that Joss had learned to live with after Dan's death, now seemed unbearable. He turned on the radio, for the background noise as he stripped out of his riding gear.

The morning traffic report came on, listing several accidents and backups and other disruptions in traffic. An accident at a familiar intersection caught his ear. There had to be an accident there at least once a week. People got impatient at the short light on the road leading up to the San Gabriels and often paid dearly for trying to run the light.

After all the hours he'd put on the bike, Joss's back, shoulders, and ass were sore. He could still feel the vibrations from his engine and the road in his arms and body. Kind of how people who'd been at sea too long still felt the movement of the ocean long after they'd gone to shore.

He fixed a basic breakfast in his boxers, not that he was hungry, but he knew he had to eat. He should have headed straight to his bed, but he wouldn't be able to keep his thoughts off Milo.

And he still didn't know what he was going to do about Derek. His friend's betrayal—because what else could he consider it?—sat almost as heavy on Joss's mind as Milo's deception.

He needed to hear what Derek had to say for himself, but like his relationship with Milo, he wasn't convinced it could survive.

But right now, Derek would be busy with work, and their conversation wasn't something he wanted to squeeze between ringing phones and priority emails.

Besides, as much as Joss hurt, he didn't want to face losing his best friend *and* the man he loved—or thought he loved—in the same twenty-four hours. There were only so many punches a man could take before they took him to his knees.

He spent the morning rebuilding the Cessna's carburetor. Fortunately, it had been undamaged when he'd hurled it across the hanger. The repair had taken twice as long as it should have, and he'd had to break out the manual, reading each sentence again and again until his addled brain made sense of all the words.

Sometime in the early afternoon, his feet aching from standing on the hard concrete for so long, Joss collapsed into his desk chair. He checked his phone for missed messages from Milo, but... nothing.

Do you really want to talk to him after what he's done?

His head said no, but his heart had different ideas.

He opened the top left drawer of his desk for his hand-written passwords he kept in a small black book, preparing to login to his maintenance log on the Otter to see if he could take advantage of his downtime to address minor maintenance. A flash of deep purple in the drawer caught his eye.

He shifted his black book and found the seven cards forwarded by the OPO. Cards Milo had sent. He knew that now.

Scooping them up, he threw them in the trash can next to his desk, turned off the overhead light, and left the room.

He didn't even make it past his workbench before he returned to his office, flicked on the desk lamp, and pulled the cards out of the trash.

Joss shifted aside his keyboard and laid the cards out in order of their postage dates, his heart catching a frantic, erratic beat. Did he really dare to open them?

Instead of ripping through the flap the way he normally would, he reached into the desk drawer and found Dan's letter opener shoved all the way to the back. One by one, he sliced through the flaps. The ripping paper sounded as if a tear had opened in this world, and he was about to travel into another, parallel one.

He pulled out the first card dated a year after Dan's death. A handwritten note and a picture fell out. The picture was of an impossibly young-looking Milo in a hospital bed, a large white bandage on his chest. His hair lay mussed on the pillow, his eyes half-lidded, a simple, crooked smile on his face as he gave the camera a thumbs up.

Joss's vision blurred, and he blinked back the rush of tears.

He brushed a thumb over Milo's sweet face, already missing his voice, his laugh… his touch.

He unfolded the note that had come with the photo.

To my donor's family,

I don't know if you'll ever read this. I'm told that some families never do. But I wanted to thank you from the bottom of my heart—my new heart—for giving me this gift. I had been given less than a week to live when I got the call.

It's now a year later, and I hope you've healed enough that you can read my words. I'm sorry for your loss, but I hope I can make it up to the universe.

I want to love and laugh and do great things. I'm not sure what that will look like yet. I need to finish high school first. I'm so far behind. But, now, because of you, I have my whole life ahead of me to figure it out.

Hugs,

Milo Malone

P.S. Thanks again!!

P.P.S. I would really like to meet my donor's family. If you would like to meet me too, please contact the OPO.

Joss gave up fighting the tears and let them fall as he read through the notes one by one. Each with an updated picture of Milo. Each one reaching out, asking for contact from Dan's family.

But Joss had never contacted him. He'd never even opened the cards.

Milo's last note, the one that had arrived not too many weeks before, had a picture of Milo with that same crooked and mischievous smile that Joss couldn't help but smile back at when he saw it.

Heart hurting, Joss unfolded the last note. It was short.

To my donor's family,

It's been seven years. Seven years I never expected I'd have. Seven years since you lost your loved one. I hope you find some solace in my updates. I hope I don't make your loss harder to bear.

But in seven years, I haven't heard back, so I'm thinking it's too hard. I guess I can understand that. I won't write again. I don't want to make this worse than it already is.

I wish you all the best,

Milo Malone

P.S. This may be weird, but did my donor like Peach IPAs? I've craved them since I woke up in my hospital bed, and I wasn't even old enough to drink. Haha.

Joss set the note aside. But Milo hadn't left it at that like he said he would in the note. He'd gone the next step and hired Derek to find Dan's family. To find *him*.

And thinking back on the weeks since Milo had come into his life, even though Joss had been lied to, he hadn't felt so alive, so *happy*, in a so very long.

In seven years.

And while he'd loved Vin, he'd always known he wasn't Vin's first choice. And knowing that had eventually eaten away at their relationship until they'd had to end it.

But with Milo, so many things were different.

And the thought of going back to his life before Milo seemed... impossible.

He gathered up the cards, photos, and notes. He stuffed

them all back into their respective envelopes and put them back into his desk drawer.

He pulled out his phone and fired off a text to Milo. They had a lot they needed to talk about. Yes, Milo had lied. Yes, Milo had violated transplant protocols on family contact. But after reading all the notes, of seeing Milo's deep need to connect to his donor's family, Joss found that he couldn't blame Milo. He probably would have done the same.

And putting all that aside, he'd made a promise to Milo that he wouldn't let their relationship get in the way of Milo's employment, and he intended on keeping that promise.

If that's what you have to tell yourself to justify texting Milo first, go right ahead.

Did he need a justification? Could he not reach out because a part of him really wanted to?

Joss: We have jumps in the afternoon tomorrow. Can I expect you back by then?

There. Straight to the point. Professional even. He could keep his work and personal life separate.

But could Milo?

He didn't get an immediate text back, not that he'd expected one.

Weary, but unable to rest, Joss glanced at the clock. By the time he got himself cleaned up and rode down to the valley, Derek should be finishing up with work.

They needed to talk.

23

THERE WEREN'T ANY CARS PARKED OUTSIDE DEREK'S OFFICE besides Derek's Roadster. But unlike per usual, Joss knocked on the office door, his heavy knocks shaking the door in the jamb, as he waited for Derek to answer. Derek would have heard his motorcycle drive up, and wouldn't be surprised to find Joss standing on the other side of the door.

Joss collected his emotions, trying to tell himself that Derek must have thought he had valid reasons to do what he'd done.

"Hey, what—" The smile slipped from Derek's face, and he studied Joss for a measured second. "Fuck. He told you, didn't he?"

Derek stepped back, and Joss stomped into the office, dropping his helmet on Derek's desk before turning around. "That was a seriously fucked up thing to do."

"You're right." Derek didn't make any excuses.

Instead, he offered Joss a drink. As much as Joss wanted one, he had flights the next day, plus he'd ridden his motorcycle to the valley, and he still hadn't had any sleep. "Cola is fine," he said as he plopped down on the armrest of Derek's sofa.

Being a PI, Derek didn't have the same kinds of restrictions on his drinking. He poured himself a generous three fingers of whiskey, pulled his desk chair around and sat across from Joss. "I should have given you a heads up about Milo."

"You think?" Joss couldn't hold back the bite.

He popped the top on the soda Derek handed him, telling himself he had no plans to stay long. Only long enough to get his grievances off his chest and see where their friendship lay after that.

Derek took a measured sip of his whiskey. "You want to know the truth?"

"No. Lie to me again."

The words came out harsh but, somehow, Joss managed a feeble smile. As wrong as Derek had been to keep that kind of information from him, deep down, Joss knew Derek hadn't done it out of malice.

"For fuck's sake." Derek raked his hand down his face and wrestled his tie from around his neck. "I guess I had that coming."

Joss assumed that was a rhetorical question. He didn't bother answering.

Derek took a fortifying gulp of his whiskey, grimaced, then sat forward, his elbows on his knees. "The truth..." He made a face as if something pained him as he took a deep breath. "First, fuck you for not telling me Dan was an organ donor."

Joss grimaced but Derek kept going. "But the truth is, I knew you were struggling, and I thought meeting Milo would help you..."

Derek made a vague motion with his hand that Joss couldn't interpret.

"Help me what?"

"Move on, isn't the word I'm looking for. Maybe find some solace? Or comfort. That knowing a part of Dan still lived would help."

Derek rubbed a hand over the center of his chest, his voice gruff when he said, "It helped me, when I found out."

Joss grunted and crossed his arms over his chest, mulling over the words. Sometimes he forgot how much Derek lost as well. Joss didn't know if he felt solace or comfort. With Dan being an organ donor, he'd known Dan's death meant others would live. He knew those people were out there, so that should have been enough.

But it hadn't been.

He hadn't realized that until right then.

Whatever else Milo was to him—and he had no way of knowing where they stood because Milo hadn't returned his text—hearing Dan's heart beating had been an existential experience.

"It's been eye-opening. That's for sure." Joss took a sip of his cola and wished it were something stronger. "And it got me to finally open those cards he'd been sending all these years."

Derek's brows rose, but he didn't interrupt Joss now that he was talking.

"Frankly... they broke my heart." Joss dropped down into the seat, set his cola on the coffee table, and scrubbed his face with his hands. "I mean, here's this kid, you know, who faced down death, who's so full of love to give the world, and I couldn't even man the fuck up and open a damn card."

"It's not about manning up. You weren't ready to read those words. There's nothing *unmanly* about that."

"*Jesusfuckingchrist.* You're not my therapist, remember?"

That damned, maddening, insightful brow went up. Only one this time. "I'm not trying to shrink you. I'm just telling you it's okay to have feelings. And it's okay to not be at a point where you can be there for other people on this one thing."

"I think I did us both a disservice. And I need to tell him that.

I owe him that much. But he's not answering my texts or returning my calls."

"You could text him your thoughts. He could read them, even if he doesn't choose to respond."

"What I have to say needs to be said face to face."

Derek swirled his glass and took another sip. "Fair enough. Do you know where he is? Maybe you can go to him."

"Foster's. I assume. But I don't want to show up at his door if he's not ready to see me yet. I was such an asshole to him. I wouldn't blame him if he doesn't want to have anything to do with me after last night."

"Give him another day. I'm sure he'll come around."

Joss stood, leaving his unfinished cola on the coffee table. "I sure as hell hope so."

Derek grabbed Joss's helmet off his desk and followed him to the door, putting a staying hand on his shoulder. "Are we good here? I fucked up. I should have turned the kid down as soon as I realized who he was looking for."

While the way Derek had handled the situation had been wrong, he'd been right about Joss needing Milo in his life. He thumped the meat of his fist to the center of Derek's chest. "Your heart was in the right place. I can't condemn you for that. So, yeah. We're good."

JOSS WENT THROUGH THE NEXT DAY ON AUTOPILOT, REFUELING after his flight. He didn't even bother repacking the parachutes in his rush to drive back down to the valley. A quick call to Derek and a ten-minute wait for the return call had Foster's address in Joss's hand. Sometimes it paid to have a best friend who was good at finding people.

Joss still hadn't heard from Milo. As stalkerish as it might be, he planned on sitting on Foster's doorstep until Milo agreed to talk to him. Milo might be stubborn, but he wasn't a reigning champion like Joss.

Already near rush hour, the ride into town was a blur of honks and taillights and middle fingers. He drove around Foster's apartment complex until he found the right building, though Dan's Jeep wasn't there.

Which was fine. He'd wait Milo out. He had to come back sometime.

He sat near the top of the steps to Foster's second-floor apartment and stood when Foster pulled into an empty spot. The man trudged up the steps, all work-rumpled in his suit and loosened tie.

"He's not here." Foster's near sneer told Joss that Milo must have told him what happened. Foster would have bumped Joss in the shoulder if Joss hadn't moved out of the way as he passed.

Joss followed Foster up the remaining two steps and didn't bother to wait for an invite as he followed Foster into the apartment. "Then, where is he?"

"I'm not his keeper. And even if I knew where he was, I wouldn't tell you."

How had Joss ended up being the bad guy here when Milo had been the one who'd deceived *him*?

Because you were an absolute dick to a vulnerable, sweet guy? Just a thought. Or—

Joss cut off his internal monologue. He didn't need a beatdown from himself as well.

"He was crazy into you." Foster looked Joss up and down, his gaze appraising, his lip wanting to curl. "I don't see what he saw in you. But Milo always listened to his heart before he listened to his head. I'm hoping maybe he's learned his lesson. I hate that you hurt him."

"I'm kind of nuts about him, too," Joss said, the words

spilling out of him, and he didn't care to have them back. He gave no shits about who knew how he felt about Milo. He had nothing to hide.

Foster shoved his hands in his pockets. "You had a great way of showing it, asshole."

This wasn't an argument Joss was going to win, and everything he needed to say, he needed to say to Milo, not his friend. "You really don't know where he is?"

Blowing out a breath, Foster said, "No. I haven't seen him since yesterday morning. I thought he wasn't answering my texts because he went back to you after I told him not to."

"Could he have gone back home?"

"I doubt it. His parents moved back east around the time Milo moved to the valley. He's got nowhere else to go."

Joss left Foster's scratching his head. Milo could be holed up in a cheap hotel somewhere.

Or out looking for another job.

But a job hunt didn't explain why he hadn't come back to Foster's last night.

He threw his leg over his bike and put a call into Derek as mild panic started to creep in. "It's me," Joss said when Derek answered on the first ring.

"Hold on," Derek told him. He must have put his hand over the mic because all Joss heard were muffled voices, then a door closed, and Derek said, "I'm back. What's up?"

"You can call me back later if you're in the middle of something." Though the tone in Joss's voice didn't match the words. That mild panic leaching in.

"It's fine. I was finishing up an interview."

"Is he cute?"

Derek's chuckle sounded tired. "I guess? But I don't know his sexual orientation. And I don't care. He's tough and charismatic and has the skills I'm looking for in a business partner."

"That's great," Joss tried to sound enthusiastic. At the pace Derek was working, he might as well start digging his grave now. He'd never been able to turn a case down if he knew he could help someone. But right then, Joss had something more important things on his mind.

"But that's not why you called. What do you need?"

"Advice. Your expertise. I don't know." At the growl of a Jeep engine, Joss glanced around the parking lot, but the Jeep that pulled in wasn't Dan's. The quick flash of hope vanished. "I can't find Milo. And Foster hasn't seen him since yesterday morning. I thought about filing a missing person's report, but he's an adult. He's allowed to disappear if he wants to. Then I thought, maybe he was arrested, or—"

"Hold up. I've got a friend with the San Fernando PD, let me see if she can find any information for me before you start filing reports. For all you know, he's holed up in a hotel somewhere, drinking you out of his head."

"I was thinking that, too."

"Give me a little bit. I'll see what I can dig up. This is going to take a bit longer than finding Foster's address, so chill out for a bit, and I'll call you as soon as I know something."

"Thanks. I'll be waiting. Sooner rather than later, yeah?"

"I'm working as fast as I can."

Joss rode through every parking lot of every cheap motel in an ever-expanding circle around Foster's apartment complex searching for Dan's Jeep.

The rush hour traffic didn't help, but on the bike, he could weave through cars or squeeze down the dashed lines between lanes to get to the front of the traffic at the lights.

A long light finally turned green, and Joss twisted the

throttle and roared ahead of the other vehicles. His phone rang in his helmet's headset, and he used his voice activation as he sped ahead to the next light.

"You sitting down?" Derek asked when the call connected.

Joss's heart stalled and went into a nosedive, taking a lungful of air with it. "I'm on my bike, so yeah."

"Pull over."

The street in front of him blurred. With his chest tight and air at a premium, Joss managed a breathless, "Is he dead?"

He couldn't help that his head jumped to the worst-case scenario because he'd already lived that nightmare once. He knew all too well it could happen again.

"Pull over," Derek ordered again, a finality to his words. Joss knew he wouldn't get any more information until he did what Derek demanded.

He dove in front of a car in the right lane and slammed on his brakes as he angled for a parking lot. There came a squeal of tires behind him and a long, angry honk. The smell of burning rubber hit him a second before the car he'd cut off grazed his rear wheel, nearly sending his bike into a dangerous slide.

Luckily, he had enough momentum to maintain control until he could come to a full stop. Feet on the ground, he killed his engine and pushed up his visor so he could get some fresh air. A difficult, if not nearly impossible, task in a hot parking lot in the middle of the valley with cars belching exhaust at the height of rush hour.

"Tell me." Fire raced through his veins as Joss braced for the worst, afraid he wouldn't hear Derek's response over the swish and swirl of blood rushing behind his eardrums.

"I found him," Derek said. "He's in ICU at Valley General hospital. He's on a ventilator. It doesn't look good."

The single light pole in front of him became two. Joss

squeezed his eyes shut and opened them to find a single pole again. "What happened?"

"Where are you?"

It wasn't lost on Joss that Derek deflected his question, but at that moment, it didn't really matter what had happened. The only thing that mattered was that Milo was in the hospital and Joss had to get there. He could find out what he needed to there.

"Corner of Balboa and Nordoff." Joss started his engine and pulled into traffic. He could have this conversation while he drove to the hospital. "But I'm headed for the hospital."

"I'll meet you there."

"Oh, and Derek?"

"Yeah?"

"Can you call Foster and let him know?"

"On it."

At the hospital, Joss parked in a motorcycle slot in front of the entrance as Derek jogged over from the parking lot and the non-descript piece-of-shit car he used when he was surveilling someone. He was dressed down in jeans and a ratty T-shirt, and Joss knew he'd pulled him off a job.

Joss gripped the mouth guard of his helmet. "You didn't have to come."

Derek clapped him on the shoulder as he walked through the sliding doors ahead of Joss. Over his shoulder, he said, "Yeah, I did. And don't worry, the bastard I'm following cheats on the regular. If I don't catch him tonight, I'll have plenty of other chances."

The woman behind the reception desk schooled her face after she caught sight of the two of them barreling toward her. He knew they looked disreputable, but Joss couldn't find his disarming smile.

Derek reached the desk first. "ICU?" He glanced around

until he found a sign and pointed down the hall to his right. "That way?"

"Down that hall. Take the elevators to the third floor and turn left. You can't miss it."

Rapping his knuckles on the desk, Derek said, "Thanks."

At least one of them still managed some social graces.

"Tell me what happened," Joss said as he kept up with Derek's ground-eating pace. The hallways were brightly lit and, at least on the first floor, the smell of disinfectant not terribly strong beneath what smelled like an industrial version of Febreze.

"He was in an accident yesterday morning. He was heading up Ridge Road. I assume heading back up to you."

Joss vaguely remembered the radio report of an accident yesterday morning, but he'd never considered Milo might have been in it.

"It sounds like the roll cage saved him, but the Jeep's probably a total loss."

"I don't care about the Jeep."

It had been Dan's, sure. But material possessions didn't matter, not in the grand scheme of things. Dan had taught him that.

"The eyewitness accounts are sketchy, but it looks like he somehow lost control of the Jeep and drifted into cross traffic. Milo was unconscious when the EMTs got to him. That's all I know."

Christ. Where the hell was the elevator? Joss jammed his finger on the *up* elevator button again and again.

"You know the elevator won't come any faster the more times you punch the button, right?"

Joss cut him a glare, his hands going to his hips as he searched for the stairs. "This way."

He pointed down the hall, and Derek jogged to keep up. Joss

took the steps two at a time, arriving on the third-floor with his heart pumping and his lungs laboring.

Derek stopped him before he opened the door from the stairwell. "Take a breath. Hell, take two. You're not going to do yourself any favors bursting into the hall and demanding to see Milo."

Joss tried to shoulder Derek aside, but Derek wasn't a small man. With a staying hand in the middle of Joss's chest, Derek said, "You hearing me?"

Knowing Derek was right, Joss nodded, but as soon as Derek backed off a step, Joss flung open the door, Derek's muttered 'motherfucker' chasing him down the hall. In front of the ICU double doors, positioned off to the side, was an unmanned reception desk that Joss took full advantage of, completely ignoring the sign to wait and check in before heading toward the ICU.

Derek caught his arm, but Joss jerked it free, slamming through the swinging double doors. Derek caught the doors as they bounced off the wall with a bang and swung back. Joss marched up to the nurses' station as an armed security guard headed his way.

He glanced around, frantic, pushing all the memories of his arrival at the hospital after Dan's accident to the back of his mind. He couldn't lose them. *Him*. Fuck. "Milo Malone. Where is he?"

24

Swinging around, Joss searched the semicircle of ICU rooms, looking for Milo. Each of the rooms had windows overlooking the nurses' station. He almost started on a room-to-room search when Derek caught his arm at the same time the security guard stepped in front of him.

"I can't let you go any further until you're cleared. You got me?" The officer tucked his thumbs behind the buckle of his duty belt and rested his forearms on the handle of his gun and taser.

Joss raised his hands. "I'm not looking for trouble. I need to find someone."

"Can I have your name, sir?" The nurse glanced up from her computer with a stern face and a raised brow. She was a thick woman with a no-nonsense attitude, and between her and the armed officer, he feared her the most.

"Joss Kincaid, I'm his—I'm his partner." Joss gave himself the relationship upgrade. If Milo were on a ventilator, he wasn't in a position to argue. "Please. I need to—"

"Joss?"

A woman stepped out of a room three doors down. Her

hair in a messy ponytail, her eyes puffy, her face blotched with red. She swiped stray strands out of her face and stepped forward, her hand outstretched. "I'm Nina Malone. I'm Milo's mother."

She had Milo's sweet eyes and slim body.

The officer stepped back as Joss skipped the handshake and pulled her in for a hug. He'd never met Milo's mother, but after that one time talking with her on the phone, he felt the instant connection. She clung on tight as Derek gave his shoulder a squeeze.

When they finally broke apart, Joss had to swipe at his eyes. The officer had gone back to standing in the corner of the ICU, and the nurse watched him with a patience he probably didn't deserve.

"How is he?" Joss managed.

Nina glanced back at the room where she came from, and the nurse said, "We'll keep our eye on him. We have your number if you want to talk in the waiting room. We'll call if there's any change."

"Thank you." Nina gave the nurse a tired, small smile. "My husband should be back any minute if—"

"I'll be sure to tell him where you are," the nurse said.

Nina threaded her arm through Joss's and led him out the double doors and into the ICU waiting room down the hall. The room was nearly empty, and they settled into chairs in a corner opposite each other, Derek at his side, a supportive shadow he didn't want to shake.

"Milo's on a ventilator," Nina said, not waiting for Joss to ask again. "He was nearly blue when the EMTs got to him. He went into respiratory arrest in the ambulance. They were able to intubate him and breathe for him. They did an EEG this morning, and he has normal brain activity as far as they can tell, so we're hoping when they get the infection under control and his lungs clear, that he'll wake up and not have any permanent brain damage."

How she held it together, Joss didn't know. She was stronger than he was. The lump in his throat was so thick he croaked when he glanced at Derek and said, "I thought he was in an accident."

"He was," Derek said. "I had a friend read me the preliminary police report."

"From the eyewitness accounts," Nina said, "we think he lost consciousness and drifted into cross traffic. He's banged up from the crash, but that's the least of his issues."

Joss slumped in his seat. "I don't understand."

"He has severe pneumonia."

"The cough," Joss said, as he put it all together.

"With the anti-rejection medication he takes, his immune system is compromised, and he's susceptible to opportunistic infections. What he has, the doctor said a normal immune system likely would have fought off.

"His father and I worried about it. He's gotten sick before and been fine, but we always knew this was a possibility. But Milo's stubborn, and we'd practically bubble-wrapped him most of his childhood, so he bristles when his father or I tell him to see a doctor."

Joss feared the answer to his next question, but needed it needed to be asked. "And his heart?"

"No signs of rejection."

Thank Christ for that. Joss blew out a breath and leaned forward, his elbows on his knees, his head hung between his shoulders, swimming, and spinning.

Derek patted him on the back. "That's good news. Really good news."

"Your partner, huh?" Nina's gentle voice cut through the fog of exhaustion and distress in his head.

Letting out a rueful laugh, Joss said, "I thought it might up my chances of the nurses letting me in there to see him. We'd just decided to become boyfriends. Then he told me about the heart transplant and... and I'm embarrassed to say that I didn't take it well." After the way he'd blown up, Joss didn't deserve a sensitive guy like Milo in his life if he couldn't hold his tongue and his emotions for one goddamn minute and see where Milo was coming from.

Of all the things he regretted in his life, pushing Milo away topped the list, right after letting Dan talk him into taking him up to try that new parachute.

But *this* mistake, he had a chance to fix.

If Milo let him.

Nina put her hand on Joss's shoulder, a soft, motherly, comforting touch. "Milo called after your argument. It was your partner who was the donor?"

The tears fell, and he let them. How he had any tears left after all these years, he had no fucking idea. "Yes, ma'am," was all he managed.

Derek laid a steadying hand on his back as she leaned over and put her arm around his shoulder. There wasn't anything she could say that would make that any better. They both knew that.

She dabbed at her eyes with a balled-up tissue from her hand. "Would you like to see him?"

Joss cleared his throat. "I really would."

He followed her back to the nurses' station, the officer's eyes on him the whole time. Since Milo was only allowed one visitor at a time, after Nina added Joss to the approved visitor list, she and Derek hung back as Joss walked those thirty feet alone.

Machines beeped. Nurses bustled by. The hiss and clunk of the ventilator were loud enough to hear from the hall. He caught his hand on the door jamb and hung on as he leaned his head in and watched the unnatural mechanical rise and fall of Milo's chest.

In those moments, he was taken back seven years, when Dan was on life support, the machines keeping him alive until Joss could give the okay for the organ donations.

This isn't Dan.

This isn't happening again.

It *won't* happen again.

Joss had to believe that if he believed anything.

He stumbled into Milo's room, his legs numbly listening to the signals his brain sent. Falling into the chair Nina had pulled up beside the bed, he took Milo's warm hand in his, his voice thick when he kissed the back of Milo's hand. "If you give me a chance, I'm gonna fix this."

IF ANYONE EVER TELLS YOU BEING ON A VENTILATOR IS FUN, RUN.

Flames licked the back of Milo's throat, and the nurse couldn't feed him ice chips fast enough to squelch the fire or soothe the burn.

He waited impatiently while the doctor evaluated him and gave orders to one of the other nurses in the room. His parents had been kicked out when the doctors finally pulled the endotracheal tube, and while he'd been told Joss had been around and was expected back soon, he hadn't seen him since he stupidly left the hangar in Dan's Jeep.

He should have stood up for himself and stayed.

He knew that now. The only thing that kept him in his bed instead of knocking the doctors and nurses down to go find Joss —besides being too weak to get out of bed—was the fact that his mother told him that Joss had only left his side while she and his father took their turns sitting with him.

If Joss had stayed so many days at the hospital, maybe that meant they still had a chance.

The nurse hung another bag of IV antibiotics as the doctor finishing writing his notes. He patted Milo on his blanketed foot. "You were damn, lucky, son. Next time you start getting sick, you have it checked out."

The man was thick around the middle and had graying hair at his temples. His gaze reminded Milo of a stern uncle. Milo nodded because it hurt too much to talk.

"I'll see you tonight on my rounds," the doctor said. "Until then, there's a very worried man who'd like to see you."

Milo buzzed the head of his bed up higher and would have tried to wrestle his hair into submission if his arms didn't feel as heavy as Sequoia trees. The doctor left. The nurses kept asking if he were comfortable and some other questions he really didn't hear as his eyes locked on the open door, waiting for Joss to appear.

Finally, the nurses dimmed the room lights and left, and his eyes drifted closed even as he tried to keep them open. Deep in his lungs, the scratchiness hadn't yet abated. Even with the oxygen flowing through his nasal cannula, breathing required conscious effort.

Then a shadow fell across the doorway, Joss's big body nearly blocking all the light. "Hey," came Joss's gruff voice.

"Hey." The word came out more of a squeak followed by a coughing fit as Joss stepped up to the bed.

"You're a fucking sight for sore eyes." Joss leaned in and pressed his lips to Milo's forehead with a huge, relieved sigh.

It took all Milo's strength, but he grabbed the back of Joss's neck before he could pull away and pulled Joss's lips down where he wanted them most.

Joss's hand went to the back of Milo's head, and Milo tried to concentrate on the tender kiss instead of the fact that his hair hadn't been washed in what turned out was nearly a week now.

Milo tried to take the kiss deeper, but it jostled his nasal cannula, and he couldn't hold back another coughing fit. He pulled back, and Joss readjusted the cannula in his nose as Milo caught his breath. He glanced down at the tented hospital gown over his crotch. "At least something still works."

"There will be plenty of time for that later if—" Joss cut himself off and blew out a breath before continuing. "If you want a later. With us. With me."

Joss acted as if he'd done something wrong when it had been Milo who'd fucked everything up. You can't build a relationship on a lie. Milo had been an idiot to think relationship rules didn't apply to him. He cleared his throat and almost started coughing again, but he managed to hold it in. Every muscle, joint, and cell in his body ached, and coughing only exacerbated it. "I'm sorry."

Sitting, Joss took Milo's hand and held it between his two beefier ones. "I know we have a lot we need to talk about, but that can wait until you're feeling better. I love you, Milo. I'm not going anywhere until then."

25

AFTER HIS DISCHARGE FROM THE HOSPITAL LESS THAN A WEEK later, Milo's parents had tried to convince him to go back to the east coast with them to finish his recovery, but Joss had put on his most persuasive smile and convinced them that he could and would take care of Milo and make sure he made all of his follow-up appointments as well as his respiratory therapy sessions.

Being on the receiving end of Joss's smile and sincerity before, Milo knew how persuasive Joss could be. His parents finally, reluctantly, relented.

In a rental car until the insurance check from the totaled Jeep came in, Joss drove Milo's parents to LAX and Milo back to the hangar.

The whole drive home into the hills, Milo couldn't get the words Joss had said to him out of his head. Sure, he'd said he loved Milo, which at the time had made his head spin—and still did. But it was his other words that made his stomach feel as if the bottom had dropped out of it, and there would be no easy landing.

The words where Joss had said, 'I'm not going anywhere until then.'

Until they'd had their *talk*, he'd meant.

In Milo's mind that meant after the talk, things could be over.

Though Milo didn't question Joss's sincerity when he'd said he loved Milo. He showed his love in the way he only left the hospital when they'd threatened to kick him out, or the way he doted on Milo, or the way his lips pressed to his forehead as Joss breathed him in.

But just because Joss loved him, and Milo could admit, at least to himself, he felt the same, didn't mean it would all work out.

That tiny, niggling thought in the back of Milo's head prevented him from seeing a clear path to their future. And a not-so-small part of Milo still questioned if maybe Joss's attraction and affection had more to do with all the things Milo said or did that reminded Joss of Dan, than Joss's true feelings for Milo himself.

Joss parked the rental next to his motorcycle that Derek had arranged to be brought back to the hangar. "Home again, home again."

Home.

Milo liked the sound of that.

Though considering the state of their relationship when he'd left, he didn't want to make any assumptions. He took his bag of medications they'd filled at the pharmacy and carried them through Joss's apartment, prepared to head to his bedroom.

"Where are you going?" Joss asked from the kitchen as Milo hit the door to the hangar.

Milo held up the bag of medications as if that made where he was going obvious. "Putting these up?"

"You're sleeping in my bed. I promised your parents I'd keep a close eye on you. I can't do that if you're on the other side of the building."

Milo walked over to the kitchen and set the bag on the island separating them, prepared to make his first foray into the status of their relationship. "Where will you sleep?"

Joss handed Milo one of the bottles of water he'd pulled from the fridge. "Here. Hydrate. Doctor's orders." He waited until Milo had taken a few gulps before he took a sip from his own bottle and pointed behind Milo. "I can take the couch."

Okay. So, they were at the sleeping on the couch phase. Milo tried to wash his disappointment down with another slug of water.

Joss planted his hands on the counter and leaned across. "I didn't bring you back here to get into your pants."

"I know that."

"Then why do you look like I took your lollipop and threw it on the ground?"

"One, it's not a lollipop I want to suck..." Milo started. One of Joss's eyebrows went up, and Joss managed to suppress most of his smile. "And two... I don't want to kick you out of your bed."

Joss rested his forearms on the counter and let them take his weight as he leaned across, his gaze assessing. "Don't want to kick me out or want me in the bed with you? Two entirely different things. Pick one."

Joss was making Milo make the first move on how their relationship moved forward. Talk about putting him on the spot.

Well, he did toss out that 'I love you' earlier, so...

Yeah. Joss had been the one to put it all on the line first. Milo could take a figurative step toward that line and try to meet him halfway.

"I want you in bed with me."

Joss nodded and tapped his hand on the counter before straightening. "Okay then."

Milo's heart lost a beat at the casual way Joss said that as if they'd agreed on a restaurant for dinner and not as if they'd taken a positive step forward for their relationship. Then Joss couldn't hold back his smile, equal parts heat and apprehension. He ducked his head to hide it, but Milo caught it before he could.

Milo's heart did a little dance in his chest, and one of the knots in his stomach loosened. There was so much that he needed to say, so much that he needed to explain, but as exhausted as he was, he knew it needed to wait until he was more coherent.

Instead of spilling all the thoughts in his head, he walked around the counter and reached up. In the time that Milo had been in the hospital, the scruff on Joss's face had grown long enough to feel soft.

Milo rose on his tiptoes, and Joss ducked his head, meeting him for the kiss.

Pouring his heart into the kiss, he tried telling Joss with his body how much he wanted to be 'all in' on them and their relationship, but until they had that conversation, he couldn't put his heart on the line.

Until then, the 'I love you, too' would have to wait.

After all, it was the only heart he had, and he had to protect it at all costs.

Joss lifted Milo onto the counter and stepped between his legs, taking the kiss deeper, but not demanding. He kept it slow and sensuous and soft. If Milo hadn't already loved him, he would have fallen then and there.

Along with almost taking his life, the infection had stolen Milo's ability to hold his breath. All too soon, he ran out of air, and he had to pull back, his chest billowing, the bottoms of his lungs still scratchy.

"I want more." And Milo didn't mean just the physical stuff.

"Same." Joss stepped back and helped Milo off the counter.

Milo slapped a hand over his mouth to cover a jaw-cracking yawn, and Joss reached for the bag of medications.

Joss shook a couple of antibiotics onto his palm and plopped them into Milo's hand and gave him the last of his water. "Take these, and we'll take a nap. You need your rest."

Milo threw the pills to the back of his throat and washed the bitter pills down. "You're coming with me?"

"I thought that was okay with you."

"It was. It is. But don't you have work to do? You've been shut down since—"

Joss took him by the shoulders and steered him toward the bedroom. "Don't worry about the business. I shut it down for two weeks, but our schedule is filling up. We're gonna be fine."

Milo hoped that their relationship would fare as well.

Joss stripped Milo to his underwear without any fanfare—which Milo found mildly disappointing even though he was in no condition to do more than kiss and cuddle—and tucked him into bed. Joss lost his clothes on the other side of the bed and climbed in, scooting to the middle and tucking Milo against his side.

Milo snuggled in, his head on Joss's shoulder. Joss picked up a book from his bedside table and leaned over and kissed Milo on the top of the head. "Get some sleep. We can talk things over when you wake up."

SCROLLING THROUGH HIS PHONE AS THE SUN STARTED TO FALL AND pitch his bedroom in shadows, Joss felt it the moment that Milo woke. Milo's steady breathing changed, and his relaxed body stiffened ever so slightly.

He could have kicked himself for sending Milo into his nap

with what amounted to a gauntlet being thrown down with the parting words, '*We can talk things over when you wake up.*'

It proved how low Milo's stamina was and how much the infection had knocked him back that he could even sleep with the pending conversation on his mind. Joss hadn't slept a wink in the four hours that sleep had pulled Milo under.

Even reading his book hadn't helped Joss shut off his brain. Since his brain had refused to go offline, he'd taken the opportunity to do a little Googling. Something he'd wanted to do in the hospital, but he'd been too tired and on too much of an emotional roller coaster to focus.

Though still exhausted from not sleeping well, being back home with Milo safe and in his bed, he read everything he could find on cellular memory. And while firsthand accounts were compelling, and research interesting, his brain still couldn't wrap itself around the concept that a donor's cells could affect the recipient beyond better health.

Though, he didn't doubt Milo's experience.

And he couldn't get past the incidences that seemed too coincidental.

"I know you're awake," Joss said, laying his phone on the mattress beside him and rubbing his fingers on his screen-weary eyes. "The conversation can wait if you need more time. I was an asshole for laying that on you before your nap."

"I'm sensing a pattern."

Joss caught Milo's head in a headlock and kissed the top of his head before letting go. "*Asshole* comes factory installed when you purchase the full Joss package. But I'm trying to lock it down and keep it to a minimum. If you want perfection, then—"

"I don't need perfection." Milo pushed against Joss's chest to help him sit up. "I need for you to try." A sly smile tipped the corners of Milo's lips. "Or get good at groveling."

"You just like thinking of ways I could make it up to you."

"Preferably while you're naked and on your knees." Milo shrugged. "But we can work that into our negotiations."

"Is this a UN peace talk now?"

Milo leaned forward and kissed Joss, pulling back before either one of them could get carried away. "Except instead of handshakes at the end, maybe we can trade blowjobs."

Joss cupped the back of Milo's neck and stole another kiss. "I think if the UN adopted blowjobs, maybe more would get done on an international level."

"Agreed. But first, I need to brush my teeth and pee. Meet you back here in a few?"

"Deal."

The shower turned on after the toilet flushed, and Joss knew it would be more than a few minutes before Milo returned. He headed for the kitchen for water, medications, munchies, and a little something he'd found at the hospital gift shop.

By the time Milo came out of the bathroom in nothing but a towel draped low around his waist, Joss had everything set up.

Milo stopped half-way to the bed, his gaze taking in the bottle of water next to two pills, the open bag of chips, the pillows propped up against Joss's headboard, and the towel laid down on the bed. "What's all this?"

Joss stood and took Milo's hand, leading him back to the bed. "I got you a little something at the hospital. I hope you like it."

Though clearly wary, Milo settled against the pillows, his feet on the towel Joss had laid down. The towel around Milo's waist fell open, exposing Milo's inner thigh and the tip of his semi-hard dick. Neither one of them bothered to fix his towel.

Maybe this wasn't such a good idea. Sitting at Milo's feet and having to see Milo's hard-on might make it impossible to say what he had to say without saying to hell with it all and violating every one of the doctor's discharge orders.

Joss sat cross-legged on the bed and pulled Milo's feet into his lap. He tossed two bottles of nail polish in Milo's lap. "Pick one."

Milo ducked his head and fuck if those weren't tears in his eyes when he glanced back up and said, "This one."

"Purple with sparkles it is." Joss took the bottle from Milo's hand and shook it.

"I want this on my fingers." Milo held up the other bottle, the deep metallic purple. "As long as you won't be embarrassed to be seen with me out in public with it."

Joss's brain immediately grabbed onto that sentence, realizing in those words, Milo had indicated a possible scenario where they were together in the future. "I've told you before, the nail polish, the makeup, is a non-issue. I don't give a fuck what people think. I care that you be you. There's nothing sexier than that."

Joss stared at Milo's legs and the parted towel revealing the cock that had started leaking precum. If Joss had known Milo considered nail polish foreplay, he would have bought the whole damn gift shop out of it.

"Besides," Joss continued, "I dare them to say something about it to me." The grin on his face said he'd welcome the fight.

Milo chuckled, making him cough, but it cleared quickly and didn't leave him nearly as breathless as it had a few days before. "I'm not sure anyone would be that stupid."

Joss didn't like to fight, and his size assured him that he didn't have to very often, but he also would fight to his last breath for Milo.

Christ. He hoped they could work their problems out. Joss couldn't imagine anyone else he'd want to spend the rest of his life with.

He took Milo's foot, but Milo yanked it away. "Wait, have you ever done this before?"

Laying Milo's foot back in his lap, Joss held up his hands, "People trust their life to my steady hands at the yoke. I think I can handle a little nail polish."

"Uh, huh," Milo said, the doubt clear in his voice. "It's not as easy as you think."

Joss scoffed and tucked the bottle into the fold of his leg behind his knee to keep it from spilling. "I'll be doing YouTube videos before you know it. *FanFabulousNails* better watch out. I'm going to knock her down a few pegs."

Milo sat up, dragging his foot away again. At this rate, the damn bottle of nail polish would dry out before a drop got on Milo. "You watched instruction videos on nail polish?"

"I had a lot of downtime at the hospital." That was the best and lamest defense he had.

Milo put his foot back on Joss's lap. "Practically a professional."

Joss started at the little toe and worked his way to the big one, hoping to hone his technique by the time he got to the largest surface. It took more precision and dexterity than he expected, and he really should have brought some tissues to clean up the excess he got on Milo's skin. *Next time.*

And look who else was thinking long term?

Joss glanced up and met Milo's eyes. "Milo, I—"

"I'm sorry," Milo blurted out. "This is all my fault."

Squeezing Milo's foot, Joss said, "We both played a part in this. I can admit that. I should have answered your letters."

"And I should have told you who I was and why I was there from the start."

Joss painted another nail, his hand shaking so badly, he got paint on the skin on all three sides of the nail.

"I was scared—"

"I was afraid—"

They both said at the same time. The tightness in his chest eased a fraction, and he let out a laugh.

Milo found his voice first. "I was scared to hurt you. Derek's warning played on rewind in my head, but I thought that I could keep not telling you. That what did it really matter if you knew the truth? I was staying for my own reasons by then, not because of Dan. And then we kissed and..."

"It got a hell of a lot more complicated."

Milo nodded. "Yeah."

Taking a deep, steadying breath, Joss started in on Milo's big toe, the polish going on smoothly, the sparkles shining in the morning light.

"I wanted to tell you," Milo said. "I almost blurted it out so many times, but then I thought that would only hurt you more, and then if you found out Derek helped me find you, it could mess up that friendship, and then I couldn't see an upside to telling you. Plus, I fucking chickened out."

2 6

MILO FELL SILENT, OUT OF BREATH FROM HIS VERBAL VOMIT. HE glanced down at his feet, waiting for Joss's response. Joss was listening, but he was also trying so damn hard to make sure he did a good job on Milo's toenails. It was so fucking cute. Joss had made a colossal mess of Milo's toes, and Milo's heart melted.

As much of a mess that Joss made of Milo's toenails, Milo was doing a much worse job at explaining his side of the situation. He'd gotten the words out but conveying what was in his heart seemed impossible. He couldn't put into words how he'd felt in those moments when he'd almost told Joss the truth, all tongue-tied, chest tight, and heart racing, his mind on the verge of full-on panic.

It those moments, it had been easy to convince himself that the truth didn't matter, that that one little... *omission* could be buried and forgotten.

Instead, it had festered and exploded in Milo's face.

"Give me your other foot," Joss said as he finished the first one and dipped the brush in the bottle and gave it a shake before unscrewing the cap again.

Had Joss even heard what Milo had said? His chest was tight, the way it felt when he held his breath and had run out of air, but if anything, his breathing came more rapidly than usual, more rapidly even for a guy who'd recently been released from the hospital.

Milo's stomach flopped, and as hungry as he was, he couldn't even look at the bag of chips Joss had brought without tasting bile at the back of his throat.

As with the other foot, Joss started with the little toe and started working his way to the big one. "Derek and I… we talked it out."

"I'm glad to hear that."

Joss nodded but didn't glance up from his task. Milo appreciated Joss's care and special attention to detail, but he wanted to see Joss's eyes. "Look at me. *Joss*."

Joss glanced up, his hand midway between the bottle of nail polish and Milo's foot, a heavy drop of sparkle-y purple nail polish forming at the tip and threatening to fall.

"I'm glad you two were able to work it out," Milo said, needing Joss to see his sincerity. As much as Milo wanted a future for him and Joss, it would have sucked big, hairy, donkey balls if Joss and Derek's friendship hadn't survived because of him. Derek's heart had been in the right place when he'd agreed to help Milo, Joss must have recognized that.

"Yeah, me, too." Joss finished up the last nail, the big toe, smoothing the polish over the surface again and again until it started to get tacky. Finally, he gave up, capped the polish, and tossed the bottle aside. "Done. What do you think?"

Milo glanced down and wiggled his toes. "Honestly?"

"Hit me with it." The words almost came out as a dare.

"They're a fucking mess, but I love them. And I love you for wanting to do them for me."

The 'I love you' fell out, and Milo couldn't take it back.

Not that he wanted to.

A shy smile shifted on Joss's face. He pulled Milo into his lap, wrapping Milo's legs around his back, the knot of Milo's towel coming undone in the process. "I'll get better at it." Joss snugged him closer and held on tight as Milo circled his arms around Joss's neck. "At not being an asshole and the nail-painting thing. If you'll give me a chance."

Around the lump the size of Mount Everest in Milo's throat, he managed, "I'd like that."

Joss brushed his lips against Milo's. "I'm sorry I blew up. I'm sorry I didn't give you a chance to explain. And I'm so fucking thankful that I have the chance to make it up to you."

"I'll be honest," Milo said, "I didn't think you would be able to get past my lies."

"When you sit in a hospital room, you have a lot of time to think. I didn't make it any easier for you to tell the truth with that bullshit 'no lying' ultimatum. And all the time I waited for you to get better allowed me the chance to hit pause on my anger and focus on what was really important."

Milo raised a brow when Joss didn't continue. "And what was that?"

"You." Joss ran his knuckles along Milo's cheek, the stubble there not as long or soft as Joss's. "Seeing you fight for every breath reminded me what Dan's death had taught me. That you can't sweat the bullshit. That hard limits can be arbitrary lines in the sand that once you cross and look back from the other side, you see the fallacy of your convictions. I'd lost sight of that. And for that, from the bottom of this bruised and beat up heart, I'm truly sorry."

MILO DROVE HOME FROM HIS SATURDAY MORNING RECHECK WITH his primary care physician, with a grin on his face. He got clearance from his doctor to resume normal activities. Which meant he was cleared for sex. It had been a long couple of weeks of recovery to get to that point. It had felt longer than that, without being able to have the makeup sex.

Not that everything in the past few weeks had been perfect, but the bumps were leveling out.

He'd parked beside Derek's Roadster, Vin's motorcycle already gone. One glance through the open hangar doors at the Otter sitting on the tarmac on the other side of the hangar told Milo that Joss had made it back from taking a couple of new skydivers up. Derek and Vin had volunteered to help with the tandem skydives with the newbies since they were both certified to do so.

Joss didn't take as many of the newbie skydivers up the way that he and Dan used to years ago, but he did it on occasion.

Coming in through the hangar, the door from the hangar to the apartment opened before Milo could put his hand on the knob. Derek walked through and hooked a thumb toward his car. "I've got to go. A call came in about a new case." He clapped Milo on the shoulder. "Good to see you on your feet."

"I just got medically cleared, so I'm hoping I won't be on my feet for long."

Derek chuckled, putting his hands over his ears as he walked to his car. "TMI, Malone."

Milo laughed as he walked into the apartment. Joss fumbled with a frame on the table, turning it upside down.

"What's this?"

"You're back early." Joss had one of those expressions on his face that told Milo that if the frame had been smaller, Joss would have whipped it behind his back and pretended he wasn't holding anything.

"No, I'm back late because everyone in Burbank decided

they had to drive up the I-5." He glanced down at the frame and bumped his chin at it. "You going to show me?"

Joss picked up a screwdriver and the clips holding the picture wire and started attaching them to the back of the frame. "I wanted to have this up before you got home."

"I could leave," Milo said, "but I'd have to take my medical clearance with me, and I don't think you want me to do that."

Joss grinned. "Oh, yeah?"

"And I've been using my recovery time *wisely* while you've been working." He pointedly looked at Joss's crotch. "I don't think size is going to be a problem."

Joss swallowed hard but didn't say anything. Had he swallowed his tongue? Moving around the table, Joss pulled out a chair for Milo. When he sat, Joss put his hands on the arms of the chair and brought his lips to Milo's, taking the kiss deep, his tongue tasting and taking. But fuck, Milo was in a mood to give.

Joss broke the kiss, stealing Milo's breath and leaving him with a raging hard-on.

"Hurry up and finish that frame so you can fuck me."

Joss's eyes smoldered. "You keep saying stuff like that, and I'm going to forget how to use a screwdriver. So, sit there, look pretty, and keep your sexy, filthy mouth shut while I finish this up."

Joss couldn't suppress his grin, but the warning hadn't been idle. Milo wondered about the unspoken *or else* because that could be hella fun. But he swallowed his retort and impatiently watched as Joss finished up the frame and turned it over.

"Let me see."

Joss set the frame on the table for Milo to see. It wasn't a fancy frame, just one of those black metal ones you could buy at any box store. It already had a pre-cut mat with cutouts for eight photos. The first seven photos were the photo's Milo had sent in the cards to Joss.

Milo's breath caught, and he glanced up. "You opened them."

Joss swiped at one of his eyes, his voice cracking when he said, "Yeah."

Joss's whole expression went soft, and Milo knew what the next words out of Joss's mouth would be. He stood and held a finger over Joss's lips. "Don't you fucking dare apologize again, you got me? We're looking forward. We're not dwelling on the past."

Wrapping a hand around Milo's finger, Joss bit the tip with a playful glint in his eyes and said, "Let's hang it."

Without letting go of Milo's hand, Joss led him to the wall of photos, and took one of the largest ones down. It was one of Milo's favorites. The one of Joss and Dan in their skydiving helmets with huge grins on their sweaty faces, their spent parachutes on the ground behind them, and Joss looking at Dan the same way Joss looked at Milo sometimes. With love. Pure and simple.

Joss replaced the frame of him and Dan with the one he'd just completed. He stepped back, looking proud. "What do you think?"

It was then that Milo noticed the eighth and final photo in the array. A selfie shot of him and Joss taken at what was becoming their favorite spot at the end of the runway. The sun was setting in the background, and all you could see was the two of them in silhouette, Joss's lips pressed to Milo's cheek.

"I love it." Milo put an arm around Joss's waist and hugged him tight. "But can we get another nail and hang it in that blank spot over by the door?"

"You don't want it here in the middle surrounded by all the other pictures?"

"I don't want to replace Dan." On the wall *or* in Joss's life. What they had was new and different. And he wanted the photos to reflect that. "There's plenty of room on this wall for the both of us. Don't you think?"

ONE OF THE MANY THINGS JOSS LOVED ABOUT MILO WAS HIS inability to feel threatened by Dan's memory. He'd dated a few people in years past who couldn't understand why he still had pictures of Dan hanging on the wall, and here Milo was arguing for a new nail. A continuation, as it were, of Joss's life.

Not a replacement of his previous one.

Joss locked his arm around Milo's neck, pressed a kiss to the top of his head, and let go. "God, I fucking love you."

Milo brought him in for a kiss. It didn't linger nearly long enough, but Joss had a clear schedule for the afternoon, so they'd have plenty of time for that later.

"I love you, too." The words seemed to come easier for Milo now. He always said it back and had said it first on a few occasions. And while he didn't doubt Milo's feelings were true, he still felt Milo held back.

Joss couldn't blame him. They continued to rebuild trust in their relationship. He'd give it more time before he pressed for answers.

"I'll be right back," Joss said as he extricated himself from Milo's arms and headed into the hangar to find a hammer and nail.

When he returned, Milo had already put his and Dan's photo in its rightful place. Joss handed over the hammer and nail and had Milo to pick his spot. Milo didn't put it off to the side from the others, setting himself and their relationship apart. Milo hammered the nail at the end, tucking the frame between a photo of him and Dan working on the Jeep and one of Dan about to jump out the Cessna back when they were still flying it.

Never had hanging a frame been so damn sexy.

"Perfect." Joss walked over and stripped the hammer out of Milo's hand, set it on the ground at their feet, and pressed Milo's back into the blank wall next to the frame.

He cupped Milo's chin and kissed him. When he finally came up for air, he picked Milo up and wrapped Milo's legs around his waist. "Do I get to have my way with you now?"

Milo's grin took up his whole face, and his eyes twinkled with devilish mischief that promised they'd both be getting off. "Oh, hell, yeah."

In the bedroom, Joss dropped Milo onto his bed—*their bed*—and reached into the bedside table drawer for the bottle of lube while Milo stripped naked in a flash. Milo got on all fours and shook his perfect little ass in the air as he grinned over his shoulder at Joss.

Tossing the lube on the bed, Joss lost his clothes and knelt on the bed behind Milo, his hand skimming the most perfect ass cheek. Goosebumps rose on Milo's skin, and his head dropped between his shoulders.

Biting one of those cheeks, Joss kissed his way up Milo's back, adding some of his weight until Milo collapsed on the bed beneath him. He covered Milo with his body, his cock lining up with the crack of Milo's ass. As much as Joss loved giving up control and being dominated and fucked by Milo, he couldn't wait to be inside him.

Joss took some of his weight on his forearms, not wanting to crush Milo in the process, though from the way Milo ground his ass against Joss, Milo didn't seem concerned about that.

"What are you waiting for?" The petulance in Milo's voice made Joss chuckle.

He shifted and rolled Milo to his back and settled between his legs, bracing himself on his hands above Milo. Their dicks aligned, and Milo reached down with one hand and stroked them both together, their dicks already leaking precum. Joss pressed into the touch and nearly forgot Milo had asked him a question.

"You sure this is what you want?"

"You need to learn to take 'yes' for an answer. Yes, I want this. I've been prepping for a couple weeks now." Milo reached over and handed the lube to Joss. "Let's see how well I've done my homework."

"You're the boss." Joss sat back on his haunches and lubed himself up. He did the same to Milo, his finger working around Milo's hole.

Milo groaned, pushing back against Joss's finger until Joss breached the tight ring of muscle. Milo's eyes drifted closed. "Fuck, that feels good. But I need more than your finger."

Removing his hand, Joss hovered above him, his dick pressed against Milo's hole. He ducked his head. Milo's mouth opened for the kiss, their tongues meeting and mating. Milo pressed against Joss's cock.

They shared a sharp intake of breath, and before Joss could ask if Milo were okay, Milo said, "Don't stop."

Slowly, Joss eased inside, goosebumps flashing across Milo's chest, the sweat beading on his forehead as Milo squeezed and relaxed around him.

"Jesus, fuck." A litany of muttered curse words flowed from Joss as the pleasure rocketed around his body, leaving him devoid of coherent thought.

And even though Joss was on top, Milo as usual, was in total control. He wrapped his arms around Joss's head, pulling him into his chest and bucking up against him, taking him deeper, faster than Joss thought possible.

Joss had planned on taking it slow, but apparently, Milo

didn't get the memo. Milo's hands slipped to Joss's hips, encouraging him to go faster. Good thing Milo had been a quick study with the butt plugs.

Or maybe he was a natural.

Either way, Joss increased his strokes, nearly pulling out before thrusting back in. He sat back on his heels, his hands wrapped around Milo's thighs for leverage. He glanced down between his legs, watching Milo's ass devour his cock. "You're so fucking amazing."

Milo's breath huffed out, and his mouth fell open as Joss reached down and took Milo's cock into his hand, the precum leaking freely. The muscles in Milo's neck strained, his eyes shut tight as Joss felt the first pulses of Milo's orgasm at the base of his cock.

Joss shifted a fraction, and Milo's breath caught when Joss hit his prostate. Milo stiffened beneath him, and Joss slowed his strokes and finished Milo off with his hand. Milo's groans of pleasure made Joss's balls tighten as Milo came all over his abdomen. A few strokes later, Joss followed, Milo's spasmodic tightening around his cock sparking his own orgasm.

His body trembled. His heart raced. His lungs worked double-time.

And the only thought going through Joss's head was how fucking lucky he'd been that Milo had shown up at his door.

He gently pulled out and collapsed on top of Milo, chest to chest. He couldn't tell where his heartbeat ended and Milo's began.

Milo's heart.

Not Dan's.

And whatever part Dan had played in Milo living, of them meeting, of them being together, while profound, Joss realized now it was also insignificant.

Milo was his own man.

Their shared history may have brought them together, but they were more than the sum of their parts.

"You good?" Joss asked as he rolled off Milo, his breath coming under control.

Milo held his hand over his heart as if keeping it from jumping out of his chest. "Never fucking better." With a half-laugh, Milo rolled to face Joss and said, "But I'd be lying if I said I'm not going to be feeling it later."

Joss pressed his lips to Milo's. "You fucking amaze me, and it has nothing to do with how well you take dick." He shifted, his softening cock sticking to his thigh. "I'll be right back."

He cleaned himself up in the bathroom and brought a warm washcloth to the bedroom and freshened Milo up. After dropping the wet cloth in the bathroom, he returned to find Milo curled up on their bed, his eyes half-mast.

He stirred and rolled to his back when Joss crawled into bed beside him. Joss snuggled against Milo's side, his arm low around Milo's waist and his head over the scar on Milo's chest. That steady beat beneath his ear a comfort, and he felt his own heart slowing to match.

With lazy strokes, Milo ran his hands through Joss's hair, his fingers making his scalp tingle. He could lay there for days and let Milo do that.

All too soon, Milo shifted out from beneath Joss, waking him from his light snooze. Joss grumbled, "Where are you going?"

Milo leaned over and kissed him. "I'll be right back."

MILO PADDED NAKED INTO THE HANGAR, NOT EVEN CARING THAT both hangar doors stood wide-ass open. As remote as they were, they rarely had visitors unless they had something scheduled.

He could still smell Joss on his overheated skin. Smell the

musk and sex and sweat. But now that they had made it to a better place in their relationship, the way Joss had curled up against him, his head on Milo's chest, Milo felt he needed to give Joss another chance to listen to Dan's heart.

He returned to their bedroom and retook his spot beside Joss. He held out the stethoscope to him. At Joss's confused expression, he said, "I thought... I thought you might want to have a listen. I kind of dropped a bomb on you the last time."

Joss took the stethoscope, but instead of putting the earpieces in his ears, he rolled over and tossed it aside. It landed on the rim of a small trash can, half in and half out, the unbalanced weight dumping the can on its side.

"What did you do that for?"

Joss rolled back over, throwing his leg across Milo's hips, holding him in place. "Dan gave you a gift. And when someone gives you a gift, it's *yours*. It's not theirs anymore."

"I understand what you're saying, but I don't follow."

"I put my head on your chest because I love hearing your heart beating. *Your* heart. Not Dan's."

And fuck it if Milo didn't feel the sting of tears prick the back of his eyes. Joss caught his chin as Milo started to look away. "And just so we're clear, I don't love you because of your taste in beer, or sandwich toppings, or your words, or tattoos. I love the man you are. Every organized, stubborn, sweet, seductive inch of you."

Joss kissed him, a light brush of lips and a contented sigh. "I love *you*," he said again. "And that has nothing to do with you carrying a piece of Dan around inside of you. You got me?"

That last little bit of reservation Milo had about his and Joss's relationship melted away as Joss's words washed over him. For such a big man, he was romantic and sappy as hell. But Milo wouldn't have it any other way. "Got it."

2 7

Seven Months Later

"Are we ready?" Milo asked as he glanced between Joss, Derek, and Foster.

It was early March, and the cool morning air was brisk and refreshing as they stood in the hangar, Joss with a tandem parachute strapped to his back, Milo already in the harness he'd use to strap himself to Joss before they—gulp—jumped out of the Otter.

As much as Milo had wanted to try skydiving, it seemed that carrying a piece of Dan around with him hadn't cured him of his fear of heights after all. Milo low-key shook as the adrenaline coursed through his system, sending an electric buzz through his veins and putting an extra kick to the beat of his heart—yes, *his* heart. Through Joss's insistence and persistence, he'd deleted the words 'Dan's heart' from his vocabulary.

"What about the birthday cake?" Foster asked. He was going up in the Otter, but he'd decided jumping out of it didn't align with his life goals.

"Maybe we should save it until we get back?" Milo's stomach flipped. If he had anything to eat before the jump, it was going to come back up, no question. He must have looked a little green because Joss said to Milo, "You don't have to do this. I appreciate you wanting to celebrate Dan's birthday this way, but you don't have to go through with this. And maybe we should practice the landing again and—"

"No. We're going." Milo had made up his mind, and as scared as he was, he wasn't backing out. "And I've had more pre-jump training than a platoon of parajumper recruits. And it's a tandem jump. You're basically doing all the work. I think I've got this."

Derek clapped his hands together as if that sealed the decision. "Let's go, boys. I'm itching to get my hands on this bird again."

They all piled into the Otter and took to the blue, cloudless sky. For Milo's first jump, Joss had insisted they land at Joss's drop zone up the hill from the airstrip instead of on the beach Dan preferred the way Milo had wanted. But he would defer to Joss on that decision. He knew all Joss wanted was to keep Milo safe.

And even though Joss had helped Milo expunge 'Dan's heart' from his vocabulary, he couldn't help but feel like this jump was his gift to Dan.

Foster sat in the cockpit with Derek, who warned him to keep his hands to himself. Foster obliged, but one glance at the cockpit and Milo saw Foster's lips moving nonstop as he talked Derek's ear off. That Derek hadn't told him to shut up was a minor miracle.

Without a headset, Milo couldn't really hear what they were saying over the drone of the propellers. Behind him, Joss scooted closer on the long bench they straddled near the jump door. Joss leaned in and raised his voice. "You still good to go?"

Milo gave him a thumbs up even though it felt like his stomach had started the skydive without him. He felt Joss tugging on his harness and knew he was attaching them together, Milo's back to Joss's front.

As they reached altitude, the red jump light at the back of the Otter turned yellow, indicating they were close to the jump sight. Joss patted Milo's leg, and they shuffled to the jump door. Joss pulled it up.

The wind buffeted them, and Milo reached up and held onto the grab bar by the door. He was really doing this. Below, even that early on a Saturday morning, a line of cars inched along the interstate ten thousand feet below.

Milo had expected his heart would go into overdrive at this moment, but an unexpected calm came over him. He knew he was in the best hands, and whatever happened next, he'd never regret it.

The jump light turned green, and Milo craned his head around, looking at Joss.

"Ready?" Joss asked.

"Ready."

They stepped out of the plane and yelled, "Time to fly!"

They fell.

Milo found freefall surreal and unexpectedly quiet except for the sound of the wind rushing by. That high up, he didn't really feel like he was falling. Joss whooped, and Milo felt his sheer joy in jumping.

Then Joss pulled the cord, and the parachute expanded, jerking Milo's harness. Using the steering lines, Joss maneuvered the parachute as they floated above the San Gabriels. They came down in large sweeping circles, giving Milo amazing views of the mountains, the valley, and the Pacific Ocean in the distance.

He spotted the road from the valley into the San Gabriels, all the way up until he recognized the hangar and the airstrip, and higher still until he focused on the landing zone.

The grassy landing zone lay covered in in big white letters that said, *Marry me?*

Milo craned his neck and stared up at Joss's big, goofy grin. But he didn't have time to say anything before Joss said, "Get ready to land. Remember what I taught you."

Milo turned back around to see the ground coming up fast. The letters in the grass growing bigger and bigger and blurrier and blurrier as the waterworks behind his eyes let loose. If Joss hadn't drilled the landing lesson into his head, he would have forgotten the instructions.

They landed in the middle of the 'y,' chalk dust getting all over them as it gusted in the air and billowed around them. "Cut me loose," Milo said, barely able to hold still long enough to allow Joss to what he'd asked.

When the last attachment point clicked free, Milo rolled over, his breath coming fast as he straddled Joss's hips and pinned him to the ground. "Are you serious?"

Joss grinned up at him. "I didn't spend three hours in the dark in the middle of the night last night writing that out as a fucking joke."

"Yes," Milo said, the word simple, to the point, and the only answer that popped into his head. "Yes, I'll marry you."

He leaned down for a kiss to seal the deal, taking it deep and using the opportunity to grind against Joss's growing erection. Milo broke the kiss and reached between them, unfastening Joss's pants before starting in on his own. He stopped suddenly with his pants and underwear below his hips. Milo didn't care that they were outside. The only people who could see them were in the air. "Please tell me you brought lube."

Joss reached into his back pocket and pulled out a couple of sachets of lube. Milo snatched them out of his hand and dropped back down for a soul-sucking kiss. "God, I fucking love you."

Derek flew past the drop zone, as he banked into the turn to make his approach to Joss's airstrip. Below him, Joss and Milo had already landed.

"Is that... are they..." Foster started as he leaned against his window to get a better look. "Holy fuck, they're—"

"Fucking?"

Foster covered his eyes with his hand. "I can't unsee that."

Derek chuckled. "I guess this means we're going to have to wait a little longer on that cake."

He lined up on the airstrip and decreased his speed as he went in for the landing. Foster had a grip on the door handle and the edge of his seat, his eyes squinting nearly closed. "I have landed this bird before, you know."

"Yeah, but we're coming in awful fast."

Derek shook his head. "It just feels faster this close to the ground."

They touched down, with only a squeak from Foster as Derek decelerated and brought the Otter to a stop near the hangar.

"We're here." Derek shut the engines down and prepped to leave. They'd worry about refueling later.

They climbed out of the plane and started walking toward the hangar. Foster glanced back at the dirt road that led up to the landing zone. "How long do you think they're going to be?"

"As long as they want. It's not every day you get a marriage propos—"

A man stepped out of the open rear doors of the hangar.

They had closed the front ones before they'd left, but the rear ones remained open.

Not *a* man. Maximilian Huff.

"Oh, hey. Who are you?" Foster asked.

Max didn't answer, and Derek didn't bother to fill Foster in. Hard to talk when the breath had been knocked out of him.

Max stood there, his thumbs tucked into the waistband of his jeans, his worn leather jacket unzipped, his reflective sunglasses covering his eyes. He'd matured in the ten years he'd been gone, but he was just as fit.

And just as sexy.

Damn him.

Max stepped in front of Derek, and when Derek stuck a hand out to push him away, Max fisted his hands in Derek's T-shirt and swung him around, his back hitting the side of the hangar.

"Whoa, hey, um—" Foster stuttered.

One withering look from Max shut Foster up. Then Max slammed his lips against Derek's, taking the kiss deep when Derek opened his mouth on a strangled, "What the fuck?"

Derek didn't fight back. He sank into the kiss, his dick immediately hard.

Max still smelled of equal parts arrogance and confidence. An intoxicating combination that Derek had never been able to resist. Max wasn't only his ex.

He was Derek's worst mistake.

His biggest regret.

His kryptonite.

Max broke the kiss first, a cocky, satisfied smile on his lips as Derek fought to regain his breath and his mental balance.

"Um... I take it you two know each other," Foster said, slowly backing into the hangar. "I'll be in here..."

Whatever else Foster said was lost on Derek as Max raised

his sunglasses to the top of his head, dark circles under his piercing blue eyes. "You never could tell me no."

Derek wanted to tell Max to fuck off. Instead, he grabbed Max by the lapels and switched their positions, cutting off Max's cocksure chuckle when he covered his ex's mouth with his. A drop of sanity—and let's be honest, *self-respect*—brought him back to himself, and Derek pulled away before the feel of Max's hard-on against his hip had him doing things he'd years ago promised himself he never would again.

"How did you find me?"

"Google. I stopped in at your office. Your partner told me where to find you."

"*Fucking hell.*" Taking on a business partner had seemed like a good idea six months ago. Derek was seriously reconsidering that now.

"You know," Max said in that low, sultry voice that had always drawn Derek's attention. "I never should have left."

Those were words that Derek had dreamt about hearing in the weeks and months after Max had disappeared. Max's eyes drifted to Derek's lips, then came back up to his eyes.

Before he could fall into another ill-advised kiss, Derek took a step back, needing the distance to give himself a modicum of clarity and to ask the important question. "Why are you here?"

Max's gaze dropped to the ground before meeting Derek's again. "I need your help."

"Fuck." A rueful laugh escaped him. "I should've known you hadn't come back for me."

A LETTER TO MY READERS

Dear Reader,

There's a lot going on in the San Fernando Valley, and Derek Watts and Maximillian Huff are in for a hell of a second chance romance adventure. And Derek's unflappable nature may have met its match when Max storms back into Derek's life.

Don't miss their story in the **Den of Thieves** coming out early 2021.

In the meantime, if you haven't caught up with the Black Stallion Studios crew, be sure to check out **One Shot** the first book in the sexy, steamy, heartwarming series.

ROMANTIC SUSPENSE

Lazy S Ranch Series
Cowgirl, Unexpectedly (Book 1)
Must Love Horses (Book 2)
Hot on the Trail (Book 3)
Cowboy, Undercover (Book 4)
Cowboy, Unbridled (Book 5)
Cowgirl, Unbroken (Book 6)

Wright's Island Series
Don't Look Back (Book 1)
In Her Defense (Book 2)

Steele-Wolfe Securities
Wyoming Confidential (Book 1)

CONTEMPORARY ROMANCE

Rockin' Rodeo Series
Luck of the Draw (Book 1)
Photo Chute (Book 2)
Reined In (Book 3)
Rockin' Rodeo Series Collection (Books 1-3)

MM ROMANCE

Black Stallion Studios Series
One Shot (Book 1)
Key Grip (Book 2)
Best Boy (Book 3)
Black Stallion Studios Box Set (Books 1-3)

Valley Boys
Art of Love (Book 1)
Flight of Fancy (Book 2)
Den of Thieves (Book 3)

ABOUT THE AUTHOR

Vicki Tharp makes her home on small acreage in south Texas with her husband and an embarrassing number of pets. When she isn't writing, you can usually find her on the back of her horse—avoiding anything that remotely resembles housework —smelling like fly spray and horse sweat.

Join my newsletter at: http://bit.ly/V-W-T
Join my street team and receive free Advance Reader Copies of my upcoming books at: http://bit.ly/S-W-S-T
You can find my website at: www.VickiTharp.com
I love to hear from readers. You can email me at vwtharp@VickiTharp.com

Or you can stalk me at:

facebook.com/VickiTharpAuthor
instagram.com/author_Vicki_Tharp
bookbub.com/authors/vicki-tharp
amazon.com/author/vicki_tharp
twitter.com/vwtharp